Intoxicating Magic

Books by Deanna Chase

The Jade Calhoun Novels
Haunted on Bourbon Street
Witches of Bourbon Street
Demons of Bourbon Street
Angels of Bourbon Street
Shadows of Bourbon Street
Incubus of Bourbon Street (Winter 2014)

The Coven Pointe Novels
Marked by Temptation (a novella)

The Crescent City Fae Novels
Influential Magic
Irresistible Magic
Intoxicating Magic

The Destiny Novels
Defining Destiny
Accepting Fate (November 2014)
Shattered Souls (Winter 2015)

Intoxicating Magic

A Crescent City Fae Novel

Deanna Chase

Bayou Moon Publishing

Bayou Moon Publishing
dkchase12@gmail.com
www.deannachase.com

Acknowledgments

Thank you to my team: Anne Victory, Red Adept, and Lisa Liddy. You make me look good. Also my Shih Tzu Duncan Donut would like to give a huge shout-out to the readers of the Crescent City Fae series for all of your kind comments about Link. If you weren't already aware, Duncan Donut is the inspiration for Link, and the two are more similar than you might think…right down to the inner wolf. Whatever you do, don't get between the Shih Tzu and his mistress. ☺

Chapter 1

"A strip club?" I shot Phoebe a sidelong glance as we stopped outside the front door of Mecca on Bourbon Street. "Seriously?"

Her black eyes danced with something close to giddy anticipation. "This is where he works. Besides, this isn't a strip club. It's a burlesque show."

"My mistake," I said, amused. Either way, the dancers took most of their clothes off.

I glanced at Link, who was sitting right in front of my feet. Smart dog, considering all the drunken spring-breakers stumbling around us. Flaring my wings, I bent to pick him up. If I pretended he was a purse puppy, they weren't likely to oust us. I could flash my Arcane badge and they'd be forced to let him in, but announcing to everyone who we were wasn't going to help Phoebe catch a rogue vampire. But I'd do it if I had to. I wasn't going anywhere near an unknown vamp without Link around.

"You can leave as soon as you sense him." Phoebe fished some bills out of her skirt pocket. "I just need to know if he's here tonight."

"No. Link and I will stay. What if the vamp has backup? The report doesn't say anything except that there've been attacks. You don't even know if the vamp's a male."

I was gifted in sensing vampires. Phoebe could drop them with one flash of her sun agate, but since vamps had mastered the art of blending in, it was damned hard to pick them out in a crowd. Especially after they'd fed.

"True enough. There could be another Clea stalking about." Phoebe shrugged, referencing a female vamp who'd tried and failed to take us both down not too long ago. "Either way, I can always use the backup. Thanks."

We both knew she could handle herself, but the vampire we were after was said to be particularly evasive and vicious. A deadly combination. I wouldn't leave her alone knowing I could do something to help. Besides, I was still her partner and an agent of the Void—the ghost branch of the Arcane, the government agency that oversees all supernatural activity.

Link snuggled into the crook of my arm as Phoebe paid our way into the club. The tall, oversized bouncer eyed Link, raising his eyebrows curiously. I smiled and scratched Link behind the ears, wishing I'd thought to put a cute doggie vest on him or something. Of course, he'd only tear it to shreds the first time he shifted, but it would've helped sell his purse-puppy persona.

"If he gets loose or distracts from the show in any way, you'll have to remove him from the premises," the bouncer said.

"Sure. Yeah. No problem. He's always well behaved." Except when he was stealing Phoebe's shoes or ripping a vampire to shreds. But then that was part of his charm.

Phoebe snorted her disbelief and took off for a table near the back, one where we'd have full view of the club. I gave the bouncer one last smile and followed her. Depositing Link on the table, I slid into a seat next to her.

"You're kidding me, right?" She curled her lip as she eyed Link. "Wouldn't the floor be a better option?"

"No. He can't see anything down there in his puppy form. It'll only make him agitated. Besides, it's not like we're eating or anything." Link was part of our team. When was she going to acknowledge that? He'd saved her ass more than a couple of times.

"He's just obvious, that's all." She turned her attention to the club, no doubt taking in every possible entrance and exit.

"Really?" I jerked my head to the side, indicating a tall man who'd just emerged from a door marked Employees Only. "As obvious as that?"

Her gaze shifted, and her scowl transformed into a shocked O. She gave a tiny shake of her head as she closed her mouth. "You might have a point."

I couldn't help the laugh that bubbled up from my throat as we both stared at the pasty-white, tall, thin man dressed in a purple leotard, a gold *lamé* belt, and matching knee-high boots. To complete his eccentric vibe, draped over his shoulder was a monkey outfitted in overalls and a lime-green tank top with a matching fedora.

"Sexy," Phoebe said dryly as she turned away from him.

The man was freaky enough, but what I found more disturbing was the gorgeous brunette who had her tongue in his ear. She was dressed to the nines, her off-the-shoulder silk dress exposing her flawless skin and toned shoulders. Everything about her was pure perfection. And he was pure freak. Please, Goddess, let them both be part of the show. Otherwise the pairing was too unbelievable for words.

"Anything?" Phoebe asked.

"Huh?" I tore my gaze from Mr. Purple Leotard and focused on Phoebe's narrowed eyes. Oh. Vampire. Right. I shook my head. "Nothing so far."

She nodded and got up. "Then I'm getting us drinks. You and Link sit tight."

As if we were going to go anywhere in the overcrowded club. The last thing I needed was to draw attention to myself while Phoebe checked out the nooks and crannies of Mecca under the guise of seeking libations. I tucked my wings against my back and sat back in my chair, waiting for the show to start.

A few moments later, the lights went out and the red velvet curtain rose, revealing a circular stage with a shiny black piano on a raised platform.

"Good evening, ladies and gents," a voice boomed over the loudspeaker. "Tonight you're in for a special treat. So grab your cocktails or grab your crotches and get ready to drool, because no one can tease you like Lady Victoooooria Gilman!"

The lights went out, leaving us in pitch-black darkness as catcalls and wolf whistles filled the smoky club. I put my hand on Link, soothing him. His little body was vibrating with the urge to shift. As a wolf, his golden eyes would be able to see everything as clear as day. As a Shih Tzu, he was as blind as I was at the moment.

"Don't worry, buddy," I whispered. "It's all just part of the show."

But even as the words slipped from my lips, I felt the heavy, sticky weight of vampire energy and stiffened. "Shit," I mumbled under my breath.

Link jumped to his feet, making the table rattle. A growl escaped from his small muzzle. I didn't even try to stop him. There was a vampire roaming the pitch-black club, and I had no idea where Phoebe was. If Link sensed enough danger to shift, then by God, I wanted him to shift. No matter what the bouncer had said.

One lone spotlight shone on the empty stage as a slow, seductive melody from the piano filled the club. The music ceased and the loud clatter of heels on hardwood pulsed through the club's sound system. Like everyone else in the room, I craned my neck, searching for the source of the footsteps. The spotlight winked out and immediately reappeared, shining on the abandoned black piano. A lighthearted giggle, followed by the quick succession of those same heels running across the stage, kept our attention as we waited for Victoria to appear. I was just as enraptured as the rest of them despite the fact I was supposed to be searching for the vampire.

"Ladies and gentlemen. We have a special treat for you this evening." Mr. Purple Leotard appeared in the spotlight. Using the piano bench as a stepladder, he climbed on top of the piano and spread his arms wide. "Prepare to be delighted and thrilled as she and her guest ratchet the heat up to blistering level. And if that means you need to shed a few layers of clothes, then all the better." His eyes gleamed as he stared out into the crowd. "You know how we like to take it off here on Bourbon."

Laughter rippled through the audience, followed by a rustling of clothing. My eyes had finally adjusted, and they widened as I realized a large number of women were stripping their bras off and dangling them from their fingertips.

Purple Leotard laughed. "That's it, my pretties. You're well trained, aren't you? I'm sure Miss Victoria will reward you for your obedience."

He snapped his fingers. The monkey climbed down his leg and scrambled up the red silk curtains covering the wall behind the stage. He swung back and forth, a huge grin on his adorable monkey face.

"Remember," the emcee said, waving to the monkey. "Chester sees all. If anyone gets out of line, your punishment is waiting."

The monkey reached behind a mirror dangling from a cable and produced a hose. With one flick of his finger, misty fog filtered out into the audience, winding its way through the club until it was so thick it was impossible to see the wooden floor.

I scooted my chair back, shivering in the air-conditioning. Link let out a low growl, but the patrons and staff were too busy cheering and eating up the emcee's words to even notice my Shih Tzu start to glow with his shift. I reached out to soothe Link, to delay him, but the vampire energy thickened and I yanked my hand back. My heart sped up. A thin sheen of sweat coated my brow. Panic took over, and I wanted nothing more than to bolt from the room.

"I know you're all squirming in your seats," Purple Leotard drawled as I frantically scanned the room.

The vamp energy intensified, pressing in on me from my left. In the next moment it shifted, coming at me from the right. He or she was on the move.

"But sit tight, because once you're under her spell, you're going to be so wet you'll need a change of drawers." His eyes glinted under the light as he stretched his arm out and pointed in my general direction. "Without further ado, I present the fabulous and incredibly sexy Miss Victooooria!"

The spotlight winked out once more. A new light flashed brighter than ever, blinding me. Squinting, I covered my eyes with one hand as I felt rather than saw Link shift. He landed with a soft thump and pressed his body against my thigh.

"Link," I whispered, automatically placing my hand on his back, keeping him from lunging. He was vibrating under my touch but wasn't growling. That was something at least.

"What do we have here?" The sultry voice of Miss Victoria filled the room. "A fae? In New Orleans? How positively delicious."

I stared up into the heart-shaped face of the most gorgeous woman I'd ever seen. Her vibrant eyes were sapphire blue, accented by her chestnut hair piled high on her head and the open, inviting expression on her face. She looked like a woman whom every girl wanted as her best friend and every man dreamed of taming. I was no exception. For some reason, when she smiled at me, it was like a drug. I wanted her attention. Wanted to be part of her inner circle.

And when she held her hand out, I took it and let her pull me out of my chair. I could barely feel the weight of the vampire's energy anymore and vaguely wondered where he'd gone. Every other thought vanished from my mind as Miss Victoria ran her delicate fingers down my neck. Tingles of something close to desire shivered through me.

Whoa. I tried to step back, but her hold on my wrist tightened just enough to keep me in place. My movements stilled as I gazed at her jeweled eyes. They were kind, indulgent.

"Where are you going, darling?" she asked into her microphone. "Don't you want me to dance for you?"

Before I could answer, she was tugging me over to the stage. My feet glided along with her, my mind clouded in a haze of excitement. And when my wings twitched with anticipation, a cheer of encouragement grew from the captivated crowd.

Victoria paused and turned back to her audience. "It's a special occasion, my lovelies. I had no idea when the night started that we'd be lucky enough to experience such a wonderful treat." She ran her fingertips through my long auburn hair. Her voice turned husky as she leaned in. "We could be twins if only I had wings."

With the mention of twins, my body stiffened and whatever spell had overtaken me shattered. The magic lifted, leaving me staring at an enraptured audience. Even Link seemed to be tamed by Miss Victoria's presence. He sat near our table, his puppy-dog eyes full of adoration for the seductress. In full wolf form, however. It was weird. I shook my head and scanned the room for Phoebe. Nowhere in sight.

"What's wrong, love?" Victoria whispered in my ear. "Did you get cold feet?"

She reached out to touch me again, but I backed away. Whatever she'd done to me and to the audience wasn't right. We were all pawns in her game of seduction. And this time the shiver that ran down my spine had nothing to do with desire.

Foreboding overtook me. Something was very wrong.

"No," I said, my voice chilly with judgment. "I don't appreciate being compelled to do something against my will."

Her eyes crinkled in amusement. "Feisty. Roberto said to watch out for you. I just didn't think it would happen so soon." She spun and opened her arms wide. "Welcome to *The Carnevale*, a place where the absurd becomes normal and the normal becomes absurd."

She snapped her fingers and the lights shifted, cascading across the room in a filtered red haze. More of the misty fog materialized along the floor, but this time it morphed into tendrils and clung to the patrons with a sinister vibe that made my skin crawl. I backed up, trying to fade into the shadows, determined to find Phoebe. Everything about this was wrong. Maybe even evil.

But Victoria crooked her finger and magic spilled over me, forcing me forward. I moved in slow motion, my eyes locked on hers.

Her lips curved up in a self-satisfied smile. "That's it, sweet Willow. Come to me."

Willow.

She knew my name. This wasn't a random, chance meeting. She'd known I'd be here. Every bone in my body screamed to walk away. To call Link to attention and to leave this place. I couldn't concentrate. Couldn't do anything but obey her command.

Teetering on my red suede pumps, I stepped forward, another tingle of pleasure winding its way through me. It wasn't sexual in nature but was intoxicating all the same. Euphoric even. My hand slipped into hers and together we glided our way to the stage.

With careful, deliberate steps, we climbed the stairs, stopping only when we were midstage, facing the rapt audience. Their faces were turned up in lustful anticipation as the lights dimmed, casting us in a soft glow.

The soulful sound of a sax filled the room as Victoria moved slowly around me, her heels showing off the sexy lines of her toned legs. She eyed me like a sleek panther, her hips swaying. A man dressed in all black materialized and let out a low, seductive whistle before taking his place at the piano.

She leaned in, her breath tickling my ear. "Where would you like me to touch you first, Ms. Rhoswen?"

My wings fluttered, and I could almost hear the soft chuckle of my friend Harrison when he'd insisted that was a sign I was turned on. Tucking my wings against my back, I tried to scowl, tried to get a hold of myself. I shouldn't be on this stage attracting attention. But I couldn't move. Didn't even really want to.

"Here?" she asked and ran a hot-pink fingernail down the side of my neck.

An uncontrollable shiver visibly shook my body. My eyes closed involuntarily, and I swayed as she ran her hands lightly down my back and over the tips of my wings.

"Yes," Victoria whispered.

Her voice was so low I barely heard her. I was too busy concentrating on the feathery kisses she was trailing along my collarbone. Equal parts horror and pleasure filled my muddled brain.

"Your scent is so sweet, so alluring. And to have you like this, in front of everyone. It's almost too much to take." Her right hand splayed over my stomach as she explored at will.

My focus was riveted on the tingling coming from her fingers digging into my hip and the soft murmur of encouragement reverberating from the crowd. They wanted us both. And Goddess above, if I didn't want to give them exactly what they craved.

I was ready. Ready to partake in whatever Victoria had in store for us both.

That is, until I felt the sharp prick of fangs press against my neck as Victoria said, "Asher will be so pleased."

Chapter 2

The spell instantly shattered as my blood turned to ice. *Vampire!*

Holy shit! How was that possible? I hadn't sensed her and her touch wasn't draining me like other vamps did. Just like David and Eadric, two vampires I'd turned into daywalkers.

But I hadn't turned her. How was she doing this? The question flew out of my head as she wrapped her stonelike arms around me. I jerked, trying to pry myself out of her embrace, but she was too strong.

Her grip tightened, pinning my arms to my sides. Her tongue darted out, lapping at my pulse. "Fighting me will only heighten my desire to taste you."

I shivered in disgust, and a second, more horrifying realization slammed into me. She'd said Asher—the vampire who'd killed my brother and was after my nephew and me.

Asher had sent her. She was here to kill me.

My heart thundered in my chest. I frantically scanned the crowd for Link or Phoebe. The room was bathed in darkness past the first few rows, and one quick glance told me the spell hadn't broken for anyone else, only me.

I was truly on my own.

"I can feel your pulse quickening." The vamp let out a low growl. "I'd enjoy the hell out of this if it weren't for your dirty, tainted blood."

Dirty, tainted blood. She was referring to the Sunshine potion I drank as a precaution to keep vampires from using my blood as a meal. To them it tasted horrendous. Anger squashed the fear consuming me and my fight reflex kicked in. "Victoria," I said, my voice laced with steel. "Allcot will kill you for this."

Her laughter rang clear as a bell through the club as she tilted her head back. I gritted my teeth and rammed my elbow into her marbled gut and ineffectively stomped down on her instep. *Son of a…* that had to have hurt me infinitely worse than it did her. Adrenaline surged through my veins, and I flared my wings with such force she actually stumbled backward, freeing me from her clutches. Relief warred with my panic as I turned in midair, afraid that if I left, she'd attack an innocent bystander.

The crowd gasped, but no one seemed to realize our actions weren't part of the show. Or they didn't care.

Victoria righted herself and gave me an amused smile. As she prowled forward, her eyes sparkled with challenge. "Oh, good, a fighter. And here I was worried the audience might be bored."

"You're crazy," I said, spitting the words out. "Is that what this is all about? Putting on a show? Why does Asher want all these witnesses?"

"So naïve." She shook her head. "For the congregation, of course. How else is he going to gain his followers?"

My mouth dropped open in shock and I was unable to form words. Asher wanted to be the savior of humans, and with my death he was going to form a religion. It was genius. Humans would follow him unconditionally. It would be a full-on vamp–human war. And what better way than by starting with killing the faery who could turn vampires into daywalkers?

Shaking myself, I stared into the cold, uncaring eyes of the vamp. "You tell Asher to go fuck himself."

Then with one pump of my wings, I sailed upward, angling for the last place I'd seen Link. But before I could clear the stage, she leaped and her iron grip clasped around my ankle, pulling me back to her.

"You bitch," I cried, unable to free myself or keep control of my flight.

The pair of us crashed to the stage floor, rolling around like hysterical mud wrestlers, me trying to break her hold. It was by pure luck that she landed on one arm, preventing her from pinning me the second we toppled to the stage.

A moment of clarity seized me, and I knew without a doubt I'd never be able to just flee from her. She was too strong, too fast. There was only one thing that would keep me alive… if I survived it. Closing down my mind, I reached out, my fingers clawing at her throat.

She growled, bucking to try to roll me over, but I clamped my hand around her neck and squeezed, using my magic to suck her life force from her vampire body. Instantly my hand began to burn, but I swallowed the urge to recoil and forced myself to hold on.

"Get. Off. Me!"

Her entire body convulsed beneath my touch. I pulled harder on her vampire energy. Scalding fire burned through my veins, making my eyes water from the intensity of it. My head swam, and I knew I was moments from passing out. If I took too much, I'd only end up killing myself. Talisen's face suddenly swam in my vision. Deep sadness took up residence in my heart. If I didn't survive this, I'd die never knowing what had really happened between us. I'd never get a chance to yell at him. Or hug him. Or tell him I loved him.

Would he even care?

That thought nearly broke me. Of course he'd care. He'd probably hate himself for the way we'd left things between us. Just like I did for letting him walk out of my life without demanding answers.

It took me a moment to notice her body had gone completely still. And when a terrified cry erupted from the audience, I scrambled back on all fours, desperate to fade into the shadows. Holy shit. Had I really just done that in front of a room full of witnesses? The director was going to kill me. Not literally, most likely, but the notion wasn't outside of reality.

Purple Leotard grabbed me roughly by the shoulder and yanked me up. My feet dangled for just a moment until he dropped me. I was too stunned to remember to use my wings, and my ankle turned when my feet hit the ground, causing me to reach out and grab onto the emcee. He was cold as ice. Vampire cold.

My eyes widened as I gasped. Another one? I hadn't felt his energy either. Was my ability broken? In pure panic, I yanked on his energy, bracing for the hellfire to come.

Only it didn't. He wasn't a vampire at all. The sweet rush of faery energy cooled the raw destruction caused by my attack on Victoria. My body craved the relief, reveled in it as my fingers clutched tighter.

"No!" I cried, ripping my hands from him and flinging myself backward as he crumpled to the floor. Pain shot through my knee when it connected with the edge of the piano. Unable to catch myself, I crumpled to the ground, horror filling me, my body shaking with fear. *What had I done?* I'd stolen the energy of a fae, a rare skinwalker who could morph into any living… or undead… form he wanted to.

It was the worst kind of intrusion. Utterly unforgiveable. It didn't matter that I'd thought he was a vampire. I shouldn't have been doing that either. Not according to our unspoken laws, anyway. But I'd done it before and I'd do it again if I needed to protect myself.

The crowd was on its feet now, worry filling their expressions as a handful climbed the stage to help Victoria.

The fae lay next to me unconscious, his face pale. I crawled to him, tears streaming down my cheeks. If he died, I'd never forgive myself, would welcome the punishment the Arcane would shackle me with. Sprawled next to him, I placed my hand over his heart and closed my eyes, settling myself. After blocking out the noise of the club, I let my magic flow, pumping his energy and mine back into him.

My stomach turned and my head spun with the effort. But I wouldn't give in until I saw his chest rise and his eyes open.

His body heated under my hand, thawing the ice-cold shell he'd been cloaked in.

"Come on," I whispered, sweat now prickling my neck. "Wake up. I'm sorry. I didn't know."

There was chaos swirling around us, but I heard none of it. My entire focus was on this odd fae in his ridiculous purple leotard as I fought to save his life.

A rush of static filled my ears and a hollow pit took up residence in my chest. I was near the end. I couldn't keep going. Not if I wanted to survive. If I'd taken this fae's life, it was only right that I give mine for his. But if there was one thing I'd learned over the past year, it was that the will to live is a lot stronger than anyone's moral compass. Even mine.

I moved to yank my hand back, but the fae jerked and in the next instant, he had an iron grip around my wrist, keeping my hold on him. A gasp ripped from my throat as I tried in vain to recoil.

His green eyes blazed up at me, fire raging in his demented gaze. "You're not going anywhere, Willow Rhoswen."

"Let her go," Phoebe said from behind me, her tone low and dangerous.

The fae jumped to his feet, dragging me with him. "I don't think so."

"I'm so sorry," I cried. "I didn't know. I'd never do that to a fae. Never." I tried to reason with him. "You'd taken on a vampire form. I was only trying to defend myself. If I'd known—"

His face morphed into a dangerous scowl. "Shut up."

Well, that pissed me off.

"You're not going anywhere until you fix whatever the fuck you did to Victoria." His eyes cut to the unconscious vampire still sprawled on the floor.

Anger burned deep in my gut. He was working with her. I'd automatically assumed he'd been undercover or something. But no, this fae was my enemy. Suddenly I didn't feel so bad for draining him, even if the very idea still made me sick to my stomach. "Put me down. Now, fae. Or else I'm going to tell the witch to unleash everything she's got."

"I said to shut up," he growled, shaking me again. "I'm not afraid of you or your witch." His eyes unfocused and a second later, he morphed into the marbled form of a vampire once more.

"Idiot," Phoebe said. Raising her hand, she unleashed a blinding ray of sunlight at the fae and me. He crumpled to the ground, taking me with him.

Pain rocketed through my kneecaps as I slammed into the stage once more. His petrified hand was still clutching my neck, forcing me forward. "Son of a... dammit." Clutching at his fingers, I finally pried a few open far enough that I was able to slip from his grasp. Rubbing my neck, I glanced up at Phoebe, grateful she'd shown up when she had. "Thanks for that."

"Anytime. Now let's get the eff out of here before we're blindsided by any other surprises."

I scrambled to my feet. "What about Victoria?" She was a vamp. We couldn't leave her where she was. What if she woke up?

Phoebe aimed her agate at the vampire and flashed a ray of magic, ensuring Victoria would stay unconscious for hours. There was a loud gasp, followed by murmurs of confusion. The spectators milled about, asking each other what had happened. They were all disoriented. The spell had finally broken.

"Done," Phoebe said. "Now the cleanup crew can take care of her. Let's go before anyone from the Arcane sees you here. If they find out what just went down, you're in for another round of testing."

I shuddered. She was probably right. The fact that I couldn't sense Victoria and hadn't turned her would be very interesting to the director.

"Did you ever find the other vampire?" I asked as I followed her. There had been at least one more. The one I'd felt.

"He slipped out just as the show started. I got a picture, though. We'll find him in the Arcane's database." She shuffled me out of the side entrance, tapping away at her phone.

"Wait." I slipped loose of her hold. "I need to find Link." He was still in there. Before she could answer, I was through the door and skirting the edges of the club. I wasn't going to leave without my dog. The patrons were still wandering around, some leaving, some rubbernecking the scene on the stage.

I was halfway to our table when I stopped dead in my tracks as my gaze landed on David. My ex. The vampire I'd turned into a daywalker and the one I'd come to trust almost enough to consider dating again. But why was he leaning against the wall, his arms folded over his chest and ankles crossed as if he was a casual observer? Had he been there the entire time? And done nothing?

Our gazes met. For just a second, I saw alarm flash through those deep, sapphire-blue eyes. What was that about? Maybe he didn't want me caught up in any more Arcane business, either. He'd know they were on their way to clean up this mess.

David pushed away from the wall, heading straight toward me. My body tensed with undeniable attraction. I hadn't seen him in over a week. And whoa if he didn't look more gorgeous than ever. Tall, sculpted vampire build, dark hair, and bronzed skin from the sun. I wasn't supposed to be attracted to a vampire, let alone date one. Not as a fae. But I'd been flirting with the idea for weeks now. Ever since Talisen Kavanagh, my best friend and almost-boyfriend, had left me to go back to California. David wasn't perfect, but he'd been by my side the past few months, making sure I was safe and protected from the Arcane and other powerful entities who'd do whatever it took to get a piece of me. He'd made me feel safe, cared for.

"Wil…" He hesitated.

I frowned. He didn't seem worried. He seemed wary or even guilty. "What is it?"

He averted his gaze, focusing on nothing. Definitely guilty.

"David?" I asked, not entirely sure I wanted to know what was going on. It wasn't as if we were dating. So if he'd been with another woman, it really wasn't any of my business. The thought made me ill, though. "How long have you been standing there?" I tried to distract myself from the thoughts swirling in my head.

His expression went blank and his jaw worked for a moment, but he didn't actually speak.

"David?"

"I arrived just as you and Phoebe entered the club. I've been here the entire time." He glanced at the stage.

I took in his nervous body language, the way he was having trouble looking me in the eye, and then placed my hands on my hips. "I'm guessing by your behavior that you weren't spelled like the rest of the club?"

This time he did meet my penetrating gaze. "No."

I had to give credit where credit was due. At least he wasn't lying. Still, that didn't stop the bile from rising in my throat as my head started to pound with frustration. "So you just stood there and let that vamp attack me? The entire club was her puppet, including Link and Phoebe, and you left me to my own devices?"

"Wil," he said again, reaching out to take my hand.

I pulled it away and took a step back, my chest feeling like it was going to burst wide open from my thundering heart. "Just don't, David. I can't imagine what your excuse is for letting a vampire almost tear my neck open while you did absolutely nothing to stop it."

"I'm sorry." His eyes softened and his face took on a tortured look, the one he wore when he was being forced to do something he didn't want to.

And then I knew this had something to do with his father. Eadric Allcot went out of his way to protect my family and me, but he was also a cold bastard who would do whatever was necessary to remain the most powerful vampire in New Orleans. "What did he order you to do this time?"

David's lips formed a thin line as he took a deep breath. "You don't understand."

"I think I do. You stood there and watched Victoria try to destroy me without so much as moving a muscle. But I know you well enough to know that you'd never let that happen.

So I'm guessing you had orders to let her. And you followed them. Am I close?"

He ran a hand through his thick hair and blew out a long breath.

That action told me everything I needed to know. "Forget it." I turned my back to him.

"Wait," he said, clasping his grip over my wrist and twisting me to face him. It wasn't aggressive, but nonetheless, Link leaped out of nowhere, snarling and snapping at David.

"You'd better let go," I said evenly, acutely aware the only reason Link hadn't torn into him already was because David and I had history.

David glanced at my wolf briefly and then slowly pulled his hand away. "Sorry," he said to Link.

My wolf growled. I placed a light hand on his head, soothing him. Then I gave David a flat stare.

He closed his eyes for a moment, resigned to the fact that he was in deep shit.

I didn't wait for him to open his eyes again. I was too damned tired of waiting around for the men in my life to explain their actions. Instead, I turned silently on my heel and left the building, Link at my side.

Chapter 3

I'd known David would show up sooner or later. I just hadn't expected to see him a mere ten minutes after Phoebe and I walked through our front door.

He stood on the front porch of my Greek Revival home, trying to talk Phoebe into letting him inside. I mirrored the stance he'd taken in the club, my arms folded over my chest and feet crossed at the ankle as I leaned against the living room wall.

"You've lost your freakin' mind," Phoebe said without any heat. There was no love lost between the two, but she'd stopped actively hating him when he volunteered himself for the Arcane testing. They'd turned me into a lab rat, studying everything from how I changed vamps into daywalkers to what effect they had on me after the change. It had been unpleasant to say the least.

I was more than grateful he'd been with me. He'd stepped in when the testing went too far and had taken care of me on the nights I'd had trouble driving due to the pain. I'd come to rely on him again, and that's what made this whole situation that much more unbearable.

"We had to know what the vampire could do," I heard David say. "I swear to God, I was there, ready to engage had Victoria gone too far."

Phoebe snorted. "Really? You didn't think almost biting Willow wasn't too far? You didn't think that Willow having to drain Victoria in front of witnesses wasn't too far? You vamps have a fucked-up sense of what too far really means."

I couldn't see David, but I imagined him wincing at her words. He couldn't argue with her assessment. Allcot and his ilk did have a distorted view of reality. But the fact he'd said they had to know what Victoria could do meant they knew about her and had been watching her. What else did they know? "Phoebs, let him in," I said.

She glanced back at me, one perfectly shaped eyebrow raised in question. "You sure?"

I nodded. "He apparently has information. And I want it."

She pursed her lips. "Yeah, okay."

The door swung open as Phoebe stepped back. She waved a hand in my direction. "If it were up to me, I would've fed you a Truth Cluster first," she said to David, her lips curling into an evil smile. "Then I would've kicked you in the nuts just for good measure."

David stared at her, his face like stone.

I laughed but sobered as I turned to face my ex. "I swear, David, every time I start to think I can trust you and Allcot, something like this shit happens. Now, what do you know about Victoria? Is she the one who's been attacking the tourists? Is she the one Phoebe and I were after? Or is it the vamp who was there and then left?"

He stood in the middle of our living room, facing me, his shoulders stiff with tension. "Yes, it's Victoria. The vampire you sensed was one of ours. He was there as backup."

My stomach sank. They should have taken her out as soon as they knew. People had *died*. I moved to my couch and sank down into the soft cushions, rubbing one temple.

David sat in the chair across from me and leaned forward, his hands clasped between his knees.

I looked him straight in the eye, knowing my next question could change our relationship forever. I couldn't... no, wouldn't... associate with vampires who used humans as bait. Using me was bad enough. I at least had abilities that meant I had some chance at escape. But regular people? Not unless they were using Tal's new superhuman-strength elixir. And that was highly controlled by the Arcane. "How long have you been investigating her?"

"Four days."

"Fuck!" Phoebe kicked a pillow Link had pushed off the couch. "Two people have died since then!"

David swallowed.

I just stared at him, my mouth open, unable to really believe this was happening. The Cryrique vampires had allowed people to die in order to investigate another vampire.

"You don't understand," David said, his voice quiet.

"You're damn right." Phoebe paced, her hands shaking with anger. She turned to me. "Can I dust him now?"

I shrugged. "Might be tough with his daywalking abilities."

"I have other ways."

David stood. "Look. I know you're both upset. And I apologize, but there are bigger forces at work here that you're not aware of, and that is what I'm here to explain. The two people who died? They were volunteers. Cryrique employees who wanted to be turned. Eadric sent them and worked it out with the club owner that they would be the chosen victims. They were not innocent bystanders."

I blanched. "You let two of your own *die*?"

"No. Well, technically yes. They were turned after Victoria discarded them. They're in transition now."

Phoebe and I exchanged a glance. Turning humans into vampires wasn't illegal if they consented to it. But it was a dangerous activity and not everyone survived. At least they hadn't really died. At least not permanently. Still, I had pretty strong feelings about turning anyone. If I had my way, no one would ever be turned again. As a life faery, death went against everything I stood for. In my opinion, immortality was more of a curse than a gift. But it wasn't my decision to make, no matter how I felt about it.

"You're saying they both survived?" Phoebe asked.

"Yes." David let out a slow breath. "Look, Victoria and that fae have been wielding some sort of weird magic we've never seen before to spellbind people. Vampires appear to be immune to it, as well as humans who've taken Kavanagh's super drug. But no one else. Not fae and not witches. That was confirmed tonight."

"Okay. If vamps aren't affected, then why didn't your crew just take her down?"

"She has other witches under her spell," Phoebe said. "There were a dozen of them in the audience. If she'd asked them to fight the vamps, they would. Right to the death." She glanced at David. "Right?"

"Yes." He sounded tired and frustrated. "We needed to know if they were following her out of choice or compulsion."

"Compulsion for sure," Phoebe confirmed. "I knew a number of those witches. They were enamored with her just as I was before the spell broke. But they'd never in a million years sit by and let Victoria torture another without intervening. I wouldn't have."

I narrowed my eyes at David, seething. "You knew of the mist and let us just walk in there unprepared?"

His weary gaze met mine. "If you'd been prepared, you could've fought it off. We needed to know what we're dealing with. I never would've let anything happen to you. You have to know that."

I stared him down for a moment. Then I sighed, just as weary. I believed him. I just hated always feeling like I was being manipulated. "Yeah. I know."

"There's something else." Emotion swam in his brilliant blue eyes, turning them dark with pain. "Three of our human guards had an interaction with Victoria five days ago. The spell didn't work on them, so her fae shot them with some sort of poisonous dart. At first they had minor flu-like symptoms coupled with minor infections at the wound site. But now they're bedridden, paler than vampires, and almost too weak to even lift their heads."

My gut began to ache. "Which three?" I asked, afraid to hear his answer. If there was pain in his eyes, that meant someone he was close to was dying. And what he described meant they were all too weak to be turned.

He closed his eyes and took a deep breath. "Harrison and his team."

Phoebe let out a curse.

My heart ached. Harrison. He'd been my bodyguard and had turned into a friend of sorts. The thought of losing him left me gutted, not just for myself but for David as well.

I leaned forward. "The healers haven't been able to help at all?"

He shook his head. "Not permanently. The three we've had over had short-lived successes, but Harrison and the others aren't getting better. We need to find out what was used in that poison to create something to reverse the effects."

We all fell silent. If I had a sample, I might be able to work out the ingredients, but not an antidote. That was out of my wheelhouse. They'd need a skilled healer for that. I blew out a breath and asked David, "What else have you learned about Victoria?"

"We've been observing for four days, and so far the only thing we know is that her spell works on everyone except vampires. Even animals." He stared pointedly at Link.

Phoebe's head snapped up. "Wait. Vampires don't have magic. How could Victoria cast it?"

"The spell was cast by the emcee. He's fae," I said. "A rare shifter who can shift into any living being. Or in this case, undead being. He had to have put the spell on the club."

"A shifting fae?" David asked. "I've heard of them before, but always in sort of a mystical sense. Not as if any actually existed now."

"My brother was friends with one back in Eureka when we were growing up." I leaned back into the couch and patted the cushion for Link to join me. "Wolf shifters like Link here are more common. The original spell came from a fae shifter. Now, through breeding, there are hundreds of them. They're regulated so you don't see them everywhere, though."

"But you knew one?" David asked, his tone laced with a hint of accusation.

I stiffened and ignored his question, unwilling to let his attitude rattle me. "Fae shifters are very powerful and very private. You find them more often in heavily wooded areas. It makes it easier to shift into other animals. Most fae shifters don't like to shift into humans or other races. It holds no appeal. Or so Beau's friend said. Was the emcee with Victoria when the attack happened on Harrison and the others?"

David shrugged. "I don't know. Maybe. He's been with her at the club this entire time, so that makes sense." He whipped out his phone and sent a text. No doubt to Allcot.

His phone buzzed again and after David read the text, he scowled and leaped off the chair, already dialing. "I'll be right back," he said as he stalked out the front door.

Phoebe rolled her eyes. "Always with the secrecy. Fifty bucks says Allcot wants you to work on this."

I took a deep breath and slowly let it out. The odds were too high that she was right. "You know I can't afford to take that bet."

She smiled, but there wasn't any amusement in her expression. The realization that she was probably right must've hit her. The door swung open again and David stood in the threshold, staring at me with an odd expression. "Father wants you to go to Eureka and bring back Kavanagh."

I scoffed. "Well, he isn't likely to get what he wants, now, is he?"

"Kavanagh will come if you ask him." David's expression had turned to stone. He wasn't any happier about the request than I was.

"Have you two forgotten that Tal isn't talking to me? What makes you think I can convince him to come back here?" I wasn't going to be of any help in that regard. My chest constricted with the idea that I might see him again. If Allcot sent for him, he might come. Who was I kidding? Tal hated the vampires. Allcot had no sway with him. Tal probably wouldn't take his calls, either.

Phoebe swiveled her head back and forth between the two of us, her eyebrows raised in interest. "Well. This certainly makes things interesting, doesn't it?"

"Phoebs..." I gave her a pointed look.

"Sorry." She tucked her feet under her and waited for the fireworks to start.

"I'll come with you," David said.

That made Phoebe laugh.

I glared at her, then turned my steely gaze back to David. "Please. Talisen left because of you and your father. Besides, bringing a vampire to Eureka, it's... just no. The fae population would run you out of town before you could even get one word out. They're not tolerant."

David squared his shoulders and frowned. "I don't think you understand the seriousness of this. We've had every healer within a two-hundred-mile radius take a look at the crew. None of them can do anything for our guys. Harrison and the others will die. The Arcane is no longer cooperating, and Father says they've refused to let any of our vampires in to question Victoria. The emcee has disappeared. He either escaped while being transported to the Arcane or the Arcane is lying. Either is plausible. We're going on nothing here. There's no time to waste."

David's phone buzzed again. He read a text, frowned, and stuffed it back into his pocket. "Father wants your brother's shifting fae as well."

"What? I barely knew him!" I jumped up out of my chair.

"Why?" Phoebe asked David, her dark eyes narrowed.

"Because we need to understand this spell to make sure this never happens again," David answered. "That spell puts everyone at risk."

"You know each fae has their own gifts, right? There's no guarantee another fae will be able to cast the same spell."

David walked to the door. "It's all we have to go on right now." He turned and straightened to his full height, his eyes determined. "Father's jet will be ready at dawn. I'll meet you and Link at the airport. Don't be late."

Then he left without waiting for my answer.

"He's lying," Phoebe said.

"About which part?"

"Why they need the other fae. What he said might be part of the truth, but my bet is they are pissed as hell to find out a fae can shift into a vampire and they want to study him so they aren't caught off guard again."

I had to admit I agreed with her. I very much doubted I could find him anyway. But I did know where to find Tal. "Looks like I'm going home."

Both of her eyebrows disappeared under her dark bangs. "You don't have to, you know. You're not Allcot's beck-and-call girl."

I shook my head. "Of course I'm not. But we both know that if I don't go, he's likely to send David or one of his other vampires. And I'm not going to let that happen. Besides, I like Harrison. If I can help in any way, I will."

"I knew you were going to say that. You want me to go with you?"

"No, but thanks." I moved toward the stairs, heading toward my bedroom. "There's nothing to worry about back home." As I climbed the stairs I mumbled, "Except maybe my heart."

Chapter 4

Early the next morning, Link and I stood on the tarmac, waiting to board Allcot's Learjet. Allcot himself was there to see us off. He was dressed in a sleek, fitted-to-perfection silk suit, every bit the high-powered corporate mob boss disguised as a respectable CEO.

"The plane will land and wait for you at the Eureka airport." Allcot handed me a business card. "As soon as you have your friend and the fae shifter, call this number and the pilot will meet you to bring you home."

I fought to keep the grimace from claiming my face. Sparring with Allcot never worked in my favor. "Didn't David tell you I don't even really know that fae? He was my brother's friend, not mine. I have no idea if he still lives there. Besides, the chances are highly unlikely that he'll want to come to New Orleans to talk to vampires."

His stone features gave away nothing. "It is imperative we speak to the fae. If you do not bring him here, we will go to him."

Shit.

Of course he would. Dammit. If Hunter was still in the area, I'd have to figure out something. Even if I had to stretch the truth a bit. The last thing my community needed was an infiltration of vampires. That was a shit storm waiting to happen.

"I'll do what I can," I said as Link and I boarded.

"Check in with me each evening, Rhoswen."

As I climbed the stairs to the jet, I scowled. Despite the fact I'd saved Allcot's life a few months ago, we still hadn't formed a relationship based on mutual respect. He ordered me around and used threats to get his way. Serious, not-in-any-way-idle–type threats. He was a coldhearted bastard to everyone, even those he loved. And it bothered me that David put up with it. I glanced at Allcot over my shoulder. "I'll check in with David." At least with him, I knew he had a heart underneath all the obligation Allcot had saddled him with.

"Fine. And remember, time's running out." With that, he turned and slipped into the back of his black Town Car.

Link and I watched the car disappear behind one of the hangars.

"Are you sure you don't want me to come?" David said from the doorway. He'd boarded to talk to the pilot and to make sure we had food and drinks for the five-and-a-half-hour flight. Since vampires didn't need food, the plane was rarely stocked with the necessities the rest of us needed. "I could stay at a hotel and just be nearby if you need anything."

I suppressed a sigh. "No. It's not a good idea."

He stepped aside to let Link and me board.

Trying to calm my nerves, I took a seat facing the cockpit. Flying always drained me. It was the metal of the plane that depleted my energy. Once I landed and was near nature, I'd be fine, but after a few hours on the flight, I'd be weak and vulnerable. My body tensed with unease from the thought. Clutching the armrests, I glanced up at David. He was so handsome standing there with the sunlight washing over him. It always shook me to see him appearing human, the way he'd been when we'd been together. Before I'd been sucked into his crazy vampire world.

"I'll call you later tonight," I said quietly.

"Okay." He hesitated at the door.

Then he took two steps and pulled me out of the chair. His arms came around me, and for once I didn't lose my breath or find myself lost in his embrace. The coolness of his skin only served as another stark reminder that he'd always be a vampire, always be tied to Allcot. If I was with him, I could never take him home to California. Never have a family of my own. Never be a part of Talisen's life. Now that I was going home to see Tal, this thing, whatever it was David and I had been dancing around, seemed too much like a betrayal. As if I'd only proven Talisen right when he'd left. My stomach twisted into a ball of knots.

"Be careful," he whispered into my ear.

"I will." Out of habit, I hugged him back, but all I wanted was for him to go so we could get this show on the road. I hadn't seen Tal in over three months. Had barely even talked to him. And I had things to say.

Finally David let me go. With one last look, he exited the plane. A crew member shut the door and within a few minutes we were in the air. In less than six hours, I'd be back home. The thought comforted me as I petted Link's Shih Tzu head lying in my lap. My eyes closed, and I tried to push away all the turmoil crowding my brain.

But it was no use. What would Tal say when he saw me? Would he talk to me? Ignore me? Spit in my face? No, he wouldn't do that. But he just might shut me out, and I was certain I couldn't handle that. Sadness started to overwhelm me. We'd had something special. We'd been best friends, had almost become lovers. Then he'd left me and cut off all communication. Getting back to even being just friends seemed impossible.

Damn him! Why was I agonizing so much over this? He'd been the one to leave. The one to not answer my phone calls or keep in touch. He was being an idiot as far as I was concerned. He'd promised we'd never let anything damage our friendship. But he had. He'd let Allcot and his jealousy over David come between us. Sure, I wasn't totally blameless, but did that give him the right to just cut me off? I would've never done that to him.

All of the anger and hurt I'd been burying for the past three months rushed to the surface, and five hours later when the plane was circling the landing strip, I was seething. I was done feeling guilty. Tal was going to hear what I had to say whether he liked it or not.

I'd been so agitated when we'd landed that Link had shifted in the plane. I hadn't even bothered to tell him to shift back. If he wanted to wander around as a wolf, fine with me. There'd been a Jeep waiting for us. I'd requested it, knowing I'd have to go into the woods to look for Hunter. But first I made a stop at Mom's nursery.

The metal from the plane had done its worst on my energy levels, and the quickest way to recovery was to be surrounded by nature. Not to mention Mom had a couple of plants I could modify for an energy boost. I'd been too rushed before I left to stop by my shop for any of my own creations.

The lush ferns lining the porch of her shop made me smile. They were twice as big as they had been the last time I'd been there. Tal was taking good care of her plants while she spent time in New Orleans with Carrie and Beau Jr.

Nervousness skittered through me. What if Tal was inside? His truck wasn't in the parking lot, so chances were slim, but if he was, I wasn't quite ready to confront him yet. I needed to replenish.

The bell chimed as Link and I poked our heads in.

"Be with you in a moment," a woman called from the back. I recognized her voice instantly: Regan, the full-time shopkeeper Mom kept on staff. She was great at keeping the retail shop thriving, but the greenhouses needed something extra. Thus the reason Tal was helping out.

"Regan," I called.

"Willow?" She bustled out of the back room, her arms full of cut flowers. "Oh, wow. I didn't know you were coming. Your mom didn't tell me anything." The flowers floated to the counter as she thrust her wings and fluttered to my side, her arms open wide.

I laughed and hugged her. She was the sister I never had. "Last-minute trip. Mom doesn't even know I'm here yet. Better let me call to tell her or I'll be waist deep in manure."

She pulled back, holding me at arm's length. "You look exhausted. Let me get you some Mocha in Motion."

I let out a sigh of relief. I wouldn't have to expend any magic to recharge. "Oh, great. I didn't know if you'd have any."

She smiled. "Your mom has your shop ship it every couple of weeks."

Really? That was interesting. I'd had no idea. My assistant Tami handled all the mail-order items. Perhaps Mom had become a little addicted since she'd come to New Orleans.

After Regan supplied me with an iced Mocha in Motion, I headed outside to sit on a giant redwood limb. Mom had placed a set of wooden stairs at the base of it years ago so any human friend of ours wouldn't have to climb the trunk. Getting to the top was a breeze for fae. Males climbed and females flew. It was my favorite place in her gardens.

Rows and rows of herbs and other greens filled the grounds. They were surrounded by large greenhouses that grew anything that required more sunlight. Everything was lush and utterly inviting for a life faery such as myself.

The sea-scented air mixed with the pungent scent of the redwood tree, calming my nerves. Link, who'd shifted back to Shih Tzu form not long after we'd come outside, lay curled at the base of the tree, sleeping soundlessly. I'd have happily stayed right where I was for the rest of the day, but Harrison's face swam in my mind. It was time to get to work. Reluctantly, I climbed down and picked Link up, carrying him back into the shop.

"Awww," Regan cooed, petting Link's ear. "He's so adorable." Her voice went high pitched as she leaned in closer to him. "Aren't you, buddy? You're mama's little wolf. So, so cute. I just wanna take you home and snuggle you all night long."

Link lifted his head and let out a small growl.

I laughed. "He's not one for being babied."

She straightened and backed away. "I guess not."

"Don't worry. He's not going to shift or anything. He likes being petted. He's grumpy 'cause he just woke up."

"If you say so." But she eyed him like he was going to eat her hand.

Maybe he was. If someone talked to me like that, I'd be growly, too. "Is Talisen at the university today?"

She shrugged. "I don't really know. Ever since he got back from New Orleans, he hasn't been very talkative. He's very private all of a sudden. You can check."

Hmm. That was unsettling. Tal was outgoing and friendly to everyone. Did he resent taking care of Mom's shop now? Crap. I hated this. "Okay, thanks. I'm sure I'll find him."

"Good luck." She handed me another Mocha in Motion and waved as Link and I scooted back outside.

The weather had turned drizzly. Perfect. Just what I needed. Rain. My hair would be frizzy and unmanageable, making me look twelve. I sighed and tucked one of the long locks behind my ear.

Within minutes, Link and I were standing outside the science building where Tal had worked for the past five years. Yet again, I hadn't seen his truck in the parking lot, but that wasn't saying much for a school that had over seven thousand students. His truck could be anywhere.

Still carrying Link, I strode into the building and headed to Tal's lab. But when I got there, I found a fae I didn't know. She had long dark hair that was piled up in a haphazard bun, secured with a pencil. Her eyes were rimmed in tortoiseshell reading glasses and she wore a stark white lab coat. She should have been the ultimate nerd, but in reality, she was gorgeous. Librarian hot with perfectly shaped lips, flawless skin that didn't need a speck of makeup, and the greenest eyes I'd ever seen besides Tal's. Not to mention her perfect figure. Ample cleavage, shapely long legs, and curves that even her tentlike white lab coat couldn't hide. How utterly unfair.

"Can I help you?" She peered at me over her glasses.

"Yeah, hi. I'm looking for Talisen. Is he working today?"

She frowned. "And you would be?"

"Oh, sorry." I set Link down and strode to her, my hand outstretched. "I'm Willow Rhoswen, a close family friend. I just got in town and it's imperative that I speak with him."

She glanced at my hand, her annoyed expression pissing me off. Could she be any colder? She'd be the perfect match for Allcot—if she didn't have wings. Then she reluctantly shook my hand.

Gods, did I have cooties or something? A booger hanging out of my nose? Or maybe she had something with Tal and was jealous? The thought made my stomach turn.

"I'm sorry. I just find it hard to believe such a good friend wouldn't know Talisen doesn't work here anymore." Her piercing stare was full of judgment.

I pulled my hand from her tight grip. "What? Since when? I thought when he got back from New Orleans he went back to work here. Did something happen?" Had this ice queen taken his job? I hit Tal's number on my iPhone even though I knew he wouldn't answer. He hadn't for the past three months. There was no reason to suspect he would now. It went straight to voice mail like it always did. Damn him.

"He did. But he quit a few weeks later. And that's all I'm going to say. I'm sorry I can't help you further. Good day, Ms. Rhoswen." She glanced back at her report and continued to scribble notes as if I'd never entered her lab.

Good day? Who the hell did she think she was? The Queen of England? Well, who cared? All that mattered was that Tal wasn't here. I just prayed he was at home, otherwise I had no idea where to look for him.

"Thank you," I said to the faery. But she didn't even acknowledge I'd spoken. Whatever. "Let's go, Link."

Chapter 5

Tal's house was on the same street as my mother's. It was the same one he'd grown up in. When his parents had moved, he'd stayed and bought it from them. Since his house was only five doors down, I parked the Jeep in Mom's driveway and slipped into her house to try to tame my wild hair and freshen up before I faced him. He was there. Or at least there was a high chance he was since his red truck was parked in his driveway.

My pulse sped up. I hadn't seen him since he'd broken my heart. If I was honest with myself, it was still bruised. He'd always been the one person I'd counted on, and he'd left without even so much as a plausible explanation. Then, to make matters worse, he'd kept his distance. I'd lost more than a potential lover that day. I'd lost family. Again.

Seeing him at his house was going to be way worse than in public. It was too personal. Too easy to say all the things we probably shouldn't say. Too many memories. I paused outside Beau's old room for a moment but didn't go in. If I did, I'd be too raw to talk to anyone. Instead, I pressed my hand to the door and said, "Miss you, brother. What I wouldn't give to have a hug right now."

Tears welled in my eyes, but I blinked them back. There was no time for blubbering. Later, after I'd spoken to Tal, I'd let it all out.

After combing and smoothing my hair, I squared my shoulders and woman'd up. Time to face the music. Link trotted beside me, his tongue wagging in happy bliss. Link loved Tal and Tal loved him. At least that reunion should go well. Except Tal's truck was no longer parked in front of his house. I scanned the street and caught the taillights of his red truck as it turned left onto an adjoining street.

"Son of a bitch," I cried and ran to the Jeep. "Come on, Link. Let's figure out where the hell he's going."

The Jeep fired to life, and I tore down the street as fast as I safely could. Right turn, and then I had a decision to make. Left toward the freeway or right toward town? I went left, figuring if I didn't see him right away, I'd turn around and search the town.

"You see him?" I asked Link, who was staring out the window. My dog didn't even acknowledge I'd spoken. As far as he was concerned, we were just out for a joyride.

I pressed on the gas, quickly passed a large four-wheel-drive yellow truck, and then spotted Tal's small truck. He was turning to head south on Highway 101. "Found him."

This time Link turned to look at me, his eyes glowing gold.

"You can shift if you want to, but we might be in this Jeep for a while. I'm thinking you'll be a lot more comfy curled into that seat as a Shih Tzu, but it's your choice."

His eyes stopped glowing and turned to amber brown.

"Good boy." I scratched his neck. He arched into my hand and closed his eyes. I smiled at him. So easy to please… unlike the other men in my life.

Placing both hands on the wheel, I focused on following Tal. After driving for about thirty miles, my muscles started to tense. Where was he going? At fifty miles, sweat broke out on the back of my neck and an ache formed in my gut. We hadn't been this far down Highway 101 since the last day we'd all been together. Me, Beau, and Talisen.

My heart raced with ever-growing dread. Even driving by that exit was bound to shatter the small grasp I had on keeping my shit together.

"Please, Tal. Don't be going where I think you're going."

But then his blinker lit up and he took the exit just south of Garberville. My breath caught in my throat as I choked on uncontrollable tears. "Why!" I cried and jerked the wheel just as a giant black truck swerved into my lane.

The asshole had the nerve to lay into his horn and send a rude gesture as he cut off the person in the lane to the left of me.

Link growled and with a flash morphed into wolf form, his teeth bared. If only I was on the street with that asshat, I'd be tempted to let my wolf tear him down a notch or two. Good thing we were confined in the Jeep. I didn't need to get arrested or worry about Link being hauled off by animal control.

Taking deep breaths, I followed Talisen down the two-lane road that left no question as to where he was headed. I hit his name on my phone again. Instant voice mail. Dammit, dammit, dammit!

We turned right onto a dirt road, me a few hundred feet behind Tal. He had to know I was behind him by now. What was he doing here? The last time we'd been to Garberville was the last time we'd seen Beau alive.

The tears flowed freely as I pulled the Jeep to a stop behind Tal's truck. As soon as I did, his door flew open and he jumped out. His face was set into a scowl as he stalked toward me.

What was wrong with him? Was he so upset about me following him that he was going to chew me out here, in the field where Beau died? I pulled a tissue from my purse and wiped at my eyes, trying to regain my composure.

His lightly streaked hair was casually styled in wavy clumps and his jaw was stubbled with at least three days' growth. Combined with his low jeans and tight T-shirt, he looked more gorgeous than ever, though the fierce irritation blazing from his emerald-green eyes wasn't at all like the man I'd known most of my life. What was going on? Why the hell had he come here?

Talisen stopped dead in his tracks, his face turning ash white. He shook his head in confusion and then walked slowly up to the window, his gaze searing through mine.

I just sat there, my heart strumming wildly in my chest. Holy hell, I'd missed him. Missed his banter, his expressive eyes, the feel of my hand in his.

He reached up and tugged on the door handle. Slowly, the door opened. Neither of us said a word as our eyes met and held. Then he scowled at me.

Link yelped and flew over me to get to Tal. Still in wolf form, he landed with a hard thump at Tal's feet and jumped up, his paws hitting Tal's chest. He bounced like a puppy, his tail wagging, desperate for attention.

Tal's lips curved into a whisper of smile as he scratched behind Link's ears. Link whined uncontrollably and lapped at Tal's face. "Down, boy," Tal said mildly.

I had to swallow my outrage. What I wouldn't give to have Tal's easygoing manner directed at me. Instead, I got the evil glare and not even so much as a hello.

Link sat perfectly still at Tal's feet, staring at me with his head tilted as if wondering why I hadn't followed his lead and slobbered all over Tal in greeting. Right. After that incredibly warm welcome. Not.

"Willow," Tal said, scowling again. "What the hell are you doing here?"

I'd stopped crying, but I had no doubt my eyes were red and my cheeks tearstained. What a jerk. I jumped out of the Jeep and struck him in the chest with both hands, pushing him backward. "What am I doing here? Is that all you have to say to me after three months of silence? Seriously?"

My body started to shake with adrenaline. Being in this place and confronting Talisen, it was more than I could take. And to have him angry at me… it was infuriating.

Talisen took a step back, deliberately putting more space between us. "You need to leave right now."

I scanned the fields, indignation fueling my simmering rage. "Really? Are you going to make me? I came here because I need to talk to you. And what do I find? You coming here, of all places, and then you have the nerve to treat me like I did something wrong? What the hell is the matter with you?" I couldn't stop myself. He'd made me so upset I stepped forward and pushed him once again with both hands. Hard.

"Willow." He growled and grabbed both of my hands, forcing them down to my sides. Something close to sympathy or maybe regret flashed through his eyes as he stepped in close, invading my personal space. He stared down at me as he pushed me back toward the open door of the Jeep. "Get in the car and go back to your mother's house, right now. You should not be here."

"Don't tell me what to do," I spat out and yanked my wrists from his hold. Damn him for making friends with my dog. Any other person on the planet would've already had a chunk of flesh taken out of him for putting his hands on me. "You shouldn't be here either. You should be back at your lab… working. I'm not leaving until you tell me what exactly is going on with you."

He flinched lightly at my words but said nothing. He stared at me, a muscle pulsing in his jaw.

"So that's it, then? I followed you all the way down here to find out you're visiting the place Beau was *murdered* and you have nothing to say other than to tell me to leave? Real nice, Tal. Real nice."

"Willow—"

"Don't Willow me. Damn you, Tal! All of this because you think I have something with David?" I swallowed the guilt trying to choke me as the memory of David brushing his lips over mine a few weeks ago flashed in my mind. "You left me. You never even gave us a chance. And now you're here treating me like some pesky stalker. Well, I've got news for you—"

"Willow!" He bent his head and ran a jerky hand through his sandy-bond hair. "I'm meeting someone here." Then he reached for me as if he was going to nudge me back into the Jeep again, but his hand fell. "You need to leave. Go back to your mom's or my house. It's not…"

When he didn't finish his thought, I placed my hands on my hips and stood my ground. "Not what, Talisen? Safe?" I eyed Link. He lay on his side, his eyes closed as he breathed deeply. The wolf was utterly relaxed. "Looks like there isn't too much to be worried about. Unless you're meeting someone you don't want me to know about." Could that be it? Was he meeting another woman there? That seemed highly unlikely. Why would he bring someone to my mother's old lavender fields over an hour away? I shook my head. The thought was utterly ridiculous.

Talisen clamped his mouth shut and averted his gaze.

"Tal?" Confusion overtook my frustration. None of this made sense. His attitude, the fact that he was no longer working at the lab, him meeting someone where Beau died. "I think you better tell me what's going on."

He straightened. "Go home, Willow. I'll come by when I'm done here."

Blood rushed to my head, and I opened my mouth to tell him exactly where he could shove his *Go home, Willow*, but Link woke suddenly and jumped to his feet, his gaze fixated on something across the field. The hair stood up on the back of his neck as he moved to stand right in front of me.

"What is it, Link?" I asked in a hushed tone.

"Willow!" Tal said harshly. "Go. Now."

I ignored him. I wasn't leaving Tal there. Not with the way he was acting. All my pent-up anger fled, replaced by an absolute certainty that I couldn't leave him alone. Not in that field and not that night. "Forget it."

Link crept forward, his head down as he tracked his prey. I retrieved my stun gun from my purse and followed my wolf.

Talisen grabbed my arm lightly.

I yanked myself free and didn't even look back. Steeling myself against all the painful memories trying to consume my every thought, I forced myself to head into the growing darkness. Wherever Link went, I was going. Maybe it was stupid, but I wouldn't leave Link any more than I would leave Tal. They both were entirely too important to me.

"Shit!" Tal said from behind me. It was the only indication he'd followed. Fae moved silently when they wanted to. It was from years of walking the forests. Soon enough he caught up to me. "You don't know what you're getting into."

"You're right." I cast him a sidelong glance. "But I have a feeling you don't either."

He gave me a humorless laugh. "Too late for me, gorgeous." His tone was filled with sad irony. But all the anger in his expression had fled, replaced by defeated resignation.

A dart of pain shuddered through me. What was going on with him?

He glanced at me as a small sigh escaped his lips, and then he reached out and grabbed my hand, his fingers tightening around mine.

My first instinct was to pull back, but his familiar touch comforted me in a way that no one else's could. I was still angry at his reaction to seeing me there, but I couldn't bear to separate from him either.

We walked in silence until Link let out a low growl and leaped forward. A flash of magic lit up the field, stopping Link in his tracks. He yelped and collapsed onto his side, whimpering.

"Link!" I ran to him, placing a light hand on his large head.

"You shouldn't have brought her here, Kavanagh," an impatient voice called from above us.

I leaped to my feet. "What did you do to Link?" I demanded, my thumb hovering over the trigger of my stun gun.

A tall, dark-haired vampire dropped from a limb, his pale skin glowing in the twilight. My gut tightened as I sucked in a sharp breath. But something was off. I hadn't sensed him at all either. Another spell? Was it possible? I backed up, but as I studied him, my eyes widened. He wasn't a vampire at all. He was my brother's friend, the fae shifter. "Hunter?"

He stared at me. "You're going to want to drop that Taser."

I clutched the stun gun harder and took a step forward. "And why is that?"

"Wil." Talisen reached out for me, but I sidestepped him.

I glanced between the two of them. "Someone needs to start talking and fast."

Hunter stared at me, his face expressionless. Then after a moment, he gave a tiny nod.

"No, dammit!" Tal shouted and lunged behind me, but it was too late.

An ice-cold hand wrapped around my forearm and twisted. Electric fire from my own stun gun shot through me just before my world turned black.

Chapter 6

A vibration combined with the rhythmic sound of thump, thump, thump clouded my consciousness as I came back to myself. I rolled and hissed when pain shot through my shoulder from the bounce of my body weight. "Ouch."

"Willow, wake up," an urgent voice coaxed. "Hurry."

I blinked in the darkness, trying to orient myself. From the rumble of an engine and the rocky motion, it was clear we were in some sort of moving vehicle. A van maybe? I was lying on the floor, my face pressed into synthetic carpet. "Who are you?" I forced out, my throat dry as I tried to fight the panic that was taking over.

"Hunter. You've got to wake up."

Two cold hands gripped my shoulders and pulled me into an upright position. His viselike grip indicated vampire. Shit! My fight reflex kicked in and my entire body tensed as I flailed, unsuccessfully trying to jerk back. "Let go!"

My heart pounded in my throat and my wings flared uncontrollably.

"Willow, it's me Hunter," he said again. "Calm down. We have to get you out of here."

I stilled and peered at him, taking in his dark hair and stunning green eyes. He reminded me of a panther. Then his words penetrated and I finally made sense of what he'd said. He was my brother's fae shifting friend, Hunter. Why then had he shifted into a vampire?

Was he working with one like the fae in the club? But if he was, he didn't seem intent on hurting me. He'd just said he had to get me out of there, hadn't he? Taking deep breaths, I glanced around, noting we were locked in the back of a van that was closed off from the driver. It was a security van with restraints bolted to the walls. If the restraints weren't for me, who were they for? Bile rose in the back of my throat as I imagined humans strapped into the van, being transported to a vamp blood bank. Or worse. "What do you want from me?"

He shook his head. "Nothing. You weren't supposed to be there tonight and now we only have a few minutes before it's too late to get you out of here."

My arms and legs were trembling. "Where are Link and Tal?" My heart ached. The last time I'd seen Link, he'd been crumpled on the ground, unmoving. Was he okay?

"Talisen is going to pick you up. He has your wolf. Now get over here and drain me so it will look like you attacked me and escaped on your own."

"What!" I glanced at the front of the van and yelped as we flew over a bump in the road.

"No time!" He scooted forward. "I'm working undercover and if you don't do as I say, I'll be compromised. So will Talisen. I can't have them finding out who I am. So drain me just as you would a vampire. Just enough that I pass out. Then when the van stops get yourself out." He pressed a key into my palm. "That will open the back."

I stared at it for a second and then the door, registering that it didn't have a handle. Holy crackers. This van was what nightmares were made of. There was no doubt in my mind another vampire was driving. What was Talisen mixed up in? And why was Hunter involved? The questions raced through my fuzzy mind. Whatever spell I'd been hit with, I still wasn't one hundred percent.

He placed my hand on his chest. "Do it!" His tone was urgent, demanding. "If you don't, they're going to kill you."

Those words sent the fear of the goddess through me. The very real possibility that my life might be ending took away all my reservations at draining the life energy of another fae. I had to in order to survive.

The van started to slow and I knew if I didn't act then, my chance would be over. Steeling myself, I moved my hand to his shoulder, unwilling to pull his life force directly from his chest, and then felt the sweet sensation of fae energy fill me. It made me euphoric. His essence was so pure. I almost craved it, especially after the time in the airplane and after being hit with my own stun gun. But as I reveled in Hunter's fae energy, my stomach turned with nausea. What I was doing was wrong.

Against our laws. Against my own moral code.

My hand started to slip from his shoulder, but he clasped his over mine, forcing me to maintain contact. "More!" he demanded. "Don't stop until I'm unconscious."

I hated what I was doing to him, wanted to use the key he'd given me to free us both. But if he was so adamant about making it look like I'd attacked him, then he wasn't willing to blow his cover yet. I couldn't mess with whatever investigation he was involved with. As far as I knew, it was a Void mission. Not that I'd ever heard of Hunter working for the Void. But then I wouldn't, would I? Not unless we were on the same operational team.

After I gave one last tug on his essence, my body vibrated with his life energy, and Hunter slumped backward against the side of the van, his stonelike vampire body hitting with a loud thump. Tears stung my eyes, but there was nothing I could do for him at that moment. I pressed my palm to his heart. The strong flutter of life pulled a sigh of relief from my parted lips. He'd be fine after he slept for a while.

Eyeing the restraints, I made a snap decision. It would look a thousand times less suspicious if he was bound when the driver of the van found him. Without hesitation, I clasped the manacles over his wrists as the van came to a full stop.

I wasted no time unlocking the door. Pausing, I stretched my wings and waited. When the van started to move again, I leaped into the night, my wings carrying me high above the van.

I watched as the door swung back and forth and then finally clicked closed with a soft thump. Hopefully the driver hadn't noticed anything. Either way, I wasn't waiting around to find out. I darted off the two-lane highway and into a grove of trees, then paused under the canopy of leaves, scanning the area for Talisen. Hunter had said he'd come for me. But waiting around on the side of the highway didn't seem like the best plan. Instead, I fluttered from tree to tree, keeping an eye on the road for Tal's red truck. The sky had turned even darker and it was all but impossible to differentiate the vehicles.

I kept going, but after a while, my heart started to sink. He was nowhere. Did he think I was still in the van? Had he been hurt? What about Link? Hunter's energy started to wear off and suddenly I was exhausted. I needed to recharge. After scanning the nearby trees, I chose one of the taller ones with a view of the highway and settled on a high limb, resting against the trunk.

The cool relief of the tree tingled over my skin and cloaked me in nature. Physically, I felt better. Mentally, I was all over the place. Where were Link and Tal? Where the hell was I? I didn't even know how to get back to my rental car. I stared up at the foggy sky. I couldn't see the stars, not that I could read them anyway.

Afraid to close my eyes, I kept my gaze trained on the ever-thinning traffic. The vehicles trickled down to one every few minutes.

My heart sank. Tal wasn't coming.

"Willow?"

I jumped and slipped off my limb, my wings fluttering double time to keep me from falling on my head. Righting myself, I fluttered to the ground, landing in front of Talisen and Link.

"Where have you been?" I cried, kneeling in front of Link to check him over. His wolf's coat gleamed under the sliver of moonlight shining through the fog.

"He's fine," Tal said in a tired voice. "Once the spell wore off, he was disoriented but not harmed in any way."

Link pressed against my side and licked my hand. I double-checked to be sure he wasn't wounded by running my hands over his body. He was perfectly fine. In fact, he looked to be in better shape than Tal did.

I stood and eyed my oldest friend. But before I could speak, he took the final step to close the distance between us and engulfed me in an all-consuming hug.

"Thank the gods you're all right," he said softly against my neck.

He was holding on so tight I could barely breathe. But I didn't care. His arms felt right. Perfect. Safe. I mirrored his embrace and inhaled his faint redwood scent.

"You owe me an explanation," I said without heat.

He loosened his grip. "I'm so sorry, Wil," he murmured and then pulled back, cupping my cheeks with his hands.

My heart stuttered. I had a feeling he was apologizing for more than the kidnapping.

"I don't know what I'd do if anything happened to you." His words came out on a whisper, desperate, filled with agony.

My insides churned with elation. He did love me. No matter what he'd done three months ago, he still loved me. I could see it in the softness swimming in his eyes. But then my pleasure at knowing exactly what I meant to him dimmed as rage-tinged frustration took over, and I couldn't keep the question locked away any longer. "If I mean so much to you, why did you leave me?"

Good Goddess. Did I really just ask that? There were so many other important things we should've been talking about right at that moment. Asking why he left me was trivial and downright selfish. I hated myself the moment the words left my lips.

Talisen flinched but didn't let go. He swallowed, visibly trying to decide what to say. Shaking his head, he ran his thumb over my cheekbone. "There's much to explain, but not right now." Leaning in, he pressed a soft kiss to my forehead. "Trust me. Please."

I couldn't remember a time I'd seen him this serious or vulnerable. At our last meeting in New Orleans, he'd been full of sadness and anger. Both versions of him were a far cry from the easygoing, happy Talisen I'd known my entire life.

The forest started to close in on me. I should've been at ease, being so close to nature. But all I wanted to do was flee. It was because Talisen was stripping me bare with his penetrating stare. The one that said he was looking straight into my soul. That he knew how much he'd hurt me and that I hadn't recovered, no matter how much I'd told myself I had.

I stepped back and crossed my arms over my chest, digging my fingernails into my forearms. "Can we go now?" I wanted nothing more than to be curled up in Mom's plant-filled study, preferably with a hot cup of tea, while Tal explained what the heck he and Hunter were involved with.

He nodded. "We need to get moving anyway." Clasping his hand around mine, he tugged me deeper into the forest. Link stayed close to me, his body rubbing lightly against my leg as we walked.

Soon my feet were aching from stumbling over roots hidden by the shadows. I fluttered my wings and flew beside Tal, who seemed to know exactly where he was going. "Where's your truck?"

"Back at the lavender fields." He pushed aside an overgrown branch, holding it out of my way as I passed.

"You walked the entire way?"

He shook his head. "No. I caught a ride with… well, someone I trust. She dropped me off a few miles from here."

She. Someone he trusted. A flicker of pain darted into my heart. Had he found someone? I clenched my teeth and forced the idiotic thought from my head. There I was, worrying about another woman, when Tal and I didn't even have a relationship. When Harrison was fighting for his life and I'd almost been killed. What was wrong with me? "Is your… uh… friend picking us up?"

He glanced at me in confusion.

I stared at the ground, embarrassed that my tone had betrayed my insecurity.

"No," he said finally. "We're headed to a safe house a few miles from here."

"What?" I stopped midflutter and dropped lightly to the ground. "But I need to get back. We need to—"

Talisen held up a hand. "Listen to me. Your life is in danger. The only reason you're alive right now is because of Hunter. If anyone else had been sent to that meeting tonight, it's likely both of us would be dead now. Or worse. The vampires know what you can do. They've known since Asher fled New Orleans."

"They? As in who exactly?" And what did he mean by worse?

"Asher's followers and some of his dissenters. They're all after you. Some to end you, some to use you. Coming to Eureka was a mistake. You should've stayed in New Orleans with Allcot." He spit the words out in barely controlled anger.

"I didn't have a choice!" Damn him for making me feel like this was all my fault.

"You always have a choice, Willow. It's your choices that got us here."

Oh, that did it. The self-righteousness written all over his face made me want to smack him. "What exactly are you saying, Tal? That it was my choice to inherit Beau's abilities? That is was my choice to throw my lot in with Allcot and David? That it was my choice for Beau Jr. to be in danger? That it was my freaking choice to be bound to the Void?"

His eyes narrowed as he studied me. "No. I didn't say that."

"You didn't have to. It's what you implied. And you know as well as I do that I wanted none of those things. I didn't ask for David to step into my life. I didn't ask to be part of the Void. I wanted nothing to do with Cryrique." My tone had risen with each declaration. Then I lowered my voice and said, "Do you know what I did want?"

He sucked in a breath and gave me a slight shake of his head.

"A life free of a thousand reminders of Beau. A shop where I could work and make my magical treats that made people happy. A chance to feel useful during a time when all I wanted to do was go to sleep and never wake up. And even though I got those things, I also got a whole host of crap that came with it. The Void and David and Allcot manipulating me. But then you were there and for some stupid-ass reason, I thought everything would be okay because we'd work through it together. But then you just left. The one person I trusted more than anyone, the only one who really understood how I felt about Beau, and you did it by cutting off all communication."

I stared into his stunned expression and remembered to breathe.

"And now I'm here because you couldn't even be bothered to answer your goddamned phone. So you can take your self-righteous bullshit and shove it. Got it?"

Talisen grimaced and his expression shifted from one of apprehension to regret. He stuffed his hands in his front pockets and hunched his shoulders forward. "You're right. I was an ass. I should've called you. But before you tar and feather me, I want you to know there's a good reason for my actions."

I curled my hands into fists and waited. "Well?"

He glanced around and then shook his head. "Not here. I promise I'll explain everything when we get to the safe house."

I blew out a breath, my patience having run out. "Fine. But this had better be one hell of an excuse."

Chapter 7

We trekked a good four to five miles through the trees and high into the foothills before we stopped at a modest deserted cabin. Debris covered the wood piled up on the side of the house and the heavy layer of dirt on the porch was undisturbed. No one had been there in weeks.

My feet ached, and I shifted from foot to foot, dying to sit down. I eyed the large three-car garage, hoping there was something that would get us to the airport. Harrison was waiting.

Talisen led us around the back. Reaching up, he ran his hand along the sloped eaves until he found what he was looking for. A second later, he unlocked the back door and replaced the key where he'd found it.

Link entered first, his nose to the ground. He circled the small room once, then curled up on a bearskin in front of the stone fireplace. That was enough for me. I strode in, pulled a sheet off a loveseat, and sat on the lumpy surface. I was so tired from the day's events I curled in on myself and closed my eyes.

But as soon as I heard Talisen shut the door, I straightened and stared up into his guarded expression. I hated that look. Hated that he was hiding himself from me. Sighing, I stood and glanced around, hoping there were keys to whatever vehicle was hidden in the garage hanging in an obvious place. "As much as I want to sit here and rest, we really need to get on the road."

"We just got here." He sat on the thick wood coffee table and started unlacing his boots.

I glanced out the window at the garage. "The longer we stay here, the worse off Harrison and the others will be."

He jerked his head up and pierced me with a stare. "What are you talking about? What's wrong with Harrison?"

Oh, right. So much had happened, I'd never gotten the opportunity to tell him why I'd come in the first place. "Allcot's security team was poisoned by a fae recently. The ones who are on your superhuman drug. Harrison was one of them. None of the local healers have been able to help them. Allcot thinks you can. I'm here to take you back to New Orleans before it's too late."

I moved to the open-concept kitchen at the back of the cabin and started searching the drawers for any sign of a key.

Talisen followed me and stood in front of the porcelain sink. He leaned against the counter, bracing himself on his hands. He was silent as he watched me.

"Did you hear what I said?" I slammed one drawer closed and yanked another one open. "Whatever's happening here, whatever you've gotten yourself into, it's going to have to wait. People need you. Now help me find the keys to the garage and whatever possible vehicle might be stored in there."

He pushed off the counter and walked over to me. Gently he closed his hands over mine, stilling my search. "You're not going to find any keys. The garage is full of outdoor equipment. In the summer this place is a recreation retreat for outdoor enthusiasts. It's what makes it a great safe house in the off-season."

I blinked. "What?"

"I'm trying to tell you that unless we walk back to the highway, we're stuck here for the night. Hunter will make sure someone picks us up in the morning."

Glancing out at the pitch-black night, I groaned. Hunter's team would be looking for me and it was getting bitterly cold. The chances of making it back to my Jeep without freezing or getting caught were too slim. It was better if we stayed were we were. They'd be hard pressed to find our trail. Tal had taken to the trees and I'd flown with Link in my arms. No way were they going to track us easily.

"Damn," I said softly and pulled away from Tal. Rubbing my temple, I moved back to the lumpy loveseat and folded myself into the corner. I knew we were far enough in the woods that cell service was unlikely, but I pulled my phone out anyway. No bars. No Internet. Just the soft glow of light. Shoving my phone back into my pocket, I glanced over at Tal. "I don't suppose there's a phone here?"

He shook his head.

Allcot hadn't said I had to get Talisen on the plane that very day, but I knew if I didn't get in touch soon, he'd send David to find out what was going on. My shoulders tensed. I couldn't let that happen.

Talisen rummaged through the cupboards until he found some energy bars and bottled water. With his hands full, he sat on the sofa to my left, twisting to face me.

I accepted the makeshift dinner with a nod and tore into the granola snack. The cardboard taste stuck in the back of my throat. Gross. After downing half the water, I got up and poured the rest into a bowl for Link. He was fast asleep, but I wanted to be sure it was there when he woke.

"Willow?" Talisen called.

"Yeah?" Weariness claimed my body, and I fought to keep from swaying with exhaustion.

He patted the couch cushion to his right. "Would you mind sitting with me while we talk?"

I couldn't deny the longing claiming my heart. I wanted to sit next to him. To feel his arm casually draped over my shoulders as we talked about anything and everything. But it was too much. Too personal, considering everything still lying between us. Instead, I moved back to the loveseat and sat on the end farthest from him.

He pressed his lips together in a firm line but didn't comment.

"I think it's time you started explaining just exactly what's going on." I held his gaze, unwilling to look away.

Nodding slowly, he leaned forward, his elbows resting on

his knees. "Before I start, I want you to know it was never my intention to cut you out of my life."

I raised my eyebrows as if to say *really?*

He ran a hand through his short hair. "I admit that at first, I needed some time. What happened between us, it… well, I didn't deal with it well."

I couldn't argue with him there.

"And knowing that Laveaux will always have a piece of your heart was too much for me to deal with. I'm not proud of that. You're a person made up of many parts, like the rest of us. I guess I just always thought of you as mine. As messed up as that sounds, it's the truth. I wasn't prepared to share you."

"Share me? What the hell, Tal? You make me sound like a sandwich or something. And news flash, love doesn't mean you own a person." His words only intensified my anger and frustration at the way he'd handled things. For the love of the goddess. He'd thought of me as his? As if he'd owned me? I pressed back into the corner of the loveseat, trying to put even more distance between us.

He shook his head. "I know. That's not what I meant. Look…" He glanced away for a moment, took in a deep breath, and met my gaze again. "I've known for a long time that you had feelings for me. Beau told me one night at the beach. He also told me that if I ever hurt you, he'd rip my heart out. And he wasn't kidding either."

"He told you!" I gasped, outraged my brother would do such a thing. Especially since I'd never told him my feelings for Tal. Though he had known me better than anyone else, even better than I knew myself most of the time.

Tal shrugged. "He was looking out for you. The thing is, ever since then, I had this image of the two of us ending up together. But then Beau died and the pain we were both going through meant you were the only person who got me. I was too scared I'd mess up any romantic relationship, and I kept it friendly so I wouldn't lose you. I meant it when I said no matter what happened between us, I'd always be here for you. Always." His voice was full of such conviction that it felt like he was making an oath right then. "And that's still true. I just needed time to work through what I was feeling after I came home."

"Three freakin' months?" I said, digging my fingers into the cushions to curb the sudden desire to strike him.

He shook his head. "No. More like a week. But by then I was already knee-deep into my contract with the Void."

Silence hung between us as I digested what he'd said. I stood on my tired feet and stared down at him. "The Void?"

That muscle in his jaw pulsed again. "Yeah."

"Why?" My chest tightened. After everything the Void had put me through, I didn't want Tal to have anything to do with them. Why had he signed their contract?

"I didn't have a choice, Wil." He rose, standing a head taller than me. "It was either that or serve time for supplying the drug to Allcot."

My breath came out in a whoosh, leaving my insides hollow. I was suddenly freezing in the small cabin, and I wrapped my arms around myself. *It's my fault.* The words played over and over in my head. Tal had come to New Orleans for me. To help me. And he'd been forced to give his superhuman drug to Allcot in order to keep me safe. He'd done it all for me, and now he was trapped working for the shadow agency of the Arcane. I'd learned some of the directors were as corrupt as Allcot himself. But the newest one I still didn't know. No one ever knew. When dealing with the Void, the best one could hope for was that good was winning over evil. "How long?"

Our eyes met again. He knew exactly what I meant. How long until his contract was up? "Five years."

Tears burned my eyes. He had never wanted anything to do with the government agency. All he'd ever wanted was to work in his lab doing research on his healing solutions and elixirs. Now he'd be exploited for his superhuman drug and would have no say in how they used it. The possibilities for abuse were endless. "All because of me."

"No, Willow. Not because of you. I'm the one who made the elixir. I'm the one who gave it to Allcot. I knew I was crossing lines. Knew there'd be consequences. I did it anyway."

"Because of me," I said again.

He reached up and pushed the hair from my eyes. "Would you have done it for me? Given Allcot your creations if it meant keeping me safe?"

There was no debate. He already knew the answer. "You know I would've."

"What makes you think I'd do anything different?" His piercing green eyes seemed to see straight into my soul.

I closed my eyes, trying to cut off the connection we were rebuilding. It had always been there and always would be. But it was making me entirely too uncomfortable because even though we were finally talking, there was still a barrier between us. "That doesn't explain why you cut off contact with me, Tal. The Void doesn't dictate who you can talk to."

"They do in this case." He took a swig of water and sat once again on the couch. "Sit with me?" he asked again.

This time I didn't resist. My skin was still tingling from where he'd brushed my hair back. That small gesture had broken down at least one barrier. Still, when I lowered myself to the couch, I bent my knees, pulled my legs up, and wrapped my arms around them to use as some sort of shield.

Tal smiled at me and shook his head as he ran a light hand down my calf. He stopped at my ankle, and ever so gently, he proceeded to strip my shoes off my tired feet. "Just relax, Wil."

Combined with his soothing voice and the spark of his healing hands, I didn't have any trouble doing as he asked. My eyelids became heavy and the tension seemed to drain from my shoulders as he worked his magic. Literally. He was a healer and just his touch was enough to soothe my aches and pains.

I watched him for a moment and when I couldn't stand not knowing any longer, I asked, "Why wouldn't the Void let you call me, Tal?"

He frowned and all the tension that had drained from me seemed to pour right into him. The set of his jaw, his rigid posture, the rhythm of his elevated breathing. "I'm working undercover."

"Okay." That was normal. Phoebe did that all the time.

"With Hunter."

The words hung in the air as he let me work out exactly what that meant. I filtered through everything I'd learned that night. I'd followed Tal to my mother's old lavender fields, the place where Beau had died. We'd run into Hunter, a fae shifter who'd transformed himself into a vampire. He was working undercover as well. Had infiltrated a group of vampires. Ones that wanted to kill me. I let out a small gasp and peered at Tal. "No," I said on a whisper.

Regret filled his beautiful green eyes as he gave me a small nod.

My head swam. It couldn't be possible.

Then Tal took my hand once more and pressed his lips to my palm. "I'd do anything for you. You know that, right?"

"But not this. You can't," I said quietly, unwilling to accept what he was trying to tell me.

He covered my hand with both of his. "I already have. You see the reason I couldn't call you, couldn't tell you, is because my end had to be real. They have to believe I want nothing to do with you. That I'm so angry that you chose Laveaux over me that I'll do anything to get revenge."

"I didn't—" I started, needing to deny his claim that I'd chosen David. I most certainly hadn't.

Tal cut me off. "I know, Willow. But I need them to think that's what happened. It's my reason for turning on you. I needed to be the scorned fae who'd been roped into working with Allcot."

I sat stunned, staring at my hands. *Please, no. Don't let any of this be true. It was too awful.*

"Wil?" Talisen used two fingers to lift my chin. "You know I didn't have a choice, right?"

I nodded, still mute.

"Then you also need to know that now that I'm on the inside, I'm going to take the organization down." His eyes narrowed with intensity. "And I won't stop until Asher is dead."

Chapter 8

A chill ran deep in my bones. Talisen had infiltrated Asher's inner circle. Asher: the daywalking vampire who thought vampires held too much power over humans and that his kind was evil. He'd killed Beau and come after me in an effort to make sure no other vampires were turned into daywalkers. Now Talisen was determined to take him down.

I was both proud and terrified at the same time. "It's too dangerous," I said, leaning in to place my hand on his cheek.

"Everything is dangerous for me now. You know what that's like better than anyone."

I did. My life had turned into something greater than myself. I'd been contracted by the Void, used by Allcot, and ruled by my heart when it came to protecting Beau Jr. I'd willingly teamed up with Allcot because I'd known he would keep my nephew safe. I was only useful in that I could turn vamps into daywalkers and that I could make Orange Influence, the chocolate treat that could control someone's actions. That was a lot of power to wield. And even though I'd so far resisted being forced to make Orange Influence for Allcot, I had turned some of his vamps.

Stale revulsion ate away at my stomach. I'd done it as part of the Void testing and those memories always made me want to vomit. The only reason I'd endured was because David had been there taking care of me. All while Talisen had been infiltrating Asher's inner circle. "Tell me everything," I said with conviction. "How did you get hooked up with them and what exactly are you expected to do?"

Tal leaned back into the couch, his legs stretched out in front of him. It wasn't lost on me that since telling me his secret, he was much more settled. As if everything would be better now that I knew.

I wasn't so sure about that, but if he'd been keeping all this to himself the past three months, he was probably more than ready to talk it out.

"Hunter. He's been a Void agent since right after Beau died four years ago. He's been working on the inside of this particular group for over three years. Three years he's spent in vampire form." Talisen visibly shuddered. "Can you imagine?"

I shook my head and wrapped my arms around myself, trying to stop the shiver from his words.

"But he's finally gained their trust," Tal continued. "So when he suggested bringing me in as someone who knows you well, they went for it on his word. It's obvious most of them don't trust me, but then I'd be shocked if they did."

Unease was circling in my gut. "How did Hunter prove himself?" I asked, too afraid to ask the same question of Talisen.

He shook his head. "You don't want to know, Wil. You really don't."

"Talisen. Tell me," I demanded. "If you expect me to trust him, I need to know how far he's willing to go."

"Shit." He glanced at the ceiling but then met my stare head on. "He brings them, uh, Void resources and feeds them information about Allcot's corporation."

"Void resources? What does that mean exactly?" Normally I wouldn't give a second thought about Allcot, but now I was worried. He had Beau Jr. in his care. Did they know that, too?

"Some of the drugs they use on other vampires to control them. A spell here and there. He walks a fine line between feeding them things and info they can use versus anything too sensitive."

I knew the drill. Phoebe was my partner and roommate, for God's sake. I'd seen her give up information when she was going after a bigger threat numerous times. But none of the stuff she'd given out had been about me. I was too close to this and was having trouble separating my personal and professional feelings. Maybe Hunter didn't even know about Beau Jr. But Tal did.

"And what about you?" I asked hesitantly. I wasn't at all sure I wanted the answer, but I had to ask anyway. "What do you give them?"

He grimaced. "Mostly stuff that's readily available to anyone who cares to look hard enough. Info on your shop, what you make, your contract with the Void. That sort of thing."

I got up and paced. He was holding something back. I could tell by the way he kept averting his gaze. "Doesn't seem like they'd bring you into their inner circle just for that."

He shrugged. "I don't tell them anything they couldn't find on their own." Then he narrowed his eyes. "Or are you thinking I told them about your nephew?"

I bit my lip.

"God, Willow. You can't be serious."

I threw my hands in the air. "Of course I didn't think you did. But I won't lie and say it didn't cross my mind. I can't help it. Three months ago, I wouldn't have even considered it. But three months ago you didn't work for the Void and were never more than a phone call away. Now… Everything's different. I'm still trying to catch up." I sat back, exhausted, and blinked away tears. The day had taken too much out of me. Learning about Harrison, coming to Eureka, being kidnapped, and hearing all this stuff I never would've thought Tal would be involved with—it all overwhelmed me. And all I wanted to do was bury my head under a pillow until we could leave in the morning.

"Link," I said as I stood.

He jumped up, his fur matted flat against one side of his face. I laughed. Doggie bed head. "Let's go out."

Talisen jumped up and shoved his feet in his boots. "Let me take him. It's cold out. Not to mention, if Asher's minions have found this place and have started watching it, I don't want you to be spotted."

"But spotting you and Link is okay?" My tone was skeptical.

"No. Not okay exactly, but I can talk my way out of that scenario. If you're spotted, it's over."

I nodded and watched as my two favorite men disappeared out the front door. A stinging chill whipped through the cabin, settling into my bones. It was early spring and normal for the temperature to drop several degrees at night. With no hope of lighting a fire, I rummaged around the cabin searching for blankets. In the one and only closet, I found an old quilt and a cotton thermal blanket. Neither were enough for one person. I closed my eyes and sighed. We were going to need body heat if either of us wanted to get any sleep.

An odd mix of excitement and nervousness made my stomach do backflips. The thought of being wrapped in Tal's arms all night made me ache for his embrace. But this wasn't the way I wanted it to happen. Out of necessity. Not to mention, I hadn't forgiven him for leaving me in the first place. Maybe it wouldn't get that cold.

Goddess, I hoped not.

I pulled the Murphy bed down from the far wall and made it up with the pillows and blankets I'd found in the closet. Then I stood there staring at the bed, my heart fluttering out of control.

The door banged open on a gust of wind. Link bounded in, shaking aggressively. White flakes of snow splattered around him.

"Damn," I muttered. Snow in the area was rare, but not unheard of.

"It's coming down pretty hard," Talisen said, brushing the flakes off his head.

I stood there, stupidly staring at his flushed face and the moisture clinging to his dark blond hair. He was so handsome, rugged with his stubble, and athletic. So alive. Nothing like the vampires I'd been hanging out with. David had a tan now, but he was too perfect. Too sculpted. Not... real. Talisen was a hot-blooded male from head to toe, and I wanted nothing more than to be wrapped in his embrace.

When I didn't speak, his eyes shifted to the Murphy bed. I watched him, fingering the hem of my sweater.

He let out an audible breath as he blinked a few times. Then his face and body relaxed. He turned to me, transformed into the easygoing Talisen I'd known my entire life. "Right or left?"

"Huh?" My throat was dry and the question came out as more of a croak.

Talisen's smile widened, and I swear I saw a sparkle of mischief in his emerald eyes. He jerked his head toward the bed. "Which side do you prefer?"

The fact that he didn't even know seemed so unreal to me. We'd been together for such a short time we hadn't even learned the most basic things about each other. At least basic intimate things. Though he did know exactly how to touch me to make me shiver. A tingle ran up my spine at the thought.

Stop that! The last thing I needed was unrealistic fantasies. Tonight definitely was the worst time to be picking at that thread. "The right," I finally said when the silence became too deafening.

He chuckled and moved to the left side, kicking his shoes off as he went. "Come on, Wil. Lighten up. It's not like we've never shared a bed before."

I scoffed. Yeah, but the last time he'd held me all night, making me feel safe and loved, had been a few days before he'd left. I didn't know if I could handle being so close to him with the mile-wide gulf still between us.

His smile vanished. "Willow?"

"Yeah?" I jerked my head up, startled out of my thoughts.

Slowly he walked over to me, holding a hand out.

I didn't move to take it.

"It's okay. I promise. I'll be a perfect gentleman. We both know that without a heat source we're going to need each other in order to keep warm tonight."

I stepped back. "I have Link."

He gave me a wry smile. "True enough." The smile vanished as his eyes turned serious. "I guess I deserve that. Maybe if Link takes the middle of the bed, that will be enough."

Disappointment claimed that deep place in my heart, the place that had been hopeful and overjoyed with an excuse to have Tal's arms around me. I cleared my throat. "Yeah. That sounds like a good idea."

No. It didn't. And I would still be cold. Tal's healing energy had the ability to warm a person from the inside out. But I sure as hell wasn't going to admit I wanted that sort of intimacy from him. Not tonight. Maybe not ever. My heart was too bruised. Too confused. I understood what he'd said about the Void and needing to maintain his distance. But he never should've left the way he did.

After brushing my teeth at the kitchen sink, using a new toothbrush I'd found in a box of supplies, I crawled into my side of the bed. With one pat of my hand, Link jumped onto the bed and over me to settle in the middle. I curled into his back and draped one arm over his lean wolf body. He twisted his head and licked the side of my face in contentment.

"Love you too, Link buddy." I adjusted my head on the pillow and closed my eyes. My breathing turned to a steady rhythm of a peaceful sleeper, but I was one hundred percent alert. Tal still hadn't come to bed. I heard him shuffling around the cabin but was too stubborn to open my eyes to see what he was doing.

And just when I thought he'd never join us, the mattress dipped with his weight. I felt him shift closer to Link and was hit with a wave of his light redwood scent. My eyes fluttered open reflexively.

He was sitting up, his shirt discarded as he stared down at me.

I swallowed, my mouth dry at his perfectly sculpted chest. He'd been working out. And oh damn, it wasn't fair. Not fair at all. Closing my eyes to rid my mind of his naked torso, I licked my lips and asked, "Something wrong?"

"The temperature is dropping."

"So get in under the covers. It's cozy in here," I lied. Cold was seeping in through the blankets. Link kept my right hand

and my chest warm, but the rest of me was complaining loudly. Damn early spring storms.

"You can keep lying if you want to, but I can see you shivering from here."

Crap on toast. Of course he could.

"Well, what would you prefer, for me to lie to myself or bitch about it?"

"Neither." He reached over and tugged the blankets up, brushing his fingers over my chin. As much as I wanted to ignore it, I couldn't. His touch sent a bolt of sweet warmth straight to my very toes.

"If you let me hold you, I can make sure you stay warm and comfortable." His expression was soft, the question clear in his gaze. Did I trust him enough? Or would I prefer to suffer rather than be forced to endure a night in his arms?

The longer the silence dragged on, the cloudier his expression got. But he never said a word. He wasn't that kind of fae. Always helpful, always stoic. He'd do anything he needed to in order to help. And he'd do it without complaint. *But that didn't mean he'd be around the next time I needed him.*

Tal slid under the covers next to Link. When he was finally comfortable, he glanced over at me. "I got the message. Really. But the offer stands. If you want me, I'm yours."

Chapter 9

If you want me, I'm yours. His words hung in the air, taunting me. When had I ever not wanted him? I lay stiff and unmoving. If I relaxed for even a moment, I might throw myself at him. Thank goodness Link was between us.

He'd stayed in wolf form. Even though only Tal and I were in the cabin, the two people he trusted most, he knew there was something more going on, that danger still lurked in the woods. But I was much more worried about what was—or wasn't—going on in the cabin. I had the covers tucked around me, and Link was providing a little bit of heat to my left side, but he was on top of the blankets, his body heat escaping into the cold room.

I turned onto my side, pressing my back to him and curling into myself. But as the minutes ticked by, I started to shiver. Link jerked his head up and placed his long snout on my shoulder. It was a comforting gesture but did nothing to warm me. My blood was too thin from living in New Orleans for so long. When my teeth started to chatter, I heard Talisen let out a long breath, but he just lay on his side of the bed… waiting.

Dammit. This was ridiculous. The wind was now whistling through the cabin. I rolled over and sat up, bringing the covers with me. "Over here, Link." I patted the right side of the bed. He moved without hesitation, and I scooted over and slid back down in the bed.

Talisen still hadn't moved. He was staring at the ceiling, not acknowledging me.

"Does the offer still stand?" I asked quietly. I knew I was being stupid and overdramatic. I could trust Tal. I just didn't know if my heart could stand being so close to him. To be touched by him.

Without looking at me, he wrapped his arm around my waist and pulled me to him. The chill in my bones thawed the moment he engulfed me into his embrace. I placed my head on his chest, my entire body relaxing against his.

"You can trust me, Wil," he whispered as one hand trailed through my hair.

"I do," I forced out as a hot tear slipped down my temple.

"Then what's the problem?" His hand moved to the base of my neck and down my spine, making me want to flare my wings in pleasure. But I kept them tucked to my back, warm under the covers.

I took a moment to just breathe, trying to get my emotions under control. He was so warm, so solid beneath me. Everything about him was familiar and comforting. The way I felt in his arms was like coming home in a way that I hadn't experienced even when I'd visited Mom's shop or her house. He was everything to me in a way David would never be. It was all clear in that moment. I wanted him. Wanted to be with him and only him. But I couldn't lose who I was to do it.

"You're afraid of something," he said into the darkness. "And I don't mean Asher or his followers. You're afraid of me."

My body tensed, but I didn't pull away from him. I couldn't. I was too weak. Wanted him too much. Finally, I sighed into his chest. "Not you," I said by way of explanation. But it was no explanation at all. Physically I knew I was safe. But emotionally I was a wreck, and in my heart of hearts, I knew it wasn't all his fault. I shared the blame just as much, if not more.

I'd had a lot of time to think about why he'd left, and I had to admit that if the situation had been reversed, I wouldn't have handled things well. If he'd put himself in danger to help a vamp who was in love with him, I'd have lost my mind. He'd had every right to be angry at me. Could I really blame him for leaving such a messed-up situation? No. But most of the resentment had been tied up in him cutting off contact. Now that I knew why, I had a hard time being angry at him.

No, the fear was coming from deep inside me, from knowing that if I gave myself over to him again and our relationship didn't work out, I'd never be the same. All I wanted right in that moment was to have Talisen back in my life. To be able to lean on him, to talk to him, to be in his inner circle. But getting romantic, as much as I wanted to lift my head and kiss him until everything else was a distant memory, was not an option. I needed my friend. I couldn't risk losing him again.

I hugged Tal and shook my head. "I could never be afraid of you," I reassured him as another tear rolled down my face. "You're my best friend."

His body relaxed beneath mine as his arms tightened around me. Letting out a soft breath, he kissed the top of my head, prolonging the motion in a tender display of relief. "Always. No matter what."

I hiccupped on a sob, unable to calm the emotions claiming me.

"Jeez, Wil. I'm so damned sorry. I should've never left you in the dark."

"No, you shouldn't have."

"Never again." He brought his right hand up and tilted my face so our gazes met. "I promise."

The sincerity in his gaze nearly broke me again, but I sucked in a breath and gave him a small nod, knowing I should promise something in return. But I wasn't sure what. I couldn't promise to stay away from vampires or that I wouldn't put myself in danger, because I would. I'd do whatever it took to protect my nephew. Even if it meant fighting for Allcot.

"Can you do something for me?" he asked.

My heart stilled. There was a time I'd have said yes to anything. But now... there were some promises I couldn't make. "What?"

He closed his eyes and curled his fingers in my hair. "It doesn't matter."

That ache was back in my chest. We'd always been able to talk to each other. This new, strained dynamic was exactly what I'd feared would come to pass. I pressed against his chest and rose up to meet his gaze. "It matters to me."

He brushed his fingertips over my cheek ever so lightly and nodded. "I know, Wil. Let's just sleep. Okay?"

Reluctantly, I nodded. He'd tell me what was on his mind when he was ready. I hoped so, anyway.

The wind was still whistling between the cracks of the modest cabin, but in Tal's arms, I was warm and safe for the time being. Before long, my lids became heavy with sleep and my breathing evened out. I was in that world halfway between consciousness and sleep when I felt Tal shift slightly. His hand wrapped around mine pressed to his heart and then, just barely audible, I heard his deep voice whisper, "Don't give up on us. I won't survive it."

My eyes flew open, but I didn't move a muscle. My breathing hitched momentarily before I made a conscious effort to keep it steady. I was certain he hadn't meant for me to hear him. My heart started to race. He had to know I was awake. But he didn't say anything further as his chest rose and fell in an increasingly steady pattern until I was sure he'd gone to sleep himself.

As comfortable as I was draped over Tal and snuggled on the other side by Link, it took me a long time to finally slip into the welcome void of sleep.

I was startled awake by a vicious growl.

"Link?" I called as I sat straight up in bed. Talisen was already moving toward the door, crossbow in hand. Where had that come from?

"Shh." Talisen pressed against the wall and peered through the slit of the curtains.

I swung my legs over the bed and wrapped the blanket around my shoulders as I stuffed my feet into my athletic shoes. Link stood on guard at the door, the hair on his back standing straight up. A shuffling noise sounded from outside and he growled again, this time jumping up on the door.

"Down, Link," Talisen ordered.

Link did as he was told, but his teeth were bared, ready to attack.

Tal glanced at me. "Get in the closet."

I eyed the small walk-in just off the kitchen and contemplated refusing but decided to do as I was told. Talisen had been right the night before. He could talk his way out of a search party, but if they saw me, all bets were off. Clenching my jaw, I slipped into the tiny utility closet and shut the door.

"Open up, Kavanagh," an angry voice bellowed through the door.

Link's growls grew more insistent.

"Relax, Macinson," Tal said easily. "It's just me and the wolf."

Peering through the crack in the door, I watched as Tal pulled the door open, revealing a man who was clearly a vampire. His features were entirely too chiseled, too perfect, to be human. Only I couldn't feel him. What was wrong with my vamp detector? What was different about this one? Another Fae? No. If he was undercover wouldn't he be working with Tal?

"What are you doing here?" The tall vampire was dressed in black thermal snow pants and a matching jacket. A ski hat was pulled down over his ink-black hair and he carried a tranq gun.

"Waiting out the storm." Tal glanced at Link. "I'd invite you in, but the wolf isn't friendly. Better if you stay outside."

Macinson flattened his hand on the partially open door and pushed, but stopped when Link crept forward. He took two steps back, giving Link the space he demanded. "Where the fuck is she?"

Tal raised one eyebrow. "Who?"

"You know damned well who. The fae. *Your friend.*"

Tal leaned his forearm against the door and swung the crossbow over his shoulder. His brows pitched together as he gave the other man a confused look. "She's with Hunter. Didn't you see her when they got back to the compound last night?"

Macinson let out a hollow laugh. "The bitch attacked him. Escaped before they ever made it up the mountain."

Tal's eyebrows shot straight up in the perfect imitation of shock. "Attacked him? Willow? You're kidding, right? But how could she overpower a vampire? That seems unlikely."

Macinson scoffed. "You're so naïve. Didn't you learn anything about her when you were banging her last winter?"

I scowled. Banging me? Had Tal been telling everyone that's how he knew me? If anyone did any research at all, they'd know we'd grown up together. Why the messed-up lie?

"Seems like you could've spent a little more time investigating her abilities and a little less time fu—"

"That's enough," Tal barked in anger. "I was there to get information on the Cryrique. Not Willow. Besides, I've known her for forever and am well aware of her abilities already."

"Idiot," Macinson said under his breath. "Well, she nearly killed Hunter. If it hadn't been for that human we stumbled upon, he'd have slipped into an unrecoverable coma. That bitch has powerful magic. Too bad you were too stupid to unravel it. Maybe then you'd be able to do more than just watch the dog."

Tal's eyes narrowed. "Human?"

Macinson shrugged. "Hunter needed blood. What's one human life compared to the war?"

Acid burned on the back of my tongue. They'd fed a human to Hunter? Had he really killed someone in order to avoid suspicion? Had he really needed human blood to recover? My knees went weak, and I clutched the shelving, hanging on for all I was worth.

If that was true, was it sanctioned by the Void? My hands went numb from clutching the nearby shelves. I had to get away from them, and I'd do whatever it took to take Tal with me.

Talisen was quiet while he seemed to gather his thoughts and compose himself. Finally he said, "As long as we didn't lose one of the team. Casualties happen."

Vomit threatened to choke me. He didn't mean it. He couldn't. But he was standing there acting as if nothing was wrong. I took a deep breath. *Calm down, Willow.* What else was he supposed to do? Blow his cover? He was only doing his job.

But it was hard to watch. I don't know why. I'd watched Phoebe bullshit her way through all kinds of scenarios, and I'd never once doubter her. Why couldn't I extend Talisen the same courtesy? Maybe because I'd never seen him play this role before. Or maybe I was still punishing him for leaving.

I hated that about myself. But there it was.

"What happened? Why did you end up here?" Macinson asked.

Tal jerked his head toward Link. "After her dog woke up, he took off. Looking for her, no doubt. I had to track him down before he became a nuisance. Once I finally did, it had already started to snow. I holed up waiting for the storm to pass."

So plausible. I never knew he was that good a liar.

Macinson eyed Link. "He's useful, then. Hand him over so we can track the girl."

Link snarled, saliva dripping from his muzzle.

"I don't think so," Tal said sympathetically. "He doesn't play nice with vampires. You'll spend more time fighting him off than you will getting him to search for his mistress."

Link inched forward, his eyes narrowed, growling low and deep.

Macinson glared at Link, then pulled a gun from the small of his back and aimed it at my wolf.

My heart nearly stopped right there in my chest. And just as I was pushing the pantry door open, Link lunged.

The loud echo of gunfire filled my ears and all I saw was red.

Chapter 10

"Link," I screamed and tore across the room toward his unmoving body. Tears blinded me, and while a small voice deep in the back of my mind told me I'd only made things worse by exposing myself, I didn't care in the least. Link, my little buddy, was hurt and the vampire on the other side of the door was the one who'd have to pay.

"Shit!" I heard Talisen bark.

"She was here the entire time?" the vampire cried and lunged for Talisen. "You fucking spy!"

A whirl of color bypassed me as I fell to my knees near Link's unmoving body. The pool of blood was coming from his hindquarters. His big amber eyes latched onto mine and suddenly he was on his feet again, going after the vampire who had his hand wrapped around Talisen's neck.

I didn't stop to think. Unadulterated rage overtook me, and before I knew what I was doing, I had Tal's discarded crossbow in my hands.

Link latched onto the vampire's leg at the same time I leveled the weapon at his chest. Only the vamp twisted, shielding himself with Talisen before I could get a shot off.

Macinson kicked out with tremendous force, dislodging my wounded dog. Blood dripped into a small pool near Link's back feet. But he was alive. The pressure eased slightly off my chest. That is until I saw Talisen's reddening face. He needed air. Soon.

"Let Talisen go," I said with deadly calm.

The vamp froze but didn't relax his grip. "Why should I do that? He's a fucking traitor. I always knew we couldn't trust him."

Talisen gasped for breath, clawing at the vampire's hand.

"If you don't, I'm going to drive this stake right into your unfeeling heart. Then while you're incapacitated, I'm going to let Link rip your limbs off while you watch." I almost couldn't believe the words were coming from my lips. My scenario was so crude. I knew I'd never follow through with such an act. I'd end his existence swiftly, but he didn't need to know that.

"Pain doesn't scare me, faery," he said, his eyes going completely black.

"It should." And then instead of firing the crossbow, I struck out and clasped my hand on his shoulder. The instant burn brought tears to my eyes as it rushed into my veins and seized my insides like fire ants at a picnic. He was definitely a vampire. Every instinct begged me to let go of the vamp, but I couldn't. Not while he had a hold on Talisen. Instead, I gritted my teeth and yanked on his toxic vampire energy, pulling until it flowed freely from him to me.

My energy fled fast. Faster than it had every other time I'd used that particular gift. And after only a few seconds, my hand slipped. I fell to my knees, gasping.

He jerked, rounding on me.

The crossbow had fallen to the side, just out of reach. But I didn't have the energy to pick it up, much less aim and fire.

He grabbed my hair and yanked my head back. Bending down, he scraped his teeth along my neck. My skin crawled as the fire scalded my flesh. I did my best to jerk away, but his hold was too strong.

"If Asher hadn't decreed you were to not be killed, I'd drain you right here and now." His tone was low, seductive, as if he were talking to a lover.

"Then it's good being Asher's favorite, isn't it?" I seethed, wishing more than anything that I'd had the nerve to just shoot his ass. But Tal had been right there and the chances of hitting him had been too great.

I heard Link clamber to his feet and let out another snarl.

"Call him off," the vamp whispered into my neck, pressing one of his sharp fangs against my vein.

I sucked in a breath. "My blood is toxic."

He laughed, his low chuckle reverberating off my neck. "The sunshine potion? That shit's nothing to me. Can drink it for breakfast, lunch, and dinner as long as the fae is ripe enough. And you, my dear, are a fucking treasure. One I'd like to— Ouff!"

His body slumped to the side, a crossbow bolt sticking out of his back. Talisen stood over us, his neck already turning purple and his eyes wild. "Tend to Link," he said quietly and then kicked Macinson until he was several feet away from me.

I didn't hesitate. I scrambled over to Link, who was already standing. The blood had stopped seeping from his hindquarter, but he wasn't putting any weight on his back right leg. Carefully I ran my hand over his thigh, applying slight pressure until he whimpered.

"I know, buddy. Just trying to find the wound." I glanced over at Tal, who already had the vampire trussed up with metal cable. The vamp was immobile, indicating the bolt was stuck in his heart. Score one for Talisen. My chest swelled with pride and gratitude for my best friend. I turned to Link. "Hold on, buddy. I'll be right back."

Staggering to my feet, I hauled myself over to the kitchen and opened the cabinet stocked with an overabundance of first aid supplies. I pulled out gauze, iodine, and medical tape. I eyed the suture kit but prayed we wouldn't need it. First I needed to see the wound. After filling a bowl with water, I grabbed a clean towel and the medical supplies and then hurried back to Link. He was still standing where I'd left him, waiting.

"It's okay now, Link. I'm gonna fix you up."

Talisen would've been the better choice for healing Link, but he was too busy interrogating the vampire. He couldn't move, but he could talk… if he wanted to. So far, Talisen was the only one saying anything.

I wetted the towel and carefully went to work on Link's wound. He stood stoically, letting me administer my care. It took a while to clean all the blood away, but after I did, I found the wound was a quarter-inch graze that ran about five inches along his hindquarter. No wonder there had been so much blood.

At least he wouldn't need stitches. "I'm so sorry, boy, but this is going to hurt a bit. Just relax now. That's it." I soothed him as I opened the iodine bottle. This was going to suck, but in order to avoid infection, it had to be done. I ran a soft hand down his back and leaned in to kiss his neck. "I'm sorry."

Then I poured the iodine over his angry wound. He stood perfectly still and howled his anguish. Right then and there I regretted not killing the vampire when I had the chance. If I'd pulled enough of his energy, he'd be snail food already. "So sorry," I whispered to Link again as I smeared a topical painkiller on the wound. When I was finished, Link nuzzled me with his nose and licked my cheek once.

"You're welcome," I said, relieved he'd only suffered a surface wound. He'd be okay after a few days' rest. Except we were out in the middle of the woods and the only way to get out of there was a five-mile trek. Shit. "Tal?" I called.

He was standing over Macinson, his face contemplative as if he was trying to figure out what to do next. "Yeah," he said without looking up.

"Can you take a look at Link? He can walk on three legs, but I'd rather he be fully functional if we're going to run into any more of these assholes today."

He finally turned and met my gaze. "Of course."

Nodding, I went to work on cleaning up the medical supplies and then stood over Macinson, seething. "How many of you are there?"

His cold eyes glared at me.

"Daywalkers are rare. Who turned you?"

His lips turned up in a sinister smile, but he didn't answer.

Anger flared to life, but I shoved it down. Now was not the time to lose my cool. Whoever the fae was that turned him, Macinson was damned happy I didn't have the information. And he'd use that to his advantage for as long as possible. The one thing I knew that he didn't, however, was that I didn't need the information that badly. There were other ways to get answers. "Gonna use that as a bargaining chip, huh? Well, good luck with that." I stepped back and folded my arms over my chest.

"It's eating you up inside. I can see it in those pathetic blue eyes of yours, cupcake."

I almost laughed at his choice of nickname. No doubt he already knew I owned The Fated Cupcake back in New Orleans. "You're deluded."

"Maybe." He gave me a tiny bob of his head. "But I have the answers you both need." His words came out short as if he was low on air. But vamps didn't need to breathe. It was the bolt lodged in his heart.

My fingers twitched, and I had to grip my forearms to keep from lashing out at him. He'd play this game all day. Maybe just to keep us busy until reinforcements arrived. "You think you can last all day, vampire?"

He gave me a flat stare.

"Ahh, so I'm right. There are no other daywalkers coming to rescue you, are there?"

"Why would I tell you that? I'm not a fucking idiot."

"Yes, you are," Tal said from behind me, his voice full of rage. "Not only five minutes ago, you talked about Hunter coming for you. Well, I've got news for you, you sick fuck. Hunter is a fae and he's never coming to help you. No one is."

Then Talisen leaped forward, grabbed the bolt, and twisted. The vamp's lips formed an O as his expression turned to one of pure shock. There weren't any traces of pain or agony. Just shock. And as I stood there, unable to comprehend what was happening, his face started to disintegrate right before my eyes. His skin decomposed into tiny granules of sand just before his body combusted into complete dust.

"Oh my God," I breathed into my shaking hand.

"You okay?" Talisen pulled my hand away from my mouth gently and kissed my palm before tucking it into his.

"I don't... know." Staring up at him in awe, the tears gathered and there was nothing I could do to stop them.

"Hey, hey. It's okay now," he said, wrapping me once again in his arms.

"I know," I said into his shirt. "It's just... just that you and Link almost died." The last word came out in a whisper as the full weight of what had almost happened bore down on me.

"We're okay." He kissed my forehead and then glanced down at Link, who was now sitting at our feet.

I nodded, blinking back my tears of relief. My fingers were rough on my skin as I wiped the remaining tears away. The only thing left of our ordeal was the metal bolt and a pile of sand. I stared at it, finally registering the barb on the end of the bolt. Metal bolts normally couldn't kill vamps, just incapacitate them. Holes in the heart healed quickly, but hearts shredded beyond repair couldn't. Tal had literally ripped the vamp's heart to shreds when he'd twisted the large bolt.

I shuddered, remembering the look of shock on his face. He hadn't seen it coming. It made me wonder what exactly he'd thought we were going to do with him. "Tal, what did you say to him while I was tending Link?"

"That his only hope of survival was if he gave up Asher's location. He steadfastly refused, as I knew he would."

"And that's why you dusted him before we had a chance to question him on other important things." Like who the other fae was who'd changed Asher's small army into daywalkers.

"No." Tal narrowed his eyes at me. "I dusted him because he was fucking with you. And he'd have kept it up until the next round of searchers found us. He was never going to give you any information. You know that. The best soldiers never do."

"You knew him well." I rested my hands on my hips and waited for the ensuing explanation.

"You could say that. I knew him before he turned vamp, back in high school. He went to a rival school. He was a cocky son of a bitch then too. Believe me, Wil. He wasn't going to give us anything. Besides, he didn't really believe we'd dust him."

"You don't think so?"

Tal shook his head. "I know so. Now let's get going before any more of Asher's goons show up."

I glanced down at Link. "How is he? Will he be okay?"

"Better than okay." Tal filled a backpack full of snack bars. "Good as new."

Link trotted across the room to stand next to Tal, staring up at him adoringly.

"You fixed him."

Tal nodded and handed me a small tranq gun he'd found in the supply cabinet.

I stuffed the gun into the back of my jeans and then closed the distance between us and hugged him with the remaining strength I had. After the plane ride and the attack on Hunter the day before, my energy was already depleted. The vamp drain had left me swaying on my feet.

"Wil, you're exhausted," Tal said after touching me. His magic meant he could sense the well-being of any living creature. And with me, he'd always been extra sensitive. To say he'd been watching over me for more than a decade wasn't an exaggeration.

I shrugged. "It was the vampire attack. I'll recover."

"I could help."

I pulled back and gazed up at him, noticing the indecision. He'd helped Link without consent, but for the first time ever, he wouldn't take it upon himself to infuse me with some of his fae magic. I could see how much he wanted me to ask him to do it. And I wanted to, but I shook my head and stepped back anyway. It wasn't that I didn't trust him. I did. It had to do with me and how much I was already depending on Tal just to survive. If I was going to battle vampires, I needed to learn how to survive after I unleashed my magic on them.

"Thank you, but no. I need to deal with this."

He stiffened and then his gaze hardened as he pulled the door open. "Then let's go. We have a long day ahead of us."

Chapter 11

Link trotted by my side through the thick blanket of snow. With the appearance of Macinson, Tal had said it was too dangerous to wait for Hunter to send someone. Asher's crew would be looking for him soon and we couldn't be anywhere near the cabin.

Talisen was well ahead of us under the guise of scouting the area. It wasn't a blatant lie. We did need to keep a diligent eye out, but normally he'd have demanded I stay as close to him as possible.

This was him purposely distancing himself from me. Frankly it just pissed me off. All because I hadn't let him help me. Couldn't he see I was just trying to learn to be strong? Being surrounded by the forest was helping a little, but not enough. The worst part was that after the first twenty minutes, my legs had become heavy and my lungs ached from lack of oxygen. I was sorely regretting using today as my day to stand on my own two feet.

My steps slowed and after a few minutes the distance between Tal and me widened until I couldn't see him anymore. I shook my head in exasperation. Was it really going to be this way? All the men in my life demanding I lean on them for everything. I sighed in exasperation and fluttered my wings until I was floating above the snow.

Link stopped dead in his tracks and growled at the exact same time Talisen came into view. He had that crossbow positioned on his shoulder and was aiming directly at a woman wearing black thermal pants and a pale blue fleece jacket. Her dark hair was piled into a messy bun on her head and she wore thick plastic glasses. I frowned. I knew her from somewhere. But where?

I glanced at Link and jerked my head, signaling for him to back up Tal. He leaped, bounding to Talisen in no time. I trailed behind, taking care to not wear myself out too much. By the time I landed softly just behind Tal, she was glaring at me. That look triggered my memory. The fae from his lab at the university.

"I told them you'd be with her," she said. "You're ruining your life, you know."

"Shut up." Talisen glared at her.

"Why?" she said, taunting him. "Afraid she's going to find out we're lovers?"

I gasped involuntarily as shock had me staring openmouthed at Tal. Lovers? What the hell?

"Don't listen to her, Willow." His voice was low and steady, full of danger. "She'll say anything to drive a wedge between us."

The brunette fae laughed, a throaty bedroom version. "Don't be so modest, Talisen. How else would I know about that birthmark on your upper thigh or the scar on your hip?"

Anger-tinged jealousy burst forward and pooled in my chest. I'd never seen the alleged birthmark, but I knew about the scar. Back when we were teens he'd slipped on a mossy log and gotten a jagged rock lodged in his hip. There was no way he'd walked away from that without a reminder.

"What do you want?" My voice was as chilly as the cold air.

Her piercing eyes bored into me. "You."

Talisen shifted so his body was completely in front of mine. "You have two seconds to get out of here before I put this bolt in your leg."

I peeked over his shoulder at the supermodel fae and had a flash of them together in bed. The contents in my stomach churned.

"You know I can't do that," she said, standing her ground. "Especially not since you ended Macinson. You know Asher's entire team is out looking for you both, right?"

How did she know about Macinson? Had Tal told her? And
how many people was the entire team? I pulled the small tranq
gun from the back of my jeans and held it behind my back. No
matter what happened, I wasn't going down without a fight.

"They might be looking, but they'll never find us." Tal took
a step forward.

"So naïve." The woman shook her head. "Do you really think
I'd come out here all by myself?" She waved a hand and three
other fae materialized from the trees. One woman and two men.

Tal didn't even look at them. He just raised the crossbow
to aim it at her chest. "Do you really think I'd be so stupid as
to take Willow to a safe house when I didn't have backup?"

I turned my back to Talisen and eyed the new arrivals. I
didn't recognize any of them. "Tal?"

"Just stick close to me, Wil. This won't take much longer."

I hated not being in the know. Tal seemed so confident.
As if he'd planned for this encounter. But I didn't see how we
were going to get out of this. As far as I knew, we were outnumbered four to two... well, three including Link. Sure, Tal
had a crossbow and I had the tranq gun, but the unfamiliar fae
could have spells or other weapons they hadn't yet brandished.

"This is getting really old, Talisen," his supposed lover said
in a bored tone. "Just hand her over and we'll let you go. No
one really liked Macinson anyway."

Talisen scoffed. "Give it up, Meredith. One would've
thought you'd have realized by now that no one is who they
seem to be."

"What's that supposed to mean?" Her voice rose as suspicion set in.

"This." I felt him move and a second later a bolt flew and
landed in the knee of the fae to our left. He let out a cry as
a burst of magic exploded from him in a cloud of blackness.

"Duck." Talisen grabbed me around the waist and pulled
me face-first into the snow. More magic flew over our heads
as the other fae turned on each other. Link stood guard, not
letting any of them advance on us.

"Move," Tal said as he pulled me up to my knees. "To the trees."

I scrambled in front of him, reaching the nearest tree just as a stream of magic flew by me. I plastered myself to the trunk and took in the magical battle. The shorter, dark-haired female was throwing electric bolts at the one Tal had called Meredith while the two males were caught in an invisible struggle, each fighting the other off in some weird energy battle. They were all manipulators of elements, while Tal was a healer and I was a life fae. Our magic required a connection, theirs didn't. They could call up their powers at will, which made them much more dangerous.

Meredith threw a stream of electricity that hit the brunette right in the chest. She went completely stiff and fell over, her unseeing eyes staring up into the bright sun. Meredith let out a whoop of triumph as she turned to Talisen. But he was up and running toward the brunette, his back to her.

Link lunged, but before he could latch his jaws onto Meredith, I gripped the tranq gun and aimed. The dart hit my target dead center. Right in her heart. She let out a loud gasp as she pulled the dart from her chest, but it was too late. Her eyes were already rolling back in her head.

I didn't waste any time. I turned to the fae Tal had hit with the crossbow bolt and pulled the trigger on the tranq gun once more. But he just waved a hand, sending the dart off into the woods.

"Shit." I ducked back behind the tree, avoiding the fireball of magic he'd tossed in my direction before he unleashed another assault on our remaining ally.

Fire and water met in the middle of the circle, each streaming from the dueling fae. I wasn't in a position to shoot again—my dart would be incinerated. So I sprinted to Talisen and the brunette. He had his hands on her chest and was so focused, so intent, that sweat dripped from his face. He was working hard to save her.

"Anything I can do?" I asked.

He shook his head, but then his eyes met mine and he said, "Help Matt."

I glanced back at the water-wielding fae to find he was being pushed back. The fire fae was much stronger.

Dammit! I needed Link. Where had he gone? I prayed he hadn't been caught in the crossfire. Knowing I couldn't stand there and do nothing, I fluttered my wings and rose into the canopy of the trees. I couldn't risk being seen or the fire fae could burn me straight to the ground. As I positioned myself over the dueling fae, it occurred to me Talisen hadn't treated me like a porcelain doll the way most everyone else had. He'd told me to help Matt. And I'd be damned if I wouldn't do just that.

The realization gave me the burst of confidence I needed and just as the fire fae was about to completely take over the water fae, I dropped from the trees and tackled him from behind. I landed on top of him, flattening him on his stomach. Fire bolted from his hands, melting the snow into a large puddle of water beneath us.

Physically I was no match for him. He must've had at least seventy-five pounds on my thin frame, but I did what I swore I'd never do again to another fae. I latched onto his neck and sucked in his life force. His energy was foreign, tainted with evil, and tasted of ash. It made me gag and my head swim. I had to let go before his evilness consumed me, but if I did, I'd be his next victim. My vision turned blurry as tears streamed down my cheeks and my insides turned over on themselves.

"Tal!" I cried, praying he was nearby. But just before I passed out, I heard the familiar growl of Link and felt his soft coat brush my skin as he attacked.

I let go and scrambled backward as Link dove directly for the fae's neck. Relentless and unforgiving, Link closed his jaws and blood splattered and seeped into the snow. He held on and shook until the fae beneath him stilled. I huddled into myself, horrified by what I'd just watched. I'd known Link was dangerous. Deadly. But I'd only ever seen him attack a vampire. Not another fae. My body started to tremble with delayed adrenaline. When had our war against Asher turned into a fae war?

"Are you all right?" a soft male voice asked from a few feet away.

I jerked back, startled.

"It's okay. I'm not going to hurt you." The water fae kneeled down, holding his hand out to me the way he would a skittish animal.

Link stalked to my side and sat in front of me, possessively claiming me as his. Normally I'd reprimand such an action, but since I had no idea who I could trust, I said nothing and glanced to where Talisen was helping the brunette to her feet.

"Thank you," Matt, that's what Tal had called him, said. "He would've burned me alive if you hadn't helped."

I glanced at the dead fae and shuddered.

"It had to be done." Matt held a hand out to me again, but I didn't take it.

I didn't know this guy. I didn't know any of them. And I sure as hell didn't trust anyone at the moment. With the exception of Tal. Even with all the crazy going on, I could never believe he wasn't on my side. Besides Phoebe and my mother, he was the only person on the green earth that I trusted at that moment.

Matt's eyes darkened. "You can trust me."

I shook my head. "Sorry. At this point, I don't think I can." I met Talisen's eyes and stood.

He scanned the length of my body as if assessing my physical well-being and then ran, catching me in his embrace. He let out a long slow breath and kissed the side of my head. "Thank the gods you're okay."

"Thank Link," I said, breathless at the display of his emotion.

"I'm so sorry, Willow. I should've known she'd show up."

"Sorry, man. She and her partner showed up this morning, hell bent on leading this hunt," Matt said. "I didn't even know she was working for Asher until today."

I felt Tal nod his understanding. And when I pulled away, I met his gaze. "Did you know?"

He nodded. "I found out a few days ago. Asher's recruiting fae in his war on vampires."

That made sense. Asher was a vigilante for humans, believing vampires had too much power in our world. Fae would be his natural allies since we weren't usually very fond of vampires ourselves.

I glanced at Meredith, who was unconscious in the snow. How had he learned she was working with Asher? Suspicion clouded my mind as I imagined the two of them in bed together. It was the perfect opportunity for him to gather intel. Other agents worked that way. Why not him?

"Hey," Tal said, searching my expression. "Everything's okay now. Matt and Samantha are Void. Just like you and me. You're surrounded by people we can trust."

I glanced at the brunette and Matt. They both appeared shaken. Then I glanced at Meredith. "What are you going to do about her?"

Samantha climbed to her unsteady feet, but appeared to be well enough after Tal's ministrations. Then she walked over to Meredith and kicked her hard in the ribs. "She's coming with us. For interrogation." She glanced at Tal. "Were you really lovers?"

Tal grimaced and looked away.

Matt whistled and I blanched. Meredith and Talisen. An air fae and a healer. The perfect complement. I wanted to strangle her. Strangle Tal after everything he'd said last night and this morning. Here I was pining for him and he was sleeping with another fae. I wanted to stab him with a tranq dart.

"We need to get moving," Talisen said, pulling me to his side. I stepped away, keeping my distance. He cast me a wary glance but didn't question me. He knew what was wrong, but we wouldn't discuss it in front of the others. We stood there as Matt picked up Meredith and slung her over his shoulder.

"What about him?" I jerked my head toward the fire fae.

"We'll send a cleanup crew," Matt said.

Samantha and Matt took off in the direction they'd come from, while Tal, Link, and I followed. After a few minutes, Talisen leaned close to me and said, "You did good back there."

"So did you. Nice aim," I said, softening despite my hurt feelings over Meredith.

"Lucky shot." He gave me a small smile.

"Lucky shot, my ass. You hit her exactly where you intended to. I know you better than that, Talisen Kavanagh. If you'd wanted her dead, that bolt would've hit her directly in her heart."

He shrugged. "Perhaps."

Right. He was the best shooter in all of Northern California. And we both knew it. "Just tell me one thing?"

"What's that?"

"Are you handing her over to the Void?"

He shook his head. "No."

I stopped and stared him dead in the eye. "You're giving her to Allcot, aren't you?"

He didn't even blink. "Yes."

Chapter 12

My mouth dropped open in shock. I'd been expecting him to say yes, to confirm he'd been working for Allcot, but hearing the confession made it all too real. That meant he was a double agent, feeding information to both the Void and Allcot this entire time.

I closed my mouth, choosing not to confront him in front of the other two fae. I had no idea if they knew or not. And honestly, I didn't want to find out just then. Too much had happened in the past twenty-four hours.

I had a multitude of questions. Starting with if he was working for Allcot, why hadn't Allcot just ordered him to New Orleans? Why had I been forced to come after him? And what exactly was going on? Why had the fae agreed to work with Asher? Last I'd heard, he'd been employing vampires and humans. Fae didn't usually get into these kinds of wars, myself excepted. But I didn't have a choice. Asher had been trying to kill me for months.

Without saying a word, I followed Matt and Sam, praying we weren't too far from civilization.

Tal fell into step beside me. In a low voice he said, "I know I owe you an explanation."

I cast him an incredulous look. "You think?"

"As soon as we get some privacy, I'll explain everything."

I snorted. "Seems like we had plenty of privacy last night."

He grimaced. "Point taken."

I stared straight ahead and didn't answer him. I'd be lying if I said I wasn't hurt. I wasn't even mad anymore. Just disappointed and confused. Tal hated Allcot and everything he stood for. Yet here he was working for him. And I didn't even want to think about what he'd been doing with Meredith.

It didn't take Tal long to notice my fatigue. My legs were heavy and I was slower than everyone else. It was from draining the vamp and the emotional turmoil. I hated that my one super skill made me weak. I vowed right then and there to learn some other way of defending myself. Eyeing Tal's crossbow, I decided to sign up for lessons as soon as we got back to New Orleans. It was better at taking down vampires than pretty much any other weapon besides a sun-agate spell. Since I wasn't gifted in that type of magic, crossbow it was.

Tal inched closer to me and placed his hand on my neck.

I stiffened.

"Wil," he said. "Relax."

That wasn't going to happen. I was too wound up, too frustrated. But then his cool healing energy skittered over my skin, giving me a jolt. My steps were lighter and it was infinitely easier to keep up with the group. His hand lingered on my neck for a few moments, and I got the feeling he was reluctant to let go.

I glanced at him and then averted my gaze, biting my lip. "Thanks. I needed that."

He nodded and then stuffed his hands in his pockets. And for just a moment, I swear I saw sadness flash through his gaze. There had been a time in our relationship when I wouldn't have hesitated to ask him to help me. But now... everything was different. And even though Tal was right next to me, I started to feel as if I was farther from him than I'd ever been.

It took us over an hour to make our way to a dirt road. There were two Isuzu Troopers parked in a clearing, both a nondescript black.

Matt dumped Meredith into one of the vehicles and then tossed Tal a set of keys. "We'll follow you," he said as he climbed into the other Trooper.

"No need." Tal hit the key fob. "We're getting on a plane to New Orleans. I'll be in touch once I'm briefed on the situation."

My eyebrows rose in surprise. One thing I knew for sure about Allcot was that he most definitely wouldn't stand for Tal briefing anyone who wasn't part of Allcot's team. Wait. Did they work for Allcot, too? Not possible.

I opened the back door and gestured for Link to climb in. He jumped up with ease; all signs of his wound were nonexistent. "Feeling okay, boy?"

He leaned his head out the window and licked my hand.

"Good."

Tal came up behind me and opened the door for me. It was a sweet gesture, but gestures were meaningless when he'd been keeping important information from me. Just like everyone else in my life. David, my mom, Allcot. I'd thought Tal was different. A little piece of my heart hardened as I stared at him.

"Get in, Wil," Tal said softly. "I'll explain on the way to the airport."

He knew I was pissed. Of course he did. I nodded and climbed into the passenger's seat, relieved we were on our way home. "I need to stop at Mom's to get my suitcase."

He shook his head as he turned the ignition. "Too risky. Asher's people will be staking it out now that they know you're in town. We'll get someone to pick it up later if there's anything important."

I shook my head. I'd only brought a change of clothes. There wasn't anything I couldn't live without.

"Good."

The ride over the dirt road was bumpy as hell. But at least we were low enough in elevation that the snow had cleared. By the time we finally turned onto a paved highway, my jaw ached from keeping my teeth from clattering together. It didn't take long for me to turn to Talisen expectantly. "Well?"

He glanced at me and let out a slow breath. "What do you want to know first?"

Had he really slept with that fae bitch? That was the first question to pop into my head? How sad was I? I swallowed it and instead asked, "How long have you been working for Allcot?"

"Since before I left New Orleans. You knew that." He added the last part quietly as if to remind me.

"Yeah. But I thought that was to only supply him with your new drug. Not to spy for him. Jeez, Tal. Do you have any idea how dangerous this all is?"

He let out a humorless laugh. "That's some question after the past twenty-four hours, don't you think?"

I just stared at him, waiting.

"Son of a... of course I know how dangerous it is." His eyes flashed with anger as he glanced over at me. "You think I want to work for him? Or the Void for that matter? Hasn't it ever occurred to you I didn't have a choice? That maybe I was forced into it by both of them? That if I'd had any real choice, I'd still be in New Orleans by your side?"

A lump formed in the back of my throat. After a few swallows, I could only say the obvious. "The Void forced you to come back here. It's their fault all this happened between us."

He stared straight ahead, his neck strained from tension. Then he slowly shook his head. "No. As far as they were concerned, I could've stayed there and just worked on my drug."

"But you said you were forced—" Then it hit me. "Allcot made you leave." I knew the statement was true deep in my bones.

Tal's hands tightened on the steering wheel until his knuckles turned white. Finally he said, "Yes."

"Why?" I breathed, clutching my throat.

Tal sent me an incredulous look. "Why, Willow? Don't be so naïve."

"You're not serious?" I gaped. "You're saying he made you leave because of David? What? He was trying to get rid of the competition or something?"

He gave me a flat stare.

I rolled my eyes. "Come on. You don't really believe Allcot cares that much who his son dates?"

Talisen shook his head and focused on the road.

"That's ridiculous," I said, unable to come to terms with what he was implying. If Allcot had asked him to leave, there must've been some other reason.

"If you say so."

Now he was pissing me off. I turned my body toward him and fixed him with a stare of my own. "What exactly did he say to you?"

Tal didn't answer at first, and just when I thought he was going to stay silent, he pulled over and turned to me. His eyes were ablaze with wild fury. "His exact words?"

I pressed back against the door but nodded anyway. I needed to know.

Tal barked out a laugh. "After almost twenty-four hours of interrogation by the Void, Allcot himself was waiting for me at my trashed apartment. There he was, sitting among the destruction in one of my kitchen chairs as if there wasn't chaos surrounding him. And when I stepped through the door, he stood, staring me down as if he owned me. Then he said, 'You're a distraction. Ms. Rhoswen is safer when you're not around. Leave. If you don't want problems for her to surface, you'll go back to your woods and investigate the murder of Beau Rhoswen.'"

My heart stopped as the breath left me. The words sounded exactly like something Allcot would say. But I couldn't believe Tal had caved to his demands. "You should've told him to shove it. We already know what happened to Beau."

Talisen frowned and closed his eyes momentarily. When he opened them, the anger was gone, replaced by wariness. "I did. But he made it clear he'd renegotiate the terms he'd secured regarding your testing with the Void. As in he'd tell them he didn't care what they did to you as long as you were kept alive. It was pretty clear he was only interested in keeping Laveaux happy. He wasn't about to let you and me keep dating. The easiest way to break us up was to force me to leave."

I was frozen in the passenger seat. David would've never stood for such a thing. But then, if Tal hadn't left and we'd stayed together, would David have fought with his father over me? When I was with another man? I couldn't be sure. "So you went. To keep me safe." My voice was small and dejected. I hated that Allcot had pulled Tal's strings.

"Yes. To keep you safe. But I won't lie and say I didn't want to go. After everything that had happened, it was tempting to come back here where life was easier." His eyes turned dark again. "*Was* being the operative word. Turns out there's more to Beau's death than we knew."

Another gasp flew from my throat. "What did you find out?" The words were so low, I wasn't sure Tal even heard me.

But then he reached over and took my hand. Squeezing my fingers, he said, "He knew Asher."

My blood ran cold. My fingers involuntarily gripped Tal's until they started to ache.

"Hunter told me Beau was on Asher's payroll, but he was vague on the details. I'm not sure he was ready to share every-thing he knows. After years of undercover work, I understand it's hard to trust anybody, but I swear on everything that's good in this world that I won't stop until we find the answers."

I sat there, stunned. Speechless. Beau had been involved with Asher? How? Why? And if his power was like mine, there was no way he didn't know Asher was a vampire. Why in the world would he have gotten mixed up with him? I wanted to scream the questions. Instead, my mind whirled in a storm of chaos. Had he known who Asher was? Had he known he was in danger? But the biggest question, the one that ate away at my heart, was why hadn't he told me?

Beau had been my other half. The one person in the world I'd told everything. He was my twin, and as time went on, it became more and more apparent he had a whole other life I'd had no knowledge of.

There was no denying it. I was hurt… and angry. He'd gotten mixed up with Asher and he'd died because of it.

When we got about ten miles from Eureka, my phone beeped, indicating multiple messages. I glanced down, sifting through half a dozen texts from David. All of them from when we'd been out of range with no cell service.

Yesterday afternoon: *Checking in. Let me know when you're on your way back.*

A few hours later: *Any luck finding him yet?*

Just before ten p.m. Pacific time: *Wil? You didn't forget to charge your phone again did you?*

Midnight: *It's late. I'm worried now. Please give me a call.*

Early this morning: *No one has heard from you. Call back ASAP.*

The most recent one: *No longer willing to wait. I'm on my way.*

"No. Dammit!"

Tal sent me a worried glance. "What is it?"

I shook my head and dialed David's number. Straight to voice mail. I checked the time of his last text. Four hours ago. Oh no. Was he really on his way to Eureka? I'd barely been gone twenty-four hours. Of course, I hadn't contacted him at all. And since I'd arrived I'd been kidnapped and caught up in a magical battle.

Grimacing, I texted: *Where are you?*

The response was almost instantaneous. *In the air. We're landing in twenty-five minutes. Where are you?*

Oh, son of a… *On our way to the airport.*

Do you have Kavanagh?

Yes.

Wait for me there.

I stuffed the phone into my pocket and flopped back against the seat.

"Wil?" Tal prompted.

There was no way I could avoid telling him. He'd see for himself shortly. "David's on his way here. He wants us to wait for him at the airport."

Tal glanced at me once, a storm in his eyes, but he clenched his jaw and didn't comment.

We rode in silence the rest of the way to the airport. When we pulled to a stop outside the hangar, he put the vehicle in park but made no move to get out.

I started to wonder if he was going to refuse to go back to New Orleans with me. I'd never known him to let anyone suffer before, but everything was so complicated now. There wasn't even anything to say. I hadn't asked David to come. In fact, I'd demanded he let me do this on my own. But if there was one thing I'd learned in the past months, it was that I had little to no influence on what the vampires of New Orleans did. Even if one of them claimed to be in love with me.

Sighing, I pushed the door open, but before I could climb out, Tal put a light hand on my wrist. "Wait."

I stared at his hand before meeting his hooded eyes. "Why?"

He withdrew his hand and ran it through his mussed hair. The loss of his touch left me feeling empty, and I gently closed the door with a soft click.

He turned his gaze straight ahead, not meeting my eyes. "I need to know."

"Know what?" I asked, totally confused.

He closed his eyes momentarily and took a deep breath. "Are you with Laveaux?"

My stomach dropped to my toes. Was he really sitting there asking if I was dating David? How was I supposed to answer that when I didn't even know? David had been my companion for the past three months. He'd helped me through a rough time. Honestly, I had no idea how I would've survived the testing without him. But that hadn't been romantic at all. No, through the testing, David had just been a good friend.

But he had kissed me. Twice. That didn't mean I was with him, did it? We hadn't even been out on a proper date. Unless you counted the times we had lunch together at my store. Could you call it a date if someone just showed up and ate with you? I didn't think so.

"Never mind," Tal said, blowing out a breath. "I think that's all the answer I needed."

He had his own door open when I grabbed his hand.

"No it isn't," I said.

He froze but didn't look at me.

"Damn, Tal. I don't know what you want me to say here."

He snapped his head up, his expression tortured. "The truth, Willow. That's all. I need to know what I'm walking into. I know I left. I *know* I hurt you. That doesn't mean I stopped loving you."

My breath got caught in my throat.

He glanced away, clearly regretting his outburst.

My eyes burned with tears as emotion churned inside me. He'd explained why he left. I understood it, could forgive him for it. I still struggled with being left in the dark, but on some level, I understood that too. If he'd told me, I would've battled Allcot and likely would've ended up making my own situation worse. Tal loved me. And it was clear by the emotion welling in my chest that I still loved him.

"David and I... Well, you know we're friends. But we're not together."

"No?" The hope in his voice made me want to cringe with guilt.

"No. Not officially. But..." I didn't want to tell him we'd kissed. That was too cruel. The last thing I wanted to do was hurt him more. "The potential is there."

Nodding slowly, he pulled his arm from my grip and then clasped my hand in his, entwining our fingers together.

"When were you with Meredith?"

His eyes widened with surprise. "Three years ago. For about a week."

Relief claimed my battered heart. I knew I'd had no right to be so upset over her when I was still dancing around a relationship with David. But the heart wasn't rational.

"Can you do something for me?"

"Of course." I brushed my thumb over his knuckles. "Anything."

"Before you decide anything with Laveaux, could you consider giving me another chance?"

Chapter 13

Tal's words were what I'd longed to hear for the past three months. But as I stood there watching David's plane land, trepidation took over. Nervous energy had me shifting from foot to foot. Before long, Link was pacing back and forth, no doubt feeding off my emotions. How was I going to sit in a plane for over four hours with both Tal and David?

I'd rather give a speech in front of a national audience, wearing that horrific giraffe-print dress Phoebe had made me try on that one time than suffer being trapped in a plane with the pair of them.

Before I knew it, David was out of the plane and striding toward me. He didn't even acknowledge Tal as he engulfed me in his embrace and planted a kiss on my temple. "I was worried," he said, though his words were gentle.

I stiffened and pushed him back, very uncomfortable with the PDA he was showing in front of Tal. To make matters worse, when he released me, he draped an arm around my shoulders and tucked me into him as if we truly were a couple. As if he were claiming me for Tal's benefit.

"We were out of range," I said, shrugging him off. I took two steps away from both of them. Link followed and sat right in front of me. That's right. He was the only male in my life I'd allow to claim me. I met David's eyes. "You should've waited for me to call you back."

He raised his eyebrows. "And do what? Wait until I got the call that Asher has you or worse? You know I can't do that."

"She was with me," Tal said, making no effort to mask the irritation in his tone.

David's eyes narrowed. I knew he was wondering what we'd been doing. But I sure as hell wasn't going to tell him. Tal's Void business was confidential. If he wanted Allcot to know, it was up to him to tell him.

They stood there, each sizing the other up.

I rolled my eyes. "Which plane are we going back on?"

The one David had flown in on was identical to the one waiting for me in the next hangar.

"This one." David gestured to the one already on the tarmac. "As soon as they get it gassed up, we'll be on our way." David headed inside the hangar to converse with both pilots.

"Allcot has two Learjets?" Talisen asked.

I shrugged. "Guess so. In fact, I bet he has more than two. Or at least the corporation does."

David reappeared. "They'll be ready in a few minutes." He placed his hand on my elbow and started steering me toward the plane.

Good Goddess, that irritated me, though I was acutely aware that if Talisen hadn't been there, I'd have been perfectly fine with it. I pulled my arm away under the pretense of having to tie my shoe. I didn't want him touching me after Talisen's confession back in the Trooper. It just felt… wrong. Like I was cheating on someone. Though I wasn't sure who.

I heard Tal let out a chuckle and then there was the click of the back door opening on the Trooper. "Laveaux, we brought your maker a present."

David stilled and then slowly turned around. "Maker?"

Tal waved at the back of the SUV and then moved to join me. The fact Tal had used "maker" instead of "father" was deliberate. He was calling out the fact that David was vampire. It was a subtle slight on any relationship David and I might have.

David peered into the Trooper. "Who's this?"

"She's one of Asher's people. Tal's handing her over to Allcot," I said, my voice flat. Who knew what Allcot would do to her to get answers? It would be ugly, and even though she would've surely killed me or handed me over to Asher, I couldn't stomach her likely fate.

David nodded to one of the flight crew. "Put her on the plane. Do whatever it takes to restrain her. I don't want any surprises midflight."

The crewman nodded. "No problem, Mr. Laveaux."

Once on the plane, Tal sat to my right and David took the seat directly across from me. We were in a cluster of four chairs that faced each other. I stared at Link, wishing I could just sit with him. Because this wasn't going to be awkward. No, not at all.

Twenty minutes into the flight, I longed for some Mocha in Motion. I was already running on empty, and the metal from the plane was only making it worse. I closed my eyes, my eyelids and limbs heavy. It wasn't long before I fell into blissful darkness.

I woke to Tal's healing energy tingling down my spine. It was so familiar and welcome. I let out a small moan of appreciation and leaned into him, not wanting the sensation to end.

"Thanks," I murmured as I opened my sleepy eyes and caught him smiling down at me.

"Better?"

"Yes." I needed to fly with Talisen all the time. Dang. He was lucky. Because he was a healer, his resources didn't get depleted the way mine did. Besides that he was also gifted in stone magic. As long as he had one or two on his person, he had all the energy he needed.

David cleared his throat, startling me. I sat straight up, having totally forgotten in my sleepy haze that he was there.

I glanced between him and Tal. To Tal's credit, he wasn't engaging in David's subtle hostility. He was relaxed, one foot resting on his knee, with Link lying in front of him.

David, on the other hand, was leaning forward, piercing us both with his eyes. "What happened in Eureka?"

I glanced at Tal, letting him take the lead. It was his mission I'd interrupted, after all.

Tal met David's gaze, unblinking, and said, "I'll discuss that with Allcot."

Oh, whoa. David was going to hate that.

David kept his expression blank, but by the stiffness in his frame, I knew he was fuming. And even though Tal had perked me up with his magic, I was still worn out from the tension in the plane by the time we landed. All I wanted to do was go home and rest in my enchanted oak and shut out the rest of the world.

But Harrison was in trouble and no way was I going anywhere until I was sure he was okay.

"Let's go," David barked and led the way to his silver Mercedes.

Tal and I glanced at each other. He smiled at me and everything inside me warmed. It was good to have him back.

"This way," David said, leading us down the marbled hallway of Allcot's Victorian mansion. We were in the heart of Mid-City where most of the vampires had rebuilt after Hurricane Katrina. But since it was early afternoon, the neighborhood appeared deserted. All the other vamps were dead to the world, so to speak.

There was an eerie silence in the large mansion. I didn't even know if Allcot was there. He had an office downtown where he spent most of his days. He was old enough that even before he'd turned into a daywalker, he hadn't needed to sleep during the day. Of course, now that he could walk in the sun, there was no telling where he was.

Heavy drapes lined the windows, and ornate wall sconces lit the hall with a soft glow. All of it seemed so incredibly formal to me. I couldn't imagine living in such a place.

"In here." David opened the double doors at the end of the hallway. The place was bright with recessed lighting and was all white, sterile like a hospital.

Three hospital beds were lined up in the large room, each equipped with monitors and IV drips. I slowed my pace, shocked by the scene in front of me. Allcot had said the guards were weakening, but I hadn't fully grasped the gravity of the situation. My eyes burned with unshed tears as I neared Harrison.

The tall, well-built, larger-than-life man I'd come to respect was now emaciated and lay lifeless in the bed. His features were ashen and gaunt as if he were wasting away to nothing.

"Oh no," I said through my fingers, barely able to breathe.

"Tell me exactly what happened," I heard Tal ask David. The concern in his voice told me he was just as shaken as I was.

I glanced back to him. He had a pad of paper out and was busy scribbling notes even though David hadn't yet said a word. His features were pinched in concentration. Turning back to Harrison, I slipped my hand over his, wishing there was something I could do for him. Taking some of his energy and pushing it back into him was out of the question. He didn't have anything else to give.

My tears spilled in silence down my cheeks. What kind of drug was this and where had the fae gotten it? I glanced at my phone and contemplated texting Phoebe. She was the most experienced witch I knew. She might have seen it used before or maybe had some sort of insight, something to help Talisen counteract it.

"Willow?" Talisen called.

I'd been so caught up in my despair and thoughts that I hadn't even realized David was done filling Talisen in on the incident.

"Yeah?" I wiped my eyes, embarrassed I couldn't seem to keep it together.

"David's going to take you to your shop so you can get me some supplies. If that's okay?"

"Of course. Anything you need."

He tore off the piece of paper he'd been scribbling on and handed it to me. "Don't be afraid to bring anything else you think will help with energy levels, strength, or even pain. If I'm close on my analysis, they might need it."

I reached out and squeezed Tal's hand. "Anything else? I have that crystal you gave me."

He stared into my eyes for a moment. "That's yours. So it's your call. If I use it for this, it will likely be worthless afterward."

"It's fine," I said without hesitation. "If it will help them, then of course I'll bring it."

"I knew you'd say that," Tal said with a soft smile.

"Because she's always willing to put everyone else first before her own safety," David said, scowling at both of us.

"And you're always the first to take her up on it, aren't you, Laveaux?"

David straightened to his full height and moved toward Tal, his expression brooding. "Watch your tone, Kavanagh. You have no idea what you're talking about."

Talisen snorted while checking Harrison's pulse. "Right. Like I'm not aware she almost died turning both you and your father. Seems as if someone who loved her would never ask her to do such a thing."

I jumped between them moments before one of them threw the first punch. "That's enough! Both of you. I'm not a prize to be fought over and this is all old news. Let's focus on Harrison and his team, okay?"

"Fine by me," Tal said, raising his hands in surrender. "I'm not the one who started this pissing match."

I was well aware that David had instigated the altercation, but Talisen sure hadn't done anything to stop it.

David inclined his head, his dark hair falling over one eye. "My apologies, Willow."

Talisen rolled his eyes at David and then turned his attention once more to Harrison. He busied himself by running his hands over Harrison's chest, no doubt trying to infuse him with some of his healing magic. I watched for a few moments, hoping to see some color blossom in Harrison's features, but there was nothing. No change.

"Let's go," David said from the doorway. "The faster we get what he needs, the sooner this will be over."

For now, but what about next time? Asher's people weren't going to stop using the poison that was so effective on their enemies. We had to stop them before the recipe became common knowledge.

For now, the only thing I could do was focus on Harrison and his crew recovering quickly. Once the immediate danger was taken care of, we could worry about the new drug, and Tal and I could get to work on finding out what Beau had been doing for Asher. Was there something more to his death than just being able to turn vampires into daywalkers?

Did the reason even matter? He'd died. But Beau was my twin, literally my other half, and something was telling me we needed to find out. That there was an answer to all the turmoil Asher was causing if only we had all the missing pieces.

David and I didn't talk on the way to his car. I'd opted to leave Link with Talisen. I didn't like the idea of Tal being in a vamp's house with no backup. Not that I thought he was in any danger—Allcot needed him. But it made me feel better having them together.

Once we were on our way to The Fated Cupcake, David glanced over at me. "Are you going to tell me what happened last night?"

Red-hot anger burned my face. "Are you serious? Do you really think that's what we should be talking about right now? For the record, I was going to spend the drive brainstorming all my ingredients just to be sure I don't forget something at the shop. You know, focus on stuff that might help my friend."

"Dammit, Willow. You know how I feel about Harrison. Don't sit there and imply I'm a coldhearted bastard just because it's driving me crazy not knowing where you were last night— with Kavanagh of all people."

"What's wrong with being out with Tal?" I asked, mostly just to piss him off. "I was sent there to bring him back, was I not?"

"You know what I mean. Stop being coy. Something happened yesterday and I want to know what it is."

I didn't care for his possessive tone. At all. Crossing my arms over my chest, I shook my head. "Talisen will fill Allcot in himself. It's not my place to discuss it."

David cast me a sidelong glance, appearing more interested than irritated now. "Really?"

"Yes. Really. Can we drop this? I need to focus."

An odd mix of confusion and curiosity mingled in his expression as he nodded. Then, to my surprise, he reached over and grabbed my hand. Squeezing, he said, "Sorry. I was just worried. It's hard having you thousands of miles away with no way to help."

It felt foreign to have my hand in his. Yesterday, before I'd gone home to Eureka, his touch had been welcome. Now my instinct was to pull away. I didn't, though. I didn't want to have to explain the change in my behavior. Especially since I didn't fully understand it myself.

Chapter 14

Thankfully David got a phone call just as we pulled up to The Fated Cupcake and stayed in the car while I went inside.

It was dusk, just before closing, and the place was packed with humans and vampires alike. Tami, my assistant, was behind the counter by herself, zooming around the shop, moving almost faster than humanly possible. If I didn't know better, I'd think she was hopped up on the street drug Candy Apple. It caused a surge in energy but was also highly addictive and dangerous for humans.

I pushed my way through the crowd and jumped behind the counter, noting the dark circles beneath her eyes. How long had she been by herself? I couldn't just grab my supplies and leave. Not with how ragged she appeared.

"Willow!" she gasped and cast me a grateful look.

"Where is everyone?" I asked as I started filling orders.

She scowled, leaned over to me, and whispered, "Out making a delivery. For the Cryrique."

"Both of them?" What the hell? Had Allcot started ordering my employees around now?

She nodded. "Two different locations. I'll fill you in after the crowd dies down."

I glanced at the growing line and nearly blew a blood vessel. That bastard had gone too far. Our shop only made deliveries in the mornings and even then only to qualified accounts. I'd never approved the Cryrique. But I couldn't expect Tami to turn him down. No one said no to Allcot. No one but me, apparently.

Ten minutes later, we had the line worked down to just a few more people when David poked his head into the shop. He caught my eye and raised an eyebrow, no doubt wondering why I was working behind the counter. I shook my head, indicating he'd have to wait.

He stepped up to the counter and said, "Wil, we have to get back."

"I know." I slammed the front case closed. "Maybe if Allcot hadn't poached my employees, Tami wouldn't have been by herself and swamped."

"It's okay, Willow. I've got it from here." Tami passed a bag of Happy cookies to the cute couple giggling at each other. "Really. I'm sure one of the girls will be back soon."

I placed a hand on her forearm. "Thanks, Tami. I wouldn't leave you if it wasn't really important."

"I know." She gave me a tired smile while she rearranged the rest of the day's stock in the front case.

David followed me into my lab where I kept my supplies. I bristled and wanted to demand he leave, go back outside, but that wasn't fair. He hadn't been the one to order my employees around. And it was likely he didn't even know what his father was up to, considering he'd been flying all day.

In less than five minutes, I had a canvas bag full of the ingredients Tal had asked for as well as my new Hibiscus Healing bars, a bag of dried hibiscus seeds, and cocoa beans. I used them in my Mocha in Motion drink. They might be of some use if Tal managed to awaken his patients.

"Ready?" David held a hand out to me.

I shook my head and bypassed him. "I need something out of my office."

His hand fell to his side as he followed me. He stood statuesquely in the doorway while I rummaged through my desk. Everything was exactly where I'd left it except for the crystal pendant Tal had given me. "That crystal was here. I swear," I mumbled.

With mounting concern, I searched each and every drawer, coming up empty. Frustrated, I flopped down into my chair and pulled the middle drawer all the way open and leaned down, eyeing the very back of the drawer. Nothing but a tin of breath mints.

"It's not there?" David asked.

I turned to find his brows pinched in concern.

"You're sure you left it in your desk?"

I nodded. "Positive. I just had it a few days ago. I put it in the middle drawer because... well, that doesn't matter. I distinctly remember putting it right here." I poked the open drawer. Then I slammed it shut and stood.

"Maybe you should ask Tami if she's seen it."

I bit my bottom lip, eyeing the top of my desk. Not one thing was out of place. I highly doubted Tami had seen the crystal. My office was my private sanctuary, and she was relentless about keeping everyone out of it. She had her own desk in the office next to my lab. Still, it didn't hurt to ask.

After handing the tote bag to David, I brushed past him and headed back into the front of the shop. Tami was busy cleaning the Mocha in Motion machine. All the customers had gone and she'd flipped the Closed sign on the front door. The shop was messier than I'd ever seen it. My fingers itched to drop everything and help her clean up.

"Tami?"

"Yeah?" She blew a lock of curly hair out of her eyes as she glanced up at me.

"Sorry." I grimaced. "I wish I had time to help you out."

"Don't worry about it." She went back to scrubbing the metal steamers. "I'll have this place whipped into shape in no time."

I knew she would. She was the best damn assistant any owner could ask for. I made a mental note to add a bonus to her next check. Just because I was tangled in vampire and Void politics, that didn't mean my shop and my employees didn't mean the world to me. "I'm sure you will," I said. "No one closes faster or more meticulously than you do."

That got a smile out of her. "Thanks."

I paused, not wanting to sound like I was accusing her of anything. "Hey. I know you don't usually go into my office, but I was looking for that crystal Tal gave me. I thought I left it in my desk drawer, but I guess not because I can't find it. You haven't seen it lying around anywhere, have you?"

A blush crawled up her tan face and she bit her lip.

"Tami?" I frowned.

"I, ah… crap." She shoved her hand in her front pocket and produced the crystal, grimacing. "I went into your office to drop off a supply request and ended up taking a phone order. I was looking for a pen when I found it. I'm sorry. I wasn't going through your stuff intentionally. I swear, I wasn't."

"I believe you. If there's anyone here I trust, it's you."

Her shoulders relaxed as she slumped against the counter. "I know. I guess I'm feeling guilty for holding on to your crystal. I know Talisen gave it to you. It's just that when I picked it up, all my aches were soothed and I had more energy than I'd had in weeks. It was enough to let me push through the day without going batshit on anyone. I'm sorry."

I took the crystal, dropped it into my purse, and then pulled her into a hug. "There's nothing to be sorry about. I'd let you keep it for the rest of the night if I could. But Tal needs it."

She hugged me back and when she pulled away, she glanced over at David, who was waiting for me near the front door. "Tal's here, then?"

I nodded.

Side-eyeing David, she gave me a conspiratorial grimace. "That must be…"

"Awkward?"

"Yeah." She chuckled.

"Little bit." I started to retreat. But then I stopped and smiled at her. "Don't stay too late. And call a few of the part-timers to come in and help tomorrow. Even if everyone shows up, you need a break."

She gave me a grateful smile and went back to cleaning the mocha machine. She worked harder than anyone I'd ever met before. Bonus. That girl definitely needed a bonus.

"Got everything you needed?" David opened the car door for me.

"Yes." No. I was worried about my staff. I'd been out playing Void agent far too much and it was taking a toll on them, which worried me. Not in the way I was worried about Harrison, but they were important to me, too.

"Good. Let's hope your friend is as good as everyone says he is."

I ignored the comment. Talisen was a damn fine healer. If any fae could heal Harrison and the others, it was him. David knew it, too. Instead, I pulled the crystal out of my purse and palmed it, letting the faint traces of magic settle into my hand. There wasn't much there at all, though I supposed since Tami was human, it felt like a lot to her.

It had been too long since Tal had charged it. I'd taken to carrying it with me while at work during the Void testing. I'd told myself it was for the healing properties. But that was mostly a lie. I'd just wanted to be close to Tal.

David reached over and caressed the base of my neck. "As soon as we drop off these things to the fae, I can take you home. Get you into your tree so you can recharge."

I pulled back and scowled. "I'm not leaving until we see improvement with Harrison."

He stared at me for a moment, then put the car in gear and took off down the crowded street. The tight expression on his face made me think he knew what I'd really meant: that I wouldn't leave without Talisen.

Maybe it was stupid. Obviously Tal could take care of himself. I just hated the thought of him being stuck in the vampire mansion under the thumb of Allcot, who wouldn't hesitate to blackmail him into various effed-up situations... using me as leverage.

David pulled to a stop in front of Allcot's Victorian and killed the engine. Before I could get the door open, he said, "I should've known."

Releasing the door handle, I looked at him. "Should've known what?"

His lips thinned and then he let out an exasperated laugh. "Jesus, Willow. Wake up."

I opened my mouth but shut it. He was talking about Tal. I sighed, knowing I was caught between the two of them... again. I'd allowed David to believe there might be something between us. And hell, if Tal hadn't come back into my life, I might have let it happen.

David shook his head and pushed the door open. I sat in the passenger's seat and watched him stride into the house without looking back.

Chapter 15

Talisen met me outside the front door, his eyes troubled. "What happened?"

I shrugged. "Nothing. It just took a little longer than expected."

His brows dipped. "I meant with Laveaux."

I paused and looked up at him. "What do you mean?"

Tal slipped the tote bag from my hand and jabbed his head toward the house. "He's pissed at you."

Closing my eyes, I shook my head. "He'll get over it." I tangled my arm through his. "How's Harrison? And the others?"

"The same." He pulled the door open for me. "But I've got a plan. Ready?"

I glanced around the entry hall of Allcot's mansion. Unease crawled up my spine. Something inside me was telling me not to go in. To not get involved with whatever Allcot had going on. But I knew Talisen had work to do. And even if he weren't obligated, he'd do it anyway. And so would I.

Blocking out that unspoken voice whirling through my subconscious, I nodded and followed Talisen down the rabbit hole one more time.

The first thing Tal asked for was the crystal. We were sitting at a stainless-steel table in the makeshift hospital ward. David was standing against the wall, his arms crossed, lording over us like some sort of mob boss. I glanced at him, but he wouldn't meet my eyes. An almost uncontrollable impulse to throw the water bottle sitting in front of me at his head overtook me.

But I didn't. I gritted my teeth and focused. With the crystal in his left hand, Tal reached across the table and left his other hand palm up, silently asking me to take it.

I did without hesitation. The crystal had been mine for a long time. It had been originally tuned to me. It would take his magic better if it was mixed with mine.

His fingers tightened around mine, so familiar. And instantly a soothing calm came over me. Tal's magic danced into my fingertips, stirring my own magic. I wanted to live with him in that moment forever. He just felt... right. Warmth spread through my limbs, bringing a spark of life to my fatigued body.

The crystal, lying in the palm of Tal's hand, started to shimmer with soft silver light. Tal held the connection until the crystal became a beacon of light, and then he placed it carefully on the table but didn't release my hand.

His healing energy had filled me up, and I tightened my grip as if I were holding on to a piece of him, unwilling to let go.

"Wil?" he said.

"Yeah?" I met his gaze and felt the intensity of it deep down in my soul.

"We're going to do this together. Trust me. Okay?"

His words brought me back to myself. He wasn't holding my hand because of some mystical connection he couldn't tear himself away from. Not like I was. He looked concerned, as if he hadn't let go because he thought I was afraid we wouldn't be able to help Harrison. "Yeah," I said again and pulled away before he had a chance to. "We will."

He sent me a reassuring smile that did nothing to ease the anxiety suddenly overwhelming me. Working with Tal was going to be torture. Especially with David watching over everything we did. I made a conscious effort to not look at David and went to work on arranging the plants I'd brought for Tal.

"Want me to alter any of them?" I asked once I had everything unpacked from the tote.

"Not yet." He shook his head and turned to David. "Have you tried them on any of her creations so far?"

David cleared his throat. "A few were administered intravenously. A liquefied hibiscus mixture and one with jasmine."

Tal glanced at me. "Hibiscus? Jasmine?"

"There's a healer who uses hibiscus seeds for healing. I've been experimenting with it and had some success. Jasmine is the main ingredient in my detoxifier energy drink. It was worth a shot."

"Any results?"

David walked over to a file cabinet and pulled out a beige folder. He placed it on the table in front of Tal. "Everything's in here."

Tal was silent as he read the report.

Irritated that David hadn't just told us, I got up and read over Tal's shoulder.

> *Hibiscus-seed injection: Slightly elevated blood pressure, rapid eye movement, and slight muscle spasms consistent across all three subjects. Harrison Camillo fluttered his eyes before settling back into stasis.*
>
> *Jasmine injection: Increased blood flow to the brain and increased oxygen levels across all subjects. No other change.*

"Hmm." Talisen scribbled a few notes on his legal pad. "Willow, can you modify your plants now? The hibiscus and the jasmine. Maybe some cocoa beans as well?"

"Sure. But I did bring some that are already modified as well."

He shook his head. "No. I want you to do it while we're connected. Basically using my energy and yours. Just like we did with the crystal."

"I strongly recommend you try your conventional healing

spells before you start experimenting," David said, clearly impatient. "We're running out of time."

Tal turned and met the vampire's gaze. He cocked his head and narrowed his eyes. "I already did that while you were busy making sure I knew you and Willow have a thing now." He paused and stood up. "You know, when you escorted her to her shop as if she were incapable of driving herself."

David straightened, seeming to grow at least two inches taller. His fists clenched as anger radiated from him. "What I do with Willow is none of your concern."

Tal raised one eyebrow. "Really? I think we both know differently. If I hadn't left town, you'd never have had even an inkling of a chance with my girl. And she doesn't need a damned babysitter."

My girl? Oh shit. My heart stilled and then pounded almost out of my chest. What was he trying to say? That if he had his way, we'd be back together?

"But you did leave." David seethed. "And now you're too late."

Too late? Was that true? I glanced at Tal, took in his long, lean frame, his corded muscles, his quiet strength. No. The word flittered through my mind. It wasn't too late. It had never been too late. Why else had I kept David at arm's length? Except for that vampire thing. I knew right then and there I wouldn't let Tal leave me again. I wouldn't let anyone force us apart. Even if all we ever were was friends, I'd make sure he was still in my life and I was in his one way or another. And he was right—I'd always be his girl.

Tal didn't look at me. Neither did David. They were staring each other down, each waiting for the other one to strike a blow.

Were they really going to do this right now?

"Tal," I said softly, placing a light hand on his arm.

He glanced at me and his expression shifted to concern. "Sorry." He took a deep breath and turned his back to David. "I'm ready to infuse the plants when you are."

"Just a minute." I glanced at David. "I think this would be better for everyone if you waited in another room."

"What?" He took a few steps closer to us. "I'm not leaving them unattended."

"They aren't." I took a deep breath, ready to scream. My footsteps were silent as I tugged him across the room and lowered my voice. "Look, I know this is awkward for everyone. But Tal and I need to focus, and I'd appreciate it if you'd wait in another room because honestly, it's too much for me to deal with right now. Send someone else in to keep an eye on us if you want. But for now, we... I need a little space. Can you understand that?"

I'd softened the request in order to get what I wanted with the least conflict necessary, but really I was ready to kill both of them. There were far more important things to deal with right now besides my love life.

David glanced between Tal and me, tightened his jaw, and then left soundlessly.

Tal raised his eyebrows at me, asking if everything was okay.

I shrugged and sat across from him again. "Let's just get moving, 'kay?"

"Sure." He took my left hand and placed the hibiscus seeds in my palm. Then he laid the crystal over the seeds and curled my hand into a fist. "Keep a loose hold on these."

"Okay." The crystal warmed my hand, and I had to actively keep from absorbing Tal's healing energy. It was like my drug. Tal's energy had always been too much for me to resist.

He reached both of his hands out, each of them covering mine. "Now, concentrate on altering the seeds."

I let out a breath and focused on the seeds poking into my palm. Picturing them in my mind, I closed my eyes and pulled in the sharp essence of the seeds. The bitterness was like fire in my veins. It was the immaturity of the plant that caused the burn, but I was used to it. I'd been working with the seeds for the past few months.

But then a rush of coolness soothed my limbs. The crystal's magic was chasing the essence of the seeds. I pulled harder, making sure I had all the life the seeds had to offer and let it mix with the coolness. Euphoria made my vision slightly blurry as peace settled over me. I felt as if I were floating over the table, overtaken by the intoxicating magic.

I felt hopeful and more powerful than ever before. I heard a small cry of joy escape my lips as a life with Talisen flashed before my eyes. We were together in my house, lying under my oak tree, me pressed to his side as he caressed my back lazily. There was a feeling of contentment, one of peace, a confidence that this man loved me. I was whole. Whole in a way that I hadn't been since Beau died.

Tal's soft voice tickled my ear as he told me of his day in his lab and asked about the shop. The joy of a normal life, a stable relationship, of knowing that I was with the one person who cherished me.

"Willow." Tal's voice broke the haze of the vision. "Send it back. Now."

His words jolted me, made the images flee, and all that was left was the incredible magic fighting to consume me again. "Return," I whispered, something I never had to do when I was altering plants. All I had to do was think about sending it back and it went. Not this time. It had too much of a hold on me.

"Return," I said more forcefully and imagined the magic flowing with ease from my palm, straight into the tiny seeds lying in my hand.

Magic rushed from my core, snapping with force back into the seeds. I slumped over, completely empty. I opened my palm and let the seeds and crystal slide to the table.

"Excuse me," I said, pulling away from Tal. I stood and wrapped my arms around my middle, trying to hold myself together. I felt as if I was going to shatter into a billion pieces.

Tal was there a moment later, engulfing me in his strong embrace. He whispered in my ear, "It's all right, Wil. I promise."

"It's not all right," I choked out on a sob. "I can't…" My body started to shiver from the magic loss.

"It is, love. I felt it, too. I know."

I grabbed his T-shirt and held on, too afraid to ask what he'd meant by that. Had he envisioned the scene in my oak tree? Or had he only felt the magic leave and was referring to the hollow feeling after infusing one's magic into something? It had to be the latter. How could he have seen into my private thoughts?

Damn him for leaving. And damn me for not moving on.

"Willow. You need to open to me. I can't help you if you keep yourself closed off."

It was then I noticed he was caressing my neck, trying to help with this healing touch. Only I was so tense, my body wasn't willing to accept it. "Sorry," I whispered and tried to relax. But it was no good. No matter what I told my body, it was in too much shock.

"No need to apologize." His touch only got lighter as he leaned in and brushed his lips over my temple. I froze, unable to move. But he didn't stop. His soft kisses trailed in a line down my cheekbone until he kissed the corner of my mouth. I turned into him, letting his lips press over mine briefly.

Then his magic rushed into me, filling all my empty places. I jumped back, my eyes wide with wonder, and I clasped my hand over my lips. "Whoa." I swallowed the lump in my throat. "Sorry. My magic got the better of me."

He shook his head, smiling at me. "Not yours. Ours. And don't apologize. You did exactly what I asked you to."

I nodded, still feeling unsettled. The image combined with the tender kisses was too much for me. I sat back down and stared at the seeds sitting innocently on the table.

"Want to try the jasmine?" Tal asked, startling me.

"What?"

"We don't have to. We can see if these work first before we move on."

My gaze landed on the seeds, then the jasmine, and then Tal. "You want to alter the jasmine?"

He frowned in confusion. "I thought that was the plan."

"Uh… yeah. I mean, I guess so." I was so disoriented because of what had happened when we'd used our magic together that I was having trouble focusing. Was I ready to try that again? Was it better to just get it over with? The allure of losing myself in the magic was too tempting, and before I could second-guess myself, I pressed the jasmine flowers into my palm and held my hand out to Tal.

Chapter 16

The jasmine didn't burn my veins like the seeds did. Its life force was mild, almost ticklish. But the effect of Tal's magic from the crystal was just as wonderful and torturous as before as I envisioned Tal and me strolling hand in hand along Magazine Street. We were checking out the local shops, browsing for new living room furniture… for our own place. The sun was shining on a beautiful spring day with a slight breeze, no supernatural nonsense in sight.

The scene was straight out of a daydream. I could've stayed there indefinitely, but the objective was there in the back of my mind: to alter the jasmine. This time Tal didn't have to pull me back from the fog. I focused on the flowers and sent our combined magic zipping back into them, leaving me somewhat depleted but not incapacitated.

But Tal seemed a little beat up when I gazed at him across the table. His brows were pinched over sad eyes and his lips were turned down.

I touched his hand. "You okay?"

He shook himself slightly. "Yeah. Fine. Sorry. Long day."

I couldn't argue with him there. My limbs had started to get heavy and my vision was going slightly blurry.

Gathering the flowers and the seeds, he stood. "Let's get these cooked down."

I followed him to the lab table and went to work on chopping the flowers first. Then I ground the seeds. In order to administer each of them, they needed to be liquefied. I dumped each into its own pot and then covered the contents with a couple of cups of water before setting them over a propane burner.

The only thing left to do was wait. Once each was boiled, we'd strain the liquid and then a nurse could administer it while Tal used his crystal to try to heal Harrison and the others.

"Willow?" Tal said as I stirred one of the pots.

"Hmm?"

"Want to talk about what happened when our magic mixed?"

I froze. No. Yes. Hell. "What do you mean?"

He leaned against the table, bracing himself with his hands. "You know. The visions."

My breath got caught in my throat as I met his serious gaze. "You, ah… saw those?"

He nodded slowly.

"What did you see?" Had he seen everything I had? More importantly, had he sensed how I'd felt about it? Blood rushed to my head and my cheeks heated. I wasn't ready to face those feelings. I sure as heck wasn't ready to talk about them or analyze them.

"Ah… well, you. Me. Link." He paused as he stared down at me.

Wait. Link hadn't been in either of my visions. "Link?"

"Yeah. Didn't you see him running on the beach?"

Beach? My mouth fell open. Tal had seen a different vision than I had. Slowly I shook my head. "You were in my vision, but Link wasn't."

His lips pressed together in a tight line. "That's odd. I swear it felt like you were right there with me. Like we were sharing the connection."

I'd been too occupied altering the plants, so I couldn't say. Shrugging, I said, "You were in mine, but we weren't at the beach. We were spending the day on Magazine Street in one and in the other we were… at my house." I'd almost told him I'd envisioned us in bed together. But that wasn't something we needed to talk about right then.

"Interesting." Tal's eyes lit up with excitement. "We'll need to compare notes to see if anything was the same and what the visions mean."

I gave him a nervous smile but said nothing. It was fascinating that we'd both had visions, but talking about what they meant? No. Just no. I already knew what mine meant. I was still hung up on Tal. It didn't take a rocket scientist to figure that out.

The door swung open and in walked David and Allcot.

"Ms. Rhoswen. Kavanagh," Allcot drawled in his cool tone. "Have you come up with a solution for my employees?"

I waved at the pots on the burners. "We're working on it."

He raised one perfectly groomed eyebrow. "And your plan?"

I bit my tongue and let Talisen explain. When he was done, Allcot narrowed his eyes at us. "And what makes you think your magic combined with Rhoswen's is going to do anything of consequence?"

Oh no. Had he really just said that? We were doing the best we could. I puffed up, ready to tell him to take a leap, when Tal's hand landed on my shoulder, sending a lazy stream of magic down my left arm. I shivered from the unexpected jolt of desire.

I clutched the edge of the table, trying to push the thoughts away. It was the magic and the fact we'd been working together. That's all. Uh-huh. I could keep lying to myself, but it wouldn't help anything.

"Father," David warned. "They both have powerful magic. I'm sure they feel that if they combine forces, they'll stumble on something that will help."

"Thanks," I mouthed to David. I had to give him credit. Lately he'd taken to standing up to Allcot when no one else would. I was starting to admire him for it.

David cracked just the barest whisper of a smile and quirked one eyebrow as if to say no problem. The smile vanished as he strode over to Harrison's side. The look of despair on his face nearly broke me. David didn't have many friends. Nate, another vampire who was one of Carrie's guards, me, and Harrison. Everyone else was loyal to Allcot.

Allcot stood near our makeshift lab table, studying our concoctions. "What is your plan if this doesn't work?"

"We're going to measure these results, and depending on what happens, I'll want to secure a few natural stones," Talisen said. "Ones indigenous to New Orleans. Preferably ones that reside on the estate of a witch family. More power. Also, there are more plants Willow can try. I think we've used the ones that are the most promising, but that doesn't mean I'll stop there. But the very best thing to do would be to analyze the ingredients in the poison the fae used. If we had that information, my job would be much easier."

Allcot pursed his lips and nodded. "Yes. Solid plan. We're working on uncovering the poison." He turned to me. "Your Truth Clusters and Orange Influence are being put to use on some of our informants and a suspect or two."

I gaped as my blood boiled. He wasn't authorized to use Orange Influence. No vampire held that privilege. I could try to fight him on it, but it would be a wasted effort. He did what he pleased, regardless of law. Besides, he already had it thanks to the order he'd placed when I hadn't been in the shop. I would've stood up to him, but my employees couldn't be expected to do that same. It was too dangerous for them.

"Keep me informed on any changes. Got that?" Allcot ordered.

Tal gave him an emotionless stare. "I've think I've got it."

"Rhoswen," he said without looking at me.

I cleared my throat. "What?"

"Make sure you keep your fae in line. I'd hate for anything to happen to him."

This time I couldn't keep my big mouth shut. He'd gone way too far and with no freakin' reason. "Was that necessary? He's here, isn't he? He's been—" Shit. I was about to say he'd been working for Allcot, his new mob boss, without complaint, but I wasn't supposed to know Tal worked for him.

"He's been what, Rhoswen?" Allcot's voice was cold and uncaring.

"Nothing." I averted my eyes.

Allcot's slicked-back blond hair didn't move an inch as he glanced between Tal and me. Finally he pulled out a cigarette and lit it right there in our little hospital area.

"Some of us are allergic to smoke," I said as clearly as possible amid a coughing fit.

"I'll do whatever I damned well please, faery." He took a long drag, savoring it as if it were a lover.

"Your house. Your rules," I said flippantly.

"My city. My rules. And don't forget it."

God, I hated his arrogant ass.

"Davidson," he snapped. "Let's go. I have a chore for you."

David didn't look at him. He only continued to watch Harrison.

"Fine," Allcot said, relenting. "Come to my office when you're done chaperoning these two fae." Allcot disappeared, the door slamming shut behind him.

Talisen turned the burners off and waved me over to the lab table. "Time to work."

"Ready?" I asked Talisen as I hung the IV bags full of magical potions on the rack.

"Yes. Who do we want to start with?"

"Harrison," David said, startling us. He hadn't said a word since Allcot had left.

"You sure, Laveaux? The first round is often the trickiest." Talisen wheeled the IV pole with him as he moved toward Harrison.

"He'd insist on it himself," David said.

I nodded, knowing David was right. Harrison always put himself on the line first, before his team.

"All right," Tal said. He pulled up a rolling stool and went to work on switching the IV line to the concoction we'd made.

"Does he know what he's doing?" David asked, eyeing Tal.

"Seriously?" I shook my head in exasperation. "He's a healer, David. Of course he knows what he's doing."

David cast me an irritated look. "He's a magical healer. The question wasn't out of line."

I refrained from rolling my eyes at him and sat on the other side of Harrison's bed, across from Tal. "Let me know when you're ready," I said to Tal. He'd asked me to participate when it was time to use the crystal. Since it held my energy as well as his, he thought the magic we unleashed would be more powerful if we did it together instead of just him.

After a few adjustments, Tal said, "Hold your hand out."

I did as he asked.

He clasped his hand over mine, trapping the crystal between our palms. Warm magic pulsed to the tips of my fingers. The euphoria spread and my wings fluttered until I was hovering just off the ground.

Amused at my reaction, Tal smiled at me. Heat crawled up my neck as I flushed in embarrassment. But I couldn't do anything about my reaction. And honestly, I didn't even care. The happiness claiming me was all too welcome.

Tal guided our hands to hover over Harrison's chest. Then he pressed the crystal and my hand over his heart and covered my hand with his, slipping his fingers through mine. "Just relax, Wil."

Right. He had no idea what he was asking of me. My body was tingling from head to toe.

"When I say go, I want you to push the magic filling you into Harrison. Got it?"

I nodded, praying that this would work.

Tal used his free hand to press two fingers to Harrison's pulse. Beneath my hand, I felt Harrison's heart skip a beat and then speed up. Whatever Tal was doing, it was having an effect on the guard.

"Ready?" Tal asked me.

"Yes."

His eyes met mine. "Go."

Because the magic from the stone had already filled me up, there was no need for me to pull at Harrison's already depleted energy. Instead, I focused on filtering the magic from the stone into Harrison while Tal worked his magic with his healing touch.

The magic pooled at my fingertips, resistant to my will. What usually flowed easily into my intended subject hit a barrier and wouldn't budge.

"Damn," I muttered.

"Don't give up," Tal said. "Force it if you have to."

I glanced up at his determined expression and strengthened my will. I'd been hesitant to do anything that might harm Harrison, such as force my magic where it didn't belong, but seeing how hard Tal was working gave me the courage I needed.

"Okay," I said, concentrating on the barrier at my fingertips. I imagined the magic bursting forth like a breach, envisioned it transferring to Harrison and healing him as if nothing was more natural.

The magic buoyed between my fingers and Harrison's breastbone, refusing to obey my mental command. Pressing harder against the crystal and his chest, I leaned into him and looked up into Tal's penetrating stare.

"You've got this."

His words of encouragement were all it took for my magic to blast through into Harrison. The force was so intense I nearly collapsed on his torso from the sheer velocity of it. Catching myself on the edge of the bed, I righted myself and forgot everything around me except the magic coursing from me into Harrison.

My mind blurred with vague shapes of muted colors. Green faded into blue and the blue faded to gray. The blurry fog lifted, and I was transformed into a world of Technicolor. CGI images splayed on a large screen as Harrison sat in a production booth with a man who shared many of his features. Dark skin, angled jaw, expressive dark eyes that were shaped the same. They were related. A younger brother, maybe? They studied each image carefully and spoke with conviction about which to use.

They were producing a movie, I realized as I watched them. Only they were dead serious about the work while also laughing and clearly having the time of their lives. There was so much joy in the room; happiness filled me up until my wings fluttered unconsciously and I lifted right off the ground. My hand slipped from Tal's and the connection was lost.

Reality crashed back into me in the form of harsh white walls and cold, sterile stainless-steel lab tables. My feet hit the floor, jarring my bones.

I blinked, trying to get my bearings. Tal was staring down at Harrison, a curious expression on his face. He hadn't seemed to notice I'd moved.

"Welcome back," Tal said with a smile. But he wasn't talking to me.

"Harrison?" I called and rushed back to his side.

The man's gaze shifted from Tal to me. But there wasn't any recognition in his dark eyes.

"Harrison?" I said again.

His brow furrowed. He turned his head to take in Tal again. "Who are you?"

"Talisen Kavanagh. I'm a healer." Tal didn't seem to be surprised Harrison was disoriented. "And this is Willow Rhoswen. You've been on her security detail for a number of months."

I opened my mouth to protest. Harrison hadn't been keeping an eye on me for a few months now, but then I closed it when Harrison shook his head.

"I don't know what you're talking about. I'm a filmmaker. I don't work... security." His face was contorted into confused irritation.

Tal waved David over. And David, still surly, scowled at Tal. Then his scowl morphed into a concerned frown as he strode to the other side of Harrison's bed.

"Harrison," Tal said conversationally. "Do you know this man?"

Harrison stared up at David. He pushed himself up on his elbows, as if trying to get a closer look or trying to figure something out. But then his body stiffened and he sat straight up, swinging his legs off the bed on Tal's side.

"Whoa." Tal placed a hand on his shoulder, keeping him from getting out of the bed. "You better stay right here for a little longer. Just until we're sure you're steady on your feet."

Harrison's gaze shot between Tal and David before he focused on Tal and leaned in toward him. He dropped his voice and whispered, "We have to get out of here."

Tal's facial expression didn't change, but his entire frame stiffened with what I'd come to know as concern. Harrison was awake, but he was far from okay.

Harrison covered the side of his mouth and jabbed his head once toward David. "I'm almost positive that man is no man at all. He's a vampire."

Chapter 17

Talisen and I glanced at each other; then in unison we turned to catch David's eye. There was no doubt he'd heard Harrison's strained words. There was a crease between his brows as he frowned.

"You're correct," Tal said evenly. "He's a vampire. Do you know who he is?"

Harrison shook his head.

"I see." Tal pulled out a notepad and scribbled something down. "Okay. Let's deal with the vamp later."

David's frown deepened, but he stayed near the lab table and didn't come closer.

"Do you mind answering a few questions for me?" Tal asked Harrison.

Harrison's expression went blank. "I guess not."

"Great." Tal gestured to me. "Do you know who this is?"

Harrison tilted his head and studied me. He nodded hesitantly. "I think so. She's familiar. Like I should know her, but I can't place her." He turned his gaze to Tal. "You, too. You're both friends of mine, right?"

"Shit," David muttered from across the room.

"We do know each other," Talisen confirmed.

I bit my bottom lip. Harrison and I were friends. Sort of. I'd stop and talk to him if I saw him on the street, but I wouldn't call him up and invite him to a dinner party. And he barely knew Talisen. Why did he recognize us and not David? Was it the spell we'd performed on him?

"But I don't recall your names." Harrison ran a hand over his face then shook his head as if trying to dislodge buried memories. He eyed David and shook his head again. "Am I supposed to know him?"

Tal nodded.

Harrison pushed himself up farther in the hospital bed and leveled a stare at Talisen. "What happened to me?"

Tal pulled up a stool and put his notebook down. He looked so much like a doctor conversing with his patient. Medical school had been out of the question. Fae just had too hard a time dealing with synthetics. But he would've made the perfect holistic healer if he hadn't gone into research. His calm nature and demeanor were perfectly suited for the profession. Watching him with Harrison, the way he was patient and soothing, made my heart swell. He was a good man.

"You were attacked by a fae, shot with some sort of poison that put you into a coma."

Harrison scowled. "What? Why?"

The room was silent. Only David knew exactly what had happened that night.

David finally crossed the room and stood next to me. He cleared his throat.

Harrison shifted away from him, eyeing him with extreme caution. "Why are you still here?"

"This is my father's house. And you're his employee. You were on a mission to investigate a fae and a rogue vampire who've been attacking humans. The fae shot you with some sort of dart and you've been unconscious ever since. We asked Mr. Kavanagh to do what he could to heal you. I can assure you we only have your best interest at heart."

Harrison opened his mouth to speak, but no words came out. He let out a huff of air and leaned back, closing his eyes.

"It's pretty normal to be disoriented after waking up from a coma," Tal said gently to Harrison. "Let's give it a few days and then we can try jogging your memory after you get your bearings."

Harrison didn't respond right away. But when I put a gentle hand on his arm, he met my gaze.

"It'll be all right now. I promise. Tal knows what he's doing." A small twinge of guilt had me biting back a grimace. This was uncharted territory, and I knew damned well we were lucky Harrison had woken up at all. Tal's idea hadn't really been founded on anything substantial. It could've just as easily backfired.

Tal smiled at me and confirmed my statement with Harrison. "Yes. You're going to be just fine. Sit tight while we attend the others." Tal waved toward the other two men lying unconscious.

Harrison slid back down in the bed. Dark circles rimmed his tired eyes as he closed them and nodded. "I'll be here."

I stifled a chuckle, surprised at my response. The worry that had been weighing me down had lifted. And while he wasn't going anywhere in his weakened condition, at least he was awake. The relief was making me almost giddy.

"Wil?" Tal tilted his head toward the next patient. "Ready to try this again?"

Squeezing Harrison's hand, I nodded at Tal. "Just get some rest," I said to Harrison. "Tal and I will be back to check on you soon."

He didn't open his eyes, but he did give me a small nod.

Reluctantly, I left his side and followed Tal. We repeated the spell on the second guard and were subjected to another vision. He was sitting with a small-framed redhead on a wrap-around porch, lightly holding her hand as they watched two small children playing in the sprinklers. They were laughing and sipping iced tea, enjoying the perfect summer afternoon. It was completely different from Harrison's flashback but also full of joy and contentment.

I couldn't help but meet Tal's eyes. He was staring at me with a longing I couldn't ever remember seeing in his gaze. I shifted, uncomfortable with the raw emotion emanating from him. Unexpected tears sprang to my eyes, and I had to blink them back before I lost control.

The guard's name was Bale, and he woke up just as disoriented as Harrison had. The interesting part was that he said he felt he knew both Tal and me, but neither of us had met him before that very day. It had to be the spell. They were connecting with us because of our magic.

A bolt of anticipation skittered through me as Tal and I went to work on K.C., the third guard. The visions we'd pulled from Harrison and Bale had been like a shot of happiness straight to the heart, and I was quickly becoming addicted to the sensation. The past months had been downright hard. It was nice to feel good about something for a change. And while I felt like we were intruding on their private thoughts, I didn't know of a way to block them out while we did what we needed to.

Tal's hand closed over mine, and even though the magic from the crystal warmed my palm just as it had before, I had a hard time pushing the magic into K.C. It hit the same barrier I'd experienced with Harrison, but no matter what I did, it wouldn't budge. Gritting my teeth, I narrowed my focus to just my hand and willed the magic to move.

Nothing.

I glanced up at Tal. "Do you feel that?"

He nodded, pressing his lips into a thin line. Then he removed his hand from mine and positioned himself near K.C.'s head. He ran a light hand across the man's forehead, and K.C.'s body flinched slightly, but he didn't open his eyes.

A worry line appeared above Tal's brows as he frowned. "He's further along than the other two were."

"Now what?" I wrapped my arms around myself, trying to stave off the sudden shiver.

Tal held out his hand to me. I slipped mine into his, instantly warmer. He tugged me around so that he was standing behind me with both his arms around me. Then he whispered in my ear, "I need you to pull some of my magic into you before you push it into K.C."

"What?" I said more harshly than I intended.

"Problem?" David interjected, striding over.

"No," Tal said, not looking at him.

"Willow?" David asked.

I waved him off. "I'm fine. Give us a few minutes." I made a concerted effort to keep my voice even, but I really wanted to demand that he just leave. Yes, Tal had his arms around me. That made me want to press into him and flee at the same time, but we were working to save K.C. And having David hovering was only making things harder.

David didn't leave, but he did step back, his jaw clenched and hands fisted.

So he was mad. What else was new?

"Ready?" Tal asked me.

I shook my head. I didn't want to take any of his life energy. "Can't you just force more magic into the stone or something?"

"I already put in as much as it will take. You have more power to force magic into living things than I do. And if you have some of mine mixed with yours, it should give you enough push to save this man." He tightened his arms around me, holding me against him, his face gently caressing mine.

How could I argue with that? I wasn't going to stand here and let the guard fade away into nothing. Not when Tal was so sure my magic would work. I took a deep breath and nodded once.

"That's my girl." Tal's words were a caress to my battered heart. He'd called me *his girl* again. In that moment I knew I'd forgiven him for leaving, forgiven the lack of communication, forgiven the anger and hurt we'd put each other through. I just hoped that once this was all over—once we were no longer under the thumb of Allcot and the Void, once Asher was neutralized—we'd be able to find our way back to each other.

I shut my eyes and focused on my hands gripping Tal's. Magic tingled from my fingertips, spreading over his in a thin layer. Magic shifted and jumped, sparking over his hands and creating a magnetic connection between the two of us.

He stood there, statuesque, letting my magic dance across his skin. I knew it had to be affecting him in some way. It could be irritating, but I was willing to bet he was enjoying the interaction. And then I felt his breath catch as his fingers gripped mine as if he was struggling for control. Yeah, he was enjoying my magical touch. Maybe a little too much.

Now wasn't the time.

Steeling myself, I pushed on my magic, nudging it into Tal. He went completely still with my invasion. I couldn't help but wonder what he was feeling in that moment. I didn't think it hurt, but it was an intrusion nonetheless. After a few moments, I tugged on my magical hold and our combined life energy slammed into me with such force I would've stumbled backward, but Tal's strong arms were still wrapped around me, holding me in place.

My breath caught as his memories flooded my mind in rapid succession. Tal and me on the beach when we were sixteen. Him leaning in close, the desire to kiss me overwhelming him. Tal staring at me from across the street as I laughed with friends, unaware that he was there. The urge to punch Jason Sweeny as I danced with him at the prom. Tal wanting nothing more than to hold me for days after Beau's tragic death. The pure pleasure of installing the enchanted tree in his New Orleans apartment a few short months ago.

"Willow?"

I heard Tal's voice from far away. I blinked, clearing the memories from my mind. Our combined magic had filled me to the point of almost bursting.

"Oh, no. Sorry!" I cried and jerked my hands from his.

Tal stumbled back a few feet, his body hunched over and his head in his hands.

"Tal?" I reached out, but before I could touch him, I pulled back. I'd taken too much. He was hurt.

"Do it now, Willow," he huffed out. "Heal K.C."

I hesitated. Tal needed help, too.

"Wil!" He waved at K.C. "He's your priority. I'll be fine."

His urgency snapped me back into action and I spun, placing both hands over K.C.'s heart. This time when I unleashed my magic, it held for just a moment before seamlessly flowing straight into the guard. He took it so easily I had to consciously hold back the magic for fear it would be too much for him.

But then I realized I wasn't getting any response from him at all. There was no change in his heart rate or temperature or any of his other metabolic responses. His monitors continued to beep on at a steady, monotonous rate.

"Come on, K.C.," I pleaded, not at all sure what else I could do. "Work with me here."

"I'm here," Tal said into my ear as he shifted behind me again, his hands coming to rest on top of mine. His healing energy slipped over my skin and merged with my magic as we both poured all our gifts into K.C.

A scene at Allcot's mansion materialized in my mind, only Allcot wasn't there. Neither was David. K.C. sat at Allcot's desk, dressed in a silk shirt, a tailored jacket, and designer jeans. His black-leather-clad feet were up on the desk, crossed at the ankles as he leaned back, eyeing the three vamps standing in front of him.

His lips turned up into a sly smile as he barked inaudible orders at his minions. They nodded automatically and filed out of the room just as Pandora, Allcot's lover, strolled in, wearing even less clothing than she normally did. He stood and leaned over the desk as Pandora pulled at the ties of her bustier, her eyes molten with desire.

K.C.'s heart rate sped up, sending the machines into a beeping frenzy.

I jerked my hand out of Tal's and held it close to my heart. K.C. had been deliriously happy in what could only be a fantasy. Pandora was completely devoted to Allcot, and there was no way in hell anyone would be stupid enough to not only take over Allcot's desk but also order his employees around.

Tal moved his hands from K.C.'s chest to my arms. He bent down and whispered, "I think that did it."

K.C. lay blinking up at us from the hospital bed.

"Welcome back," Tal said.

"Back?" K.C. croaked.

"Yes. You were poisoned and ended up in a short-term coma."

The guard glanced around the room, finally focusing on David. "Wasn't real," he muttered to himself. "Fuck me."

Chapter 18

Tal and I had just walked through the front door of my house in the Lower Garden District when his phone buzzed with an incoming text. He glanced down and frowned.

"What's up?" I tossed my keys on the side table and glanced around for my roommate, Phoebe. The place was quiet, no sign of her. Link bounded through the house, no doubt checking for any unwelcome guests the way he usually did.

"I've been summoned to the Void office." Tal blew out a breath as he shoved his phone back in his pocket.

I raised my eyebrows. "Any idea what it's about?"

He shrugged. "Could be anything. But I'm not going anywhere before we eat." Moving to the base of the stairs, he held his hand out to me.

I took it without any hesitation. Neither of us had eaten a proper meal since the day before. Tal took the lead up to my second story, where the kitchen was located. He slowed as he passed my bedroom door. It stood open, everything left untouched, sitting exactly as I had left it. It was neat, but the bed was unmade and called to me. Before I could stop myself, I said, "Bedroom picnic?"

He turned to me, a mischievous grin on his face.

My heart squeezed. It was exactly the expression I would've expected from him prior to our breakup.

"You sure you can handle it, being in bed with such an irresistible—"

I held up my hand, laughing. "I'm after the energy boost, thank you very much."

His right eyebrow rose and he let his gaze wander the length of my body. More than just my face heated at his careful perusal. "An energy boost, huh? Is that what you call it?"

Giggling, I swatted his arm. "Stop. You know I'm talking about my tree. If you're gonna act like a fifteen-year-old, maybe we better stick to the kitchen table."

His grin widened.

"Oh, shut up," I said, not able to stop my body from shaking with laughter.

"The table works for me." He winked and slid his arm around my waist, pulling me tight to his firm body. Then he lowered his voice, letting it go husky. "Forget dinner. Let's head straight for dessert."

My mouth went dry as I stared up into his heated expression. *Yes.* The word was on the tip of my tongue. Who needed food when he was offering me everything I'd ever wanted?

His gaze shifted to my mouth and I swear we both stopped breathing. If I moved one tiny inch toward him, I knew we'd never make it to the Void office. We'd be lost to each other.

Clearing my throat, I stepped back. "We should eat," I said reluctantly.

Still staring at my mouth, he nodded slowly. "Yeah. We should."

Every single one of my muscles was taut with tension. Why was I resisting what was so clearly arcing between us? I no longer knew or even cared about my reasons. My heart was bursting with desire for this man. But something held me back. Nerves?

No. That wasn't it.

You're afraid.

The words were a silent whisper in my mind. I didn't want to get hurt again. Talisen had the power to break me. I trusted him with my life, but not my heart. Not yet anyway.

Sucking in a steadying breath, I held out my hand.

Tal took it, his thumb brushing gently over mine. Sparks of intense need shot from his hand and touched me deep in my soul. The contact nearly broke my resolve. Instead, Link appeared behind him, wagging his tail, and the spell was broken. I tugged on Tal's hand and led him into my kitchen.

He followed willingly. As did Link. But when I stopped in front of the refrigerator, Tal didn't release me. He moved closer and cupped my cheek with his free hand. Our eyes met, his green ones searching mine. "I won't let you go this time, Wil."

Emotion clogged my throat. I swallowed, afraid if I tried to speak I'd cry.

"I'm not going to lie and say that your relationship with Laveaux doesn't bother me, because it does. Knowing that you have a connection to him tears me up inside. It's not something I can compete with, nor do I want to. Not anymore, anyway."

"You don't—"

He held up his hand. "Let me finish. I was a fool. I never should've let any of them, Allcot or the Void, dictate my relationship with you. The truth is, if I hadn't let my pride get in the way, I never would've in the first place. Being without you the past few months, it's been hell on earth. I know we weren't together for very long, but I've known for years you're the one I want to be with. And once I finally let myself believe it was possible, all my defenses were blown apart. I want you. I need you. And whatever I have to do to convince you that we're meant to be, that's what I'll do."

I stood there, staring at him, all his defenses stripped away. He'd bared everything to me. I didn't know what to say. Didn't know what I should say. Was that a question? Was he asking me to be with him? My hand shook as I reached up to brush a lock of hair off his forehead. At my touch, his eyes closed and he took in a shuddering breath.

Trailing my fingers down to his jaw, I leaned in, stopping just before my lips touched his. "Tal?"

His eyes opened. His intense gaze seared through me. "Yeah?"

"I've loved you since I was sixteen years old."

His expression softened with something I couldn't quite put my finger on. Then his other hand came up and he pressed his thumb lightly to my parted lips. "I've missed you."

I closed my eyes and gently kissed his thumb, reveling in the tender moment. He was mine again.

He slid his fingers down my neck as he closed the distance. Then his lips were on mine.

My heart nearly exploded in my chest. *Mine,* I thought as he gentled the kiss, taking care to be sure I wanted him as much as he wanted me. But he shouldn't have. I wanted this more than he knew.

Fisting my hand into his shirt, I pulled him closer and opened my mouth, welcoming him. Our tongues met and more electricity sizzled straight to my toes. I was lost in his embrace, needing to feel him against me. To know he was real. That we were real.

"Willow," he murmured, pulling my hand from his chest. His fingers slid between mine, holding on tight. His kisses moved along my jawline to my neck until I felt his heated breath just below my ear. "I love you, too," he whispered.

There was no stopping the tears then. They welled and rolled unchecked down my cheeks.

"Ah, babe. I'm so sorry." He pulled back, releasing my hand. Both arms went around me and I pressed my face into his shoulder, happy to just be held.

We stood there in my kitchen as he stroked his hand through my thick mane of hair while I held on to him. He was my lifeline, the one who understood me like no one else.

I needed him. "I can't do this without you."

"You can. We both know that. But you don't have to anymore."

I shook my head. He couldn't know that. The Void owned both of us. Neither one of us had full control over our lives anymore.

He took a step back, holding my shoulders with both hands. "I'm not leaving you this time."

"How can you say that? You have a contract with the Void. If they make you go back to Eureka, you go."

He sighed. "But that doesn't mean I'll leave you. Even if I have to physically be somewhere else, I'll still be here with you." He touched my chest just over my heart. "I won't shut you out again. Ever. Got it?"

I nodded, knowing I was being overly dramatic. But dammit, now that I had him back, I didn't want to let him go for anything. "What about your undercover mission?"

"I don't know. I suspect that's what the director wants to talk about." His hands slid down to my wrists. "It's probable that since I was seen with you, my cover has been blown. I guess we'll find out tonight what my next assignment is."

A pit of unease coiled in my stomach. I didn't like the sound of that. If his cover was blown, then there was nothing stopping Asher's people from coming after him. And they would. There was no doubt about that.

He smoothed my brow. "Stop worrying. We're safe for now."

"For now," I echoed.

Smiling, he pulled me to him and kissed me again, leaving me completely breathless when he finally released me. "Food. Then more kissing."

"You're…" I searched for what I wanted to say.

"What? Gorgeous? A genius? Making you want to rip my clothes off?"

I laughed and shook my head. Then I threaded my fingers through his again and kissed the back of his hand. "Mine."

All of the humor left his face. He gazed down at me, his eyes serious. "That's right. I am."

The fridge was shockingly empty. I considered ordering takeout, but the idea of even letting a delivery driver into our private little world was too much. In the end, I made spaghetti and opened a bottle of wine. Due to our dinner choice, we skipped the bedroom picnic and ate at the table. Link lay at our feet, content with the meatballs I'd dished into his dinner bowl.

"This is good," Tal said after inhaling two forkfuls of pasta.

"It's okay." It wasn't anything special. Just noodles, jarred sauce, and some garlic meatballs. It was one step above bachelor food.

"*It's good*," he stressed and refilled my wineglass.

I could take a hint. "Thank you."

"You're welcome. Now pass me the bowl. I need another helping."

I didn't touch the second glass of wine as I watched him shovel in enough food for three people. Instead, I switched to the Mocha in Motion for an energy boost. "When is the last time you ate a real meal?" I asked when he finally pushed the plate away.

"No idea." He reached down and scratched Link's belly, who was lying at his feet, his paws in the air.

"Tal?"

He looked up. "Yeah?"

"Are you going to fill me in on exactly what you've been doing with Asher's people these last few months?"

He nodded. "Later tonight I'll tell you anything you want to know. But right now I have to get to the Void office. They're getting antsy." He held his phone up to me, displaying three texts from none other than the director herself.

"Jeez. Impatient much?"

"They probably just want to make sure I didn't sell their secrets to the other side." He stood. "Mind if I borrow your car?"

"I'll drive you." After clearing the dishes, I darted to my room to grab my keys and a car charger. My phone had died a long time ago. There was no doubt people had been trying to reach me. David and Phoebe for sure. And there was no way I was lucky enough that the Void wouldn't want to see me if they had any idea of what had gone down in California.

I met Tal and Link at the front door. "Ready?"

Tal shook his head.

"Forget something?"

"Yeah. This." Without warning, he bent and kissed me, one arm going around my back. His lips claimed mine, possessing me with his heated intensity. Every inch of me tingled from his touch, and the rest of the world around us faded away into nothing. When we finally parted, we were both breathless.

"Wow," I said softly.

His lips curved up into a self-satisfied smile. "There's more where that came from."

"I hope so."

We both chuckled, but then as our laughter died, a foreboding settled over me from out of nowhere.

Tal studied me. "What's wrong?"

I met his worried expression with one of my own. "Why do I feel like once we leave this house, everything is going to change again?"

Chapter 19

"You worry too much," Tal said as he opened the passenger door for me.

"And you're a typical male who doesn't worry enough." I gave him a small smile to let him know I was joking. He was anything but typical.

"Maybe. But the only thing I'm worrying about is how long it will be before I can get you back to your house and into that magical bed of yours."

There was that mischief in his eyes, again. I knew he was trying to tease me out of my downer mood. I just couldn't help it. There was something inside me telling me that whatever happened tonight at the Void would be a game changer. I shook off the sense of doom and gave him a sly smile. "I'm not sure we need my bed for our time together to be magical."

His expression turned serious as he clasped my hand in his. "No truer words have ever been spoken."

Our gazes met and held for a moment before he kissed the back of my hand and then let go to make his way to the driver's seat.

I busied myself plugging in the car charger for my phone while Link curled up in the back seat of my Jeep.

A few moments later, Tal put the car in gear and took off down the street. I was watching the text and phone call notifications pop up on my phone when Tal said, "So… K.C.'s vision was interesting, don't you think?"

I glanced up, startled by the comment. We hadn't talked about what we'd seen while working our magic on the guards. "Uh... yeah."

"We should probably warn Allcot... or Laveaux... that they have a guard with such high ambition."

I scrolled through my texts, grimacing when I saw three of them were from the director. I'd been summoned as well. Good thing we were on our way. The director was going to be pissed I hadn't answered her. I turned to Tal. "You think those visions are actual ambitions?"

He nodded. "Sure seemed like it to me. Or desires."

Heat crawled up my neck as I remembered the way I'd felt seeing my own vision. "So you're saying Harrison's biggest desire is to be a filmmaker?"

"That's my guess. The emotions were too strong to just be daydreams. Wouldn't you say?"

"Yeah," I said almost to myself. Tal had said both Link and I were in his vision. But he hadn't said what we were doing. What if he was saying good-bye to me? My heart stuttered. Shaking my head, I focused on K.C. If Tal was right, and I had a feeling he was, that meant K.C. was a live wire, one that needed to be watched. "It's odd K.C. knew who David and Allcot were while the others didn't. You think that's because his deepest desire is to be Allcot?"

"That's a solid theory. He was pretty confused about everything else, so I think you're on to something there."

"I'll tell David to watch out for K.C."

Tal made a right and pulled into the parking garage attached to the Void building. I sat there in my seat, frozen. Every instinct told me not to go into that building.

"Wil?" Tal's voice was full of concern. "What's wrong?"

My breathing became shallow and my hands got clammy. I squeezed my eyes shut and pictured the redwoods with the sound of the ocean breaking against the coastline. It was my happy place. The place Beau and I had escaped to as kids when life was too overwhelming.

Talisen's light touch trailed over my wrist and a faint trace of calm followed. "Just relax, Wil. It's only a little PTSD. You can do this."

I recognized what he was saying. Knew he was right. I'd spent three months in this building being tested, or tortured more like it, while the Void studied how I reacted to a vampire's touch and what happened when I turned them into daywalkers. It had been hell on earth. And ever since the day the testing stopped, I hadn't been back, opting to take any orders over the phone or by courier.

"I can do this," I said, willing myself to calm down. I was with Tal. Only going to meet with the director. Nothing to be afraid of.

Tal exited and came around the car to help me out of my seat.

I let him, craving his calming touch. He was definitely putting some of his healing energy into it, otherwise I never would have made it.

Dammit! I hated that I was reacting this way. I'd been through way worse. Why was I ready to break down right there in the parking lot? I climbed out of the car and wasn't surprised to see Link had shifted into wolf mode. Of course he had with the way I'd reacted. He pressed his body against my leg, his way of lending me his strength. I smiled down at him. "Thanks, boy."

"Let's go," I said to Talisen, and then with my shoulders back, I led the way into the building. I strode past security without being asked to step through the magical neutralizer. Because I'd been subjected to testing for the past three months, it had been imperative that I have full use of my powers. The guards still hadn't gotten the memo that testing had ended, and I wasn't going to be the one to tell them. The neutralizer was just this side of torture. Being without my magical gifts was bad enough, but having them zapped felt like being sent through a faery-sized microwave.

Link and Tal weren't so lucky. Link came out of the neutralizer in his Shih Tzu form, his hair standing on end as if he'd been electrocuted. Tal fared better, but he still had that dazed look everyone gets when their magic is sucked from them.

I held my hand out to him and led the way to the director's office.

Her receptionist gave us an impatient look and hurried us to the door. "She's been waiting."

Well, God forbid we make the director wait more than an hour or so.

"She's been riding my ass for the past two hours," her receptionist said, apparently reading my thoughts.

"We've had an eventful day," Tal said by way of explanation and then strode inside.

He wasn't kidding. It was late, eight or so in the evening. Frankly I was surprised the receptionist was still there. Director Halston must've made her stay late.

"You're trying my patience," the gray-haired fae said from behind her desk. She stood, her small five-foot frame taking up more space than should be possible.

Tal said nothing. I shrugged.

"Sit." She pulled out two folders. One was marked Transfer, the other Assignment.

I bit my lip as the foreboding I'd felt earlier slammed back into me. Transfer. My first thought was that I'd be split from Phoebe again. My second was that Tal would be transferred back to New Orleans and the pressure on my chest eased. I glanced at him, noting his eyes were glued to the folder that Halston had just slid in front of him. Transfer.

She held on to the other one. "I assume you don't mind that Rhoswen is here for this conversation. She'll learn about it either way."

"It's fine," Tal said stiffly.

"Good. Your contract has been transferred to the Cryrique. You'll serve out your term working for Allcot while supplying the Arcane with your superhuman elixir, only you'll be more of a contractor for us now. Your permanent service to us is now terminated."

"What?" I stood, unable to keep still.

"Sit down, Rhoswen. You are here out of courtesy only. If you cannot control yourself, I will have to ask you to wait outside." Her piercing gaze all but burned a hole in my head.

My wings twitched out of sheer frustration, but I forced them down and sat on the edge of my chair, studying Tal.

His jaw was clenched as he read the orders in front of him. When he finally looked up at Halston, his eyes were green fire. "You sold me to a vampire organization?"

Her expression was one of cool nonchalance. "It's nothing personal. Your cover was blown with Asher's circle in California. You can't go back there. Hunter has left word that if you do, they'll kill you the first opportunity they get. You were seen boarding the plane with Rhoswen." She cut her gaze to me and gave me a look that said she'd deal with me later. Turning back to Tal, she added, "They know you have ties to Cryrique. We don't have a use for you now. This way not only did we trim the budget but we made a tidy sum to help us cover some special projects. You turned out to be more useful than we thought."

"So you've forced me to work with him for the next four years." Tal's voice was laced with a dangerous edge.

"Please, Mr. Kavanagh. Do not take me for a fool. I already know you're working with Allcot. This just frees up your time and mine." She waved a hand. "Now, please be so kind as to wait outside while I discuss business with Ms. Rhoswen."

Tal stood, his arm muscles bulging with tension. "You just tied me to him. Put me in a contract I can't negotiate. This is unacceptable."

Her eyebrows rose in mild curiosity. "Did you not understand the contract you signed with us? That truly is unfortunate. I'd thought you were more intelligent than that. Pity. Maybe you should hire an attorney next time before you sign over your soul for someone else."

Her gaze darted back to me, making it clear whatever choice he'd made was because of me.

Tal didn't glance in my direction, but his eye did twitch. She'd hit the nail on the head, and he was more than pissed she'd dared call him out on it. Without speaking, he scooped up the folder and stormed out.

Would he wait for me? Or take off to confront Allcot right away? There was no doubt he'd be questioning David's father. Jeez. What the hell had he been thinking? Did David know? Hard to say. If so, I bet he wasn't any happier about it than Tal was.

"Rhoswen," the director said, eyeing me.

"Yes?" I stayed perfectly still, trying not to let on how nervous I was. New orders given to me and not to Phoebe was disconcerting. Phoebe was the muscle behind our duo, the one with all the training. The director never gave me information she could give Phoebe.

"I have a task for you."

"So I see." I nodded at the folder.

She slid it along the table. "You're to investigate the background of the fae you took out at the burlesque club the other night."

I was in the processes of flipping open the folder but glanced up before I could read the directive. "What? Why? Isn't he here?"

"Yes. We have him in custody, but he's disoriented and not talking. Your partner is investigating the vampire, Lady Victoria. Meanwhile, we need you to bring us everything you know about the fae shifter."

So, the director had lied to Allcot about the fae escaping. No surprise there. I sat back, ignoring the folder. "You do know I'm not trained in this sort of thing? Right? All I do is back Phoebe up. I didn't even go to the academy." I'd been hired specifically because I could sense vampires and could help keep fellow agents out of danger. I didn't have tracking skills or magical spells that neutralized predators like Phoebe did.

"Don't be so modest, Rhoswen. I'm privy to the research you've conducted on your plants for your shop and those magical treats you spend so much time making. We're shorthanded here and need someone to take on this project. Since he and Victoria both have ties to Asher's sect, we believe you're the best person for the job."

I narrowed my eyes. It was highly unusual for her to put me on any path that involved Asher or his people. They liked to exploit my gifts too much. Or had they decided it wasn't such a loss if Asher did kill me? They didn't exactly want me turning any more vamps. It wasn't a question I was willing to ask, though. I was happy to be useful. Grabbing the paperwork, I stood.

"One more thing," Halston added. "I expect you to work with Laveaux on this."

I froze, startled. The Void rarely worked with the Cryrique vampires. Neither side trusted the other. "Why?"

She gave me a flat stare. "Because Laveaux has information he's keeping from me but he'll tell you. I expect a report on my desk in forty-eight hours."

Of course she did. "I'll do my best." Then I bent down and scooped up Link, who'd fallen asleep at my feet, and strode gracefully out of the office, determined to keep my cool. "Laveaux," I mumbled under my breath. "Just fucking perfect."

Chapter 20

"Head to Allcot's place," I said to Tal as soon as we climbed back into the Jeep.

"Was already planning on it." He caught my eye. "But want to tell me what's got you so worked up?"

I stroked my hand down Link's back, trying to keep my temper under control. It wasn't working, though. "I have orders to specifically work with David to track down information on the fae who poisoned Harrison and the others."

"You're kidding?" He stepped on the gas and took a right down St. Charles.

"Nope."

"Well, this is awkward," he said with a wry smile. "You, me, Laveaux, and Allcot. Happy foursome."

"Ugh." I pressed my hand to my forehead. I had to tell David about Tal and me. And soon.

Tal sighed. "I'm sorry."

I turned in my seat, studying him. "Why?"

"Because I know this is hard for you. Laveaux still thinks he has a chance, and now you're forced to work with him. It's a shit situation. The last thing I want to do is make it worse. But I won't lie. It's going to be real hard watching you work closely with him. I'll do my best to not turn into a world-class ass again."

I glanced out the window, barely noticing the lights of the passing cars. Then I turned and gave him a ghost of a smile. "That means a lot. Thanks." Reaching across the Jeep, I placed my hand on his knee. "Do something for me?"

"Anything."

"Remember that no matter what happens, I chose you?"

He cleared his throat and covered my hand with his own. "I will, but don't think that won't stop me from losing my shit on a regular basis."

I pulled my hand away, my body suddenly stiff. "About David? Because there's no reason for that. And—"

He put a hand up to stop me and swerved to the side of the road. After putting the Jeep in park, he turned to me. "Not David. Not anymore, anyway. Do you realize I'd do anything I could to give you a normal life? One free of Allcot, the Void, and people like Asher? I'd gas up this car and drive to the middle of nowhere, USA, right now if I thought it would help."

I huffed out a breath. "But it won't. And you know I'd never leave my family."

"Of course you wouldn't. The thing is, I had this vision of us living in the redwoods, you running your bakery and me a holistic-health center. Two point five children and a couple of dogs. The pair of us growing old together."

My heart squeezed. The picture he was painting was too much. I wanted it too. Ached for it.

"The thing is, I know now that's not the life you were meant to live. At least not right now," he continued, his voice hoarse with emotion. "You have gifts that are unparalleled. People who crave power are always going to be trying to get to you. Our time apart made me realize that no matter the path, all I want in this world is to be by your side." He reached over and gently wiped the tears leaking from my eyes. "You know the vision I had today?"

I nodded, mute, unable to even respond to what he'd just said.

"It was of you, me, and Link," he said softly. "We were living here in New Orleans and we were working side by side. Not just at your shop or in the lab, but also on patrols with Phoebe and missions for the Void."

"That sounds… lovely," I choked out and smiled at him.

Joy filled all the empty places inside me. He wanted to be my partner, not my protector, unlike everyone else in my life.

He let out a low, ironic chuckle. "It was almost possible. Before I was sold to Allcot."

The euphoria of finding out he saw me as an equal disappeared as anger took over, sending ripples of white-hot fury through my veins. Sold. To Allcot. All because of budget concerns and because Halston saw no use for him outside of his superhuman drug, which he was still obligated to supply them. I hated the Void almost as much as I hated Asher. Though surprisingly, I had trouble finding fault with Allcot. He was shady as hell, but at least he was up front about it.

"Dammit, Tal. I don't know what to do about that. Maybe we can work out some sort of deal with Allcot."

He gave me a dubious look. "You know just as well as I do that isn't going to happen. He bought my contract. There's no getting out of it."

I bit the side of my cheek. I couldn't argue with that. But Allcot would deal if I could find something he wanted badly enough. Now that he'd already turned daywalker, I had no idea what that would be. He was rich enough to buy practically anything he wanted already. "We'll just have to look for an opening or wait it out. If there's anything I've learned this year it's that nothing is permanent."

The frustration drained from his face as his expression went soft with emotion. "Some things are." He took my hand and placed it over his heart. "What I feel for you is real and always has been. That won't change."

Tears stung my eyes again, but I didn't let them fall. Instead, I leaned over and pressed my lips to his, wordlessly showing him that I was his once and for all. All I needed to do was tell David. I'd do it tonight. Right after I got some answers.

Tal was two blocks from Allcot's mansion when my phone buzzed with an incoming text.

Phoebe: *Need you now. Backstreet Tavern.*

"Turn around," I told Talisen.

He did what I asked without comment.

I texted back. *Be there in ten.*

Phoebe: *Hurry. Vampires were spotted. Need your senses.*

Me: *Be there in five.*

"Step on it," I told Tal.

Tal glanced at me but sped up, ignoring the posted speed limit.

"Phoebe's on a job and needs backup."

"No problem."

Link jumped up, standing on all fours. I lifted him and put him in the back seat just in case he shifted right there in the car. The Void's neutralizer would've worn off by now. Link bounced back faster than fae and witches did. Tal was probably still under the influence. That worried me a little, but there was nothing to do about it.

I directed Tal until he pulled up in front of the uptown college bar. Link and I scrambled out, Link in wolf form. "Meet us inside?" I said to Tal.

He nodded. "Be careful."

"Always." I slammed the door shut and cast the Jeep a fleeting glance as Tal darted around the corner looking for parking. A tingle of pleasure warmed me with the knowledge that he trusted me to handle myself. There was no way in hell David would've let me go anywhere near the club without him had we been together. Maybe that had been the problem from the start. We'd never been on equal footing.

A group of coeds, dressed in skintight camisoles, barely there skirts, and heels so high their ankles wobbled, stumbled out of the front door. They each held Styrofoam cups, no doubt full of daiquiris, clutched in their hands.

It was the perfect hunting ground for hungry vamps. I stifled a shudder and slipped into the open-air bar. The only problem was I didn't sense any vamps anywhere. Was I even in the right place? I whipped my phone out and checked Phoebe's message. Yeah. Right place. I tapped out a quick text.

Me: *I'm here. Where are you?*

Phoebe: *At the bar. All the way to the right.*

I glanced up, searching, but the crowd was too thick. "Let's go, Link."

He was on full alert, his scruff raised on the back of his neck. He sensed something, but he hadn't spotted it yet. I stayed close to his hindquarters and followed him. The crowd parted easily for us. Faeries weren't exactly a dime a dozen in New Orleans. Neither were wolves. It was a good thing we weren't trying to be inconspicuous.

If I hadn't seen Phoebe in a hundred different disguises over the years, I might not have recognized her. But there she was, leaning over the bar and wearing a dirty-blond wig, skintight black leggings, knee-high boots, and a purple sequined tank top. Not exactly a wallflower, but she blended well enough with the crowd. And her boots had thick heels, perfect for kicking ass.

I glided up to the bar and ordered an Abita Amber.

"Beer?" Phoebe asked by way of greeting.

"It's been a long-ass day. Cut me some slack."

The bartender pulled the tap, filling a plastic cup until the head ran over.

"Feel anything?" she asked as she leaned against the bar, scanning the crowd.

"Nope." I sipped at the beer, reveling in the crisp freshness. "Dang, that's good."

She stared at me. "I can't believe you're drinking right now."

I supposed it wasn't the best decision. But holy crow, I needed it after the day I'd had. Link paced in front of us, creating a barrier between us and the crowd.

"Link, sit!" Phoebe commanded.

He immediately dropped his rear and cocked his head, listening.

I set my beer down, watching him. "He senses something."

Phoebe nodded. "But you don't?"

I shook my head, catching sight of Tal as he walked into the bar. His gaze landed on me instantly. It was as if he sensed where I was. My insides turned to jelly just looking at him.

Phoebe let out a low whistle. "Golden boy is back, I see."

"Yeah." The word came out sounding shy.

She laughed. "Good. I assume that means Laveaux is kicked to the curb?"

I gave her a dirty look.

"Well? You can't date both of them, and judging by the look on both your faces, elf boy is in and vamp boy is way out."

I rolled my eyes. "Do you have to be so flippant about it?"

"Ha! I knew it. Finally." She wiggled her fingers at Tal. "Hey tall, blond, and sexy."

"Phoebs," he said with a nod and wrapped his arm around my shoulder.

It felt so odd to be hanging out in a bar with my two most favorite people as if Tal weren't indentured to Allcot and Phoebe and I weren't on a vampire hunt. But we were, and even though all of us acted as if we didn't have a care in the world, it was just that, an act. Despite my wings and the wolf at our feet, the crowd had ceased paying attention to us. We were just a few more patrons out for a good time. How wrong they were.

Tal's phone buzzed. He frowned as he read the message.

"What is it?" I asked, unease inching up my spine.

"Our cure didn't work. Harrison and the others are getting weak again and their wounds aren't healing. The only consolation is they haven't slipped back into a coma… yet."

"How is that possible?" Frustration hit me hard. I'd known we still had to work on healing their wounds, but damn. I hadn't expected them to relapse so soon. "We just woke them up a few hours ago."

"It's the poison. We have to find an antidote as soon as possible. After we're done here, I'll need to consult some healer texts." His lips thinned into a tight line. "Maybe we'll get lucky."

I matched his frown. Research could take days. The guards didn't appear to have that long. I turned to Phoebe, anxious to help her catch her vamp so we could leave. "How long's it been since you last saw the vamp?"

"Thirty, forty minutes. And it wasn't just one. It was two. A male and a female. They were over there." She pointed to the other side of the bar's courtyard. "But by the time I got through the crowd, they'd terrorized one coed and then disappeared."

"Did you see anyone leave?" I was almost positive at least one of them was still around. Link was entirely too agitated.

"Not with either one of them." She frowned. "I just can't figure out where they went." Her frustration was boiling over. Nothing pissed her off more than when an innocent was attacked. "That was the third time I'd spotted them, too. I don't know where they're going, but they haven't left. I'm sure of it. Being out in the open isn't helping. It's too easy for them to disappear into a neighboring building and reappear somewhere else."

Yeah, that would be a problem. I eyed the rooftops of the three buildings surrounding the bar and courtyard. They were each three stories high, but that was nothing for a vamp. They could leap to any one of the terraces and get into just about any apartment. I shuddered, imagining an empty apartment with drained humans. "What about the coed? Where is she?"

Phoebe tilted her head toward a girl sitting at a picnic table in what appeared to be an employee area a few yards behind the bar. She'd been the one Phoebe had been talking to when I'd walked in.

"I'll be right back." Leaving Tal and Phoebe, I slipped behind the bar and sat next to the girl. She was staring into a plastic cup of water. "Hey. You doing better?"

Her eyes widened as she took in my wings. "You're fae."

I smiled. Way to state the obvious. "Nice to meet you."

She flushed and held out her hand. "Hi. I'm Cameron."

"Hi, Cameron. I'm Willow." I shook her hand, pleased when her grip tightened around mine. Just my talking to her seemed to be giving her some confidence back. "Want to tell me what happened with the vamps?"

Her eyes narrowed. "They were trying to convince me to go back to their house for an evening of fun. Like they were swingers or something." She visibly shivered. "Only I've seen them before and I know a few girls who've gone home with them in the past."

"And?"

"Let's just say those girls don't go clubbing anymore."

My blood pressure skyrocketed. That could mean anything from a nonconsensual feeding to sexual assault. I glanced at Phoebs and Tal. They both had their backs to us as they continued to scan the bar, searching for the rogue vampires.

"And what did they say when you turned them down?" I asked her.

She clamped her lips together and shook her head.

Damn. She was done opening up to me. "Well," I said carefully. "See my friends over there? You've already met the blonde." I pointed to Phoebe. "We're not leaving until we track them down. So any info you have on them would be most helpful."

Her expression turned wary and then skeptical as she eyed me. "Don't take this the wrong way, but you look like someone they might eat for breakfast."

I laughed at that. She wasn't wrong. No one ever pegged me as a vamp hunter. I definitely didn't look the part. Long auburn hair, hands better suited for baking than fighting, and I was dressed in a long, flowing skirt and ballet flats. I looked every bit the pacifist I longed to be. It just wasn't in my cards. "Good luck to them," I said and winked. "They aren't likely to get past my wolf, but if they do, I have a few tricks up my sleeve."

She glanced at Link, who was still pacing in front of Phoebe, and her skeptical expression turned into a small smile. "That's some nice protection right there."

"You can say that again." I grinned and then touched her hand lightly. "If you have any other information you want to share, I'll be right over there." I pointed once again to the place where Phoebe and Tal were talking, heads bent.

She nodded.

I gave her one last long look before I thanked her for her time and headed back in the direction of my friends.

"Willow?" she called.

I spun. "Yes?"

"I don't think your wolf is going to help you now."

"Wh—"

Someone slammed into me from behind. I stumbled forward, certain I was headed to the floor face first. But then a line of fire grasped me around the neck and jerked me back up and onto my feet. My entire back screamed in protest as a thousand pinpricks of pain consumed me to the point my vision blurred.

Vampire!

The word flashed in my mind like a neon light. Where had he come from? More importantly, why hadn't I felt him? Just like I hadn't felt Victoria. Was my gift broken? A vampire shouldn't have been able to sneak up on me like that. Not unless I'd turned him into a daywalker, but then their touch couldn't hurt me.

I bucked, kicking my feet out, trying my damnedest to break free, but it was useless. The vamp had a viselike grip on me and my energy was draining at a rapid rate. *Phoebe! Tal!* I tried to call to them, but I couldn't get enough air to get the words out.

Blackness danced at the edge of my vision. Heat was consuming every inch of me. And the last thing I saw before I felt the whoosh of air around us was the coed's face sneering up at me as the vampire leaped, taking me with him through one of the nearby open windows.

Chapter 21

"Get in!" The vampire kicked me in the back, forcing me into a souped-up electric-blue car with giant wheels.

I gasped for breath and curled into a ball, my body shaking uncontrollably. The trauma from being touched by the vampire was too much, and my muscles twitched from his assault. Too late—I clutched at the door handle, but the car was already in motion, speeding down the streets of New Orleans.

"Where are you taking me?" I forced out between shallow gasps of air.

A woman vampire I'd never seen before turned around in the front seat and gazed at me intently. I was lying on my side, my head bouncing against the vinyl seat.

"You don't look like him," she said, her brows pinched in concentration.

"Who?" I squeezed my eyes shut and winced as we flew over a river of potholes.

"Shut up, Talia," the driver barked.

My eyes popped open and I watched Talia hiss at him. He ignored her displeasure. Her deep blue eyes flashed with irritation as she tied her long bronze hair up into a haphazard bun. "Speak to me that way again, and I'll rip your little toy's throat out before you have your way with her."

Your little toy? Was that bitch talking about me? Now that I wasn't blindsided, we'd see how far she got. I'd drain her life even if it killed me before I'd let either of them lay a hand on me again.

He whipped his hand out and caught her around the throat in one quick movement. "Don't test me." The words came out low and controlled, but the way his muscles were flexing, he was one step away from breaking her neck. Not that it would kill her. But it would hurt like a son of a bitch.

I pushed myself up, trying to get my bearings. I wasn't going to be able to do anything curled into the fetal position.

"Sure, Vince," Talia whispered.

He flexed his fingers, squeezing harder for a moment, then flung her backward, causing her head to bounce against the window with a loud thunk. "Think before you speak next time."

She slumped in her seat, clutching her head. Then I saw her cast a look of pure hatred his way. It was there for just a moment, then disappeared when she sent him a twisted smile. "You know it turns me on when you manhandle me that way."

My stomach turned. Watching the disturbed way they interacted made my skin crawl. The only upside was I knew if I could get her alone, it wouldn't be too hard to get her to talk. It was obvious to me that she hated him and was playing along for some reason. Most likely she worked for him. They weren't professional enough to work for an organization like Cryrique. More likely they were street vamps hired by someone who didn't want to get their hands dirty. But who?

Asher? He made the most sense, especially since as far as anyone knew, he wasn't in New Orleans. If he'd heard what happened in Eureka, he could've put a contract out on me. But why not sooner? What had changed? I needed to get a few minutes with Talia.

Vince sent her a wolfish smile. "Later, my pet. I'll let you bite me just the way I like it."

Oh, what an ass. My desire to knock the shit out of him almost got the better of me. Instead, I slid closer to the door, planning my escape. I was certain that wherever they were taking me would be infinitely harder to escape from than the back of the souped-up gangster car.

Talia rolled her eyes at Vince, who only laughed and grabbed her upper thigh.

I kept my eyes riveted to their exchange as I inched my hand over to the door handle. The hard metal cooled my hand as I curled my fingers around the latch and waited for my opportunity.

Three blocks later, the light flashed red. My muscles tensed with anticipation. This was my chance. I glanced around, noting the lack of street lamps. The night was dark, filled with shadows. The houses looked deserted and no one was around. We were definitely in gang territory. Double damn. That wasn't going to stop me, though. I had to get out of there. I glanced around once more and spotted a familiar street sign. I'd been here once before. Phoebe had a safe house not too far away. If I could just get out and disappear into the darkness, I might make it.

The car jerked to a stop and I seized the door handle.

Nothing.

The male vampire whipped around, his arm lashing out, but I ducked and slammed my body against the door. It flung open, and I toppled out headfirst. The cool night air whipped around me in sweet relief just before I hit the asphalt. Hard.

I heard the tearing of fabric but had no idea if it was my clothing or someone else's.

Vince swore loudly and I heard the smack of flesh on flesh. He'd hit Talia. Holy mother of fae. I'd barely gotten to my knees before he unfolded himself from the car and loomed over me.

Shit. He was too fast. I hadn't had time to get my ass out of there.

The door was still half ajar, and I clutched it, intending to use it as a shield, but then Talia reared up behind Vince, her fangs extended, her dark eyes fixed on me. "Run!" she demanded, her voice hoarse from fury.

Vince reached back and grabbed her by her hair just as her fangs sank into his neck, ripping open his carotid artery. His face contorted to rage as they both fell forward against the open door.

I scrambled backward just out of their reach and thrust my wings, taking flight. My feet lifted off the ground, but then my wings stalled, too weak to carry my weight. The day's events and being attacked by the vamp had finally taken their toll.

The vampires were grappling, each of them seemingly trying to kill the other. Who knew how long it would last or who their altercation would attract? I had to hide. Fast. I took off at a dead run, my legs weighing me down like lead. The air constricted in my chest as I rounded a corner and spotted a small park.

It wasn't safe. Not in this neighborhood. But it did have trees. And that was what I needed more than anything at that moment. A chance to replenish some of my strength before I collapsed in the street.

I felt the tree's life energy surrounding me when I was only a few feet away. It calmed me and ordered my thoughts. Talisen. Phoebe. I had to get in touch with them. There was no telling if they'd seen the vampires take me or what that bitch coed had told them. The vamps had probably hired her to bait me. I groped through my pockets for my phone but came up empty. I knew I'd had it on me when we'd gotten to the bar. I'd texted Phoebe. Had I lost it in the struggle? Or in the back seat of Vince's car? It was even possible they'd stripped it from me when I was passed out.

Blowing out a frustrated breath, I pushed my hair back and started to climb. I needed the tree more than ever, and standing at the base of it in clear view of the entire neighborhood was asking to be shot. Or worse.

It was slow going. Trees weren't usually much of an issue. When I didn't fly, I was just as skilled as the next fae in climbing into the canopies. But this time I slipped twice before I got to a limb large enough to stand on. Thank the goddess for my wings. If I hadn't been able to fly, I would've ended up splattered on the ground below me.

I was winded, breathing heavily, but safely tucked high in the tree against the trunk when I saw the three pimped-out cars circling the block. Oh no. Someone had seen me. The gang members were coming after me.

They slowed as they reached the park, the windows down and each car armed, at least one gun barrel poking out of the windows. The hair stood up on the back of my neck. I couldn't do anything about a gun. My only defense was my energy-stealing touch. I didn't even have my stun gun with me.

I held my breath and let it out when they slowly eased by.

Then I heard the rapid fire of gunshots followed by a scream and wheels squealing as the cars sped off down the street.

I sat there staring at the corner where the cars had disappeared. My body started to tremble with the realization that I'd never felt so utterly alone in my life. Not even when I'd been locked in a cage in the Arcane. Link had been there then. He been locked in his own cage, but he'd been there.

I leaned back against the trunk of the tree and fingered a nearby leaf. The smooth foliage was cool and sent electric shocks of its energy straight to my magical core, giving me exactly what I needed to recharge. I pulled in as much of the tree's replenishing energy as I could and then took a deep breath. It was time to see what I was really made of.

Listening carefully, I made my way down the tree, trying my best to stay camouflaged in the leaves. Just because the cars were gone didn't mean there wasn't someone out there watching. In fact, it was likely. In a neighborhood like this one, they couldn't count on the local police to answer a call of distress. They were pretty much on their own.

After landing at the base of the tree, I glanced down at my bright blue shirt and grimaced. Not exactly undercover wear. Nor was my skirt. I should have been in jeans and a skintight T-shirt, sporting a leather jacket. Then I'd blend in. Of course, my wings were a dead giveaway. I tucked them close to my back and kept to the shadows of the small park.

If I remembered correctly, Phoebe's safe house was three blocks away. I knew getting there unnoticed would be a small miracle in and of itself. And even if I did, there was also the problem of breaking in. Phoebe had all kinds of wards protecting that place. I could only hope she'd used the same ones she used on our house. Maybe then I'd have a chance of not tripping any of them. It was unlikely. Why would she worry if I could get in? I never went there. Except for that one time I'd been with her.

I pushed the thoughts from my head. There was nothing I could do but try. The safe house was a hell of a lot closer than any other place I might find help. And if I did manage to get in, I'd be safe.

The deserted streets seemed to close in on me as I skirted around haphazardly parked cars and fallen garbage cans, ducking when dogs barked, alerting their masters to intruders. My heart pounded, and I prayed if anyone did see me they wouldn't shoot first and ask questions later. Maybe it was a good thing I was wearing a skirt. Better than an outfit that said I could kick ass.

I'd made it two blocks when a floodlight went off, lighting up what felt like half the block. Loud voices carried from inside the house, one of them demanding to know who dared to intrude on Xavier's territory.

Without thinking, I flattened myself to the pavement and rolled underneath the nearest car. Who was Xavier?

My heart pounded and then nearly beat out of my chest when I heard the double pump of a shotgun. Holy shit. He wasn't messing around.

"Get up, chica," he said in a thick Spanish accent. "Or else you can wait for me to drag you out by your hair."

My throat went dry and sweat beaded in my palms. Maybe it was better to let him drag me out. At least then I'd be close enough to touch him, inflict some damage of my own. Or would that only piss him off more? Could I reason with him? I didn't want any trouble, and no doubt he had a bunch of brothers who'd back him up even if I did manage to take him down.

I sucked in a shaky breath and inched toward the street on the opposite side of where the man stood.

But just as I was about to give up my cover, a girl huffed out, "Jesus, Daddy. We were just watching the stars. Give Miguel a break, huh?"

"I told you," he growled, "that I don't want you seeing that *boy*." The way he stressed the word boy indicated his true feelings for Miguel. As if he'd be happy to feed the kid to the gators before he'd let his daughter date him. "You know who his father is."

There was the sound of feet hitting the pavement and a cry of disgust from the girl. "You can't control who he's related to. God! You'd think you of all people would understand that." Her steps echoed into the night as she stomped off. Then I heard the slam of what must've been a screen door.

There was silence and then the boy said, "My apologies, sir. Vanessa and I, well, she's my friend and I just needed someone to talk to tonight."

There was a long pause followed by a snapping of someone's fingers. Footsteps and then the sound of flesh hitting flesh and a grunt from... Miguel?

"I told you to stay away from her," the dad said, his tone low and dangerous. "I meant it. Next time Kia will do more than blacken your eye."

There were grumblings and a few chuckles of laughter as the footsteps faded up toward the house. I lay perfectly still, watching the white tennis shoes of Miguel fade away into the night.

When the floodlight went out and everything was silent again, I crawled out from under the car, still shaking from delayed adrenaline. The street was deserted. I placed my hand over my heart and closed my eyes for just a moment. That had been a close one.

"One more block," I whispered to myself and turned to the left... right into the chest of the bulkiest man I'd ever laid eyes on.

"Miss Rhoswen," he said.

Startled, I stepped back and stared up at a man who had a dragon tattoo covering the right side of his face from temple to jawline. Vibrant green tears dripped from the dragon's anguished eye.

"You didn't think you'd actually get out of our neighborhood unseen, did you?"

I shook my head. Of course I hadn't. But I'd hoped.

His lips curled into a knowing smile. Then the smile vanished and he nodded at someone behind me. "Cuff her."

Chapter 22

"No!" I held up my hands. "No need to cuff me. I'll cooperate." It was a bold-faced lie, but I had to try.

Dragon Face narrowed his eyes at me. "I don't think so."

The person behind me grabbed my wrists and forced them down behind my back, making it impossible for me to unleash my magic on him. He moved quickly, expertly binding them together in what had to be zip ties.

Dammit. The only saving grace was that my captors weren't vampires. Or was it? Maybe gangbanger humans were worse. At least I usually knew what vamps wanted from me. A myriad of unspeakable crimes flashed through my mind, followed by the horrible thought that they might actually work for Asher. My mouth went dry with fear. No matter what, I was in deep shit.

"Put her in the back," Dragon Face ordered and waved, gesturing to a vehicle behind me.

I twisted and my eyes went wide when I saw the young man who'd tied my hands. He was medium built, white skin with multiple dragon tattoos, blond hair, and had piercings up and down both ears. I glanced down and noted the white shoes I'd seen walking away from the Russian's house. The stargazer was kidnapping me. And I knew him. Jasper Miguel.

He'd applied for a job at The Fated Cupcake a couple of months ago. I'd even interviewed him... and liked him. The only reason he hadn't been hired was because of a schedule conflict. I'd needed more afternoon hours and he wanted to work the early mornings.

"Jasper?" I said, incredulous. "What are you doing? I thought you were going to school?" Meaning why the hell was he gang-banging when we both knew he had ambitions of being a chef and owning his own restaurant someday. He'd been on his way.

"I was. Couldn't keep up with tuition." He cut his gaze away from me as he carefully guided me to a blue SUV. He popped the back hatch and waved. "Get in."

I glanced at the cargo area and raised an eyebrow at him. "Can't I sit in a seat like a regular person?"

He turned serious eyes on me. "Sorry, Willow. You aren't a regular person."

That made my wings flare in agitation.

"Get in, Ms. Rhoswen, or I'll order Jasper to do things you won't like."

Jasper's face went even paler than it had been, but instead of saying anything, he just pressed his lips together in a tight line and stared straight ahead.

I glanced between the two, feeling a crap-ton of guilt for not hiring the nice kid when I'd had the chance. Maybe, just maybe, it would've kept him from falling in with this crowd. It was unlikely, though. Kids who grew up in the neighborhood always seemed to get sucked back in.

But it could have, a voice whispered in my head. Just one hand up was all it took sometimes.

"Get in, faery," Jasper barked.

I stiffened and glared at him.

But when his cold blue eyes softened and he sent a panicked look at his boss's back, I did as I was told and turned to sit in the cargo hold, lifting my knees up to try to crawl in. It wasn't so easy with my hands bound. I fell sideways and curled into a ball, making sure my body was completely in the SUV.

"I'm sorry," Jasper whispered and slammed the back shut. A moment later, Dragon Face and Jasper climbed into the front. The door locks clicked and any hope I had of escaping this time vanished.

My hip and shoulder ached by the time we stopped in front of a modest house just on the edge of Mid-City. I squinted, wondering if we were entering a vampire lair. It was hard to tell. Usually the vamps preferred larger places with more privacy. Human? One who wanted to be turned? Perhaps. But living near the vamps only meant your chances of being eaten rose about a thousand percent.

"Let's go," Dragon Face said.

I uncurled my aching limbs and stood on shaky legs.

"Don't try anything unless you like pain. Got it?" He leaned down and whispered, "I know what you're capable of, and if you even think about draining anyone, I'll have Jasper shoot you in the kneecap." He let his gaze wander the length of my body. "Or a wing. I hear that's a bitch to heal."

I forced myself to not visibly cringe. He was right. My left wing had been injured not too long ago and it still bothered me at times. I had no doubt he meant what he said, though I had trouble believing Jasper would shoot me in cold blood.

Or not.

He was standing near the door, a silver handgun trained right at me.

I nodded at Dragon Face. "Fine. But can you tell me what we're doing here?"

"Getting paid," he said.

Jasper reached out and pressed the buzzer in three rapid motions. It didn't take long for the door to pop open. Thick, honeyed vampire energy rooted me where I stood as a short vampire appearing to be in his early twenties answered the door. He grinned when he saw Jasper, but the smile faded when he spotted Dragon Face. "Fuck," he said. "What are you doing here?"

"We're here to see Rox. I've got a delivery." Dragon Face pushed me forward into the light.

I stumbled from the heaviness claiming my limbs. Could this day get any worse?

The vamp's eyes went wide and then his fangs elongated. Crap. This was going to be ugly. The only upside was his energy was lighter than most. He must've been a younger vamp. In this town, that meant he wouldn't have much power and was probably hungry for it.

"It's her." Shorty gaped at me, excitement dancing in his dark eyes. "We've been waiting a long time for this day."

Something told me he wasn't fanboying over my Kiss Me chocolates.

Jasper glanced at me, confusion lining his face. "What are you talking about?"

The vamp shook his head and opened the door wide. "Bring her in. Rox is going to lose his shit."

Dragon Face pushed me forward. Jasper still had his gun trained on me, but the hardness in his face had vanished. Now he appeared downright confused.

"What's going on?" I heard him ask Dragon Face as he fell in step behind me.

"We're collecting our bounty. Now shut up and let me do the talking."

Collect a bounty? Holy crap on a cracker. I was being sold to these vampires? Had they put a price on my head? Who were they? So far I hadn't recognized anyone except Jasper.

The house was a double shotgun that had been converted to one home. Each room was stacked against the other. We walked through the entry and straight into an office and then into a sitting room that spanned the entire width of the house. Two more vampires were sitting on a sectional, both holding a console game device as they shot at each other on the screen. The female let out a loud groan while the other one threw his controller down and raised his arms in victory. "Take that, you loser. Five-zero. You owe me a lap dance now."

She cast him a sidelong glance, running her plum-colored fingertip over his jawline. Her lips curled up into a predator's smile. "Now, in front of our guests?"

Gods. I hated vamps. They were so predictable. Always putting on the sex show for the humans, or in my case, fae.

"Later." He brushed her off and stood, noticing me for the first time.

"Rhoswen?" he asked Dragon Face.

My captor nodded. "In the flesh."

Undisguised lust lit the vamp's eyes as he stalked toward me. He was tall with thick black hair and a slender basketball player build. "She doesn't look like him," he said.

That was the second time I'd heard that today. "Look like who?" I asked, a hard edge in my tone.

"Who?" the female said with a sardonic laugh. "Who do you think? Beau, your twin."

"You knew my brother?" I asked on a gasp.

"Shut up, Grace."

"You shut up, Rox." The redhead stood, placing her hands on her slender hips and scowling. "I'm not your fucking whore that you can order around. If it wasn't for me, you wouldn't even know about her."

"Not now," he said through clenched teeth.

Dragon Face cleared his throat. "If it's not too much trouble, we'll just take our payment and be on our way."

Rox gestured to the vamp who'd opened the door. "Get the package."

Shorty nodded and disappeared into the back of the house.

"Any sign of Talia and Vince?" Rox asked Dragon Face.

Dammit! Those were the two who'd kidnapped me from the bar. Son of… crappity crap crap crap. I'd torn up my shoulder forcing my way out of the car and for nothing. I was right here with the same vamps I likely would've ended up with anyway.

"They're hiding out across town." Dragon Face shrugged. "They probably don't want to explain how two vamps managed to lose the fae or what they were doing in my neighborhood in the first place."

Rox made a sound in the back of his throat. "We both know why they were there."

Dragon Face didn't say anything, leaving me to wonder why.

"Dumb bastard," the female said. "Those street drugs are eating his brain."

Dragon Face nodded as Shorty reappeared with a large manila envelope. Rox took it, checked the contents, and then handed it to Dragon Face, who didn't even look inside. He just thanked them and left with Jasper on his heels.

Shorty, Rox, and Grace stared at me.

I stared back. "Well? Seems you paid a high price to get me here. Now what exactly is it that you want?"

Rox's dark eyes narrowed as he studied me. Then after a moment he started laughing. "Doesn't look like him and sure as hell doesn't act like him."

I felt my nostrils flare as anger built in my chest at the mention of Beau.

Rox glanced at Shorty and then gestured to me. "Undo her cuffs."

He raised an eyebrow. "You sure about that?"

The leader scowled. "We're three vampires. If we can't stop her from leaving or kicking our asses, we have bigger problems to deal with."

"It's not a matter of keeping her here," Grace said, staring at her fingernails. "It's about not having to work so hard all the time." She sat back down on the couch and slumped forward, appearing weary. "Can't we just live our lives for once without worrying about this BS?"

Rox shook his head. "We're owed this, Grace," he said quietly. "It's the only reason I'd agreed to turn. It's either this or…"

The look on her face said she already knew what he was going to say and she didn't like it. In fact, it terrified her.

Rox glared at Shorty. "I said undo her cuffs."

Shorty jumped and ran into the back again.

"My apologies, Ms. Rhoswen," Rox said. "I imagine your day hasn't been exactly pleasant."

"No," I said slowly. "Pleasant isn't the word I'd use."

Grace sat up and faced me. "Was Vince... I mean, did he hurt you at all?" There was real concern in her voice.

I narrowed my eyes, trying to figure them out. They'd hired people, paid what looked like a lot of money, to get me here. And now they were concerned as to whether I'd been hurt?

"I can imagine your confusion," Rox said, his tone apologetic. "If you give us just a little bit of time, we'll explain everything."

Shorty arrived with a pair of scissors before I could answer the strange vampire.

"Hold still," Shorty said as he grabbed one of my hands.

I jerked forward, trying not to cry out from the fire engulfing my fingers.

"Let her go," Rox demanded.

Shorty released me instantly.

I dipped to my knees, unable to cradle my singed hand.

"What happened?" Rox asked, kneeling in front of me.

I glared at him but said nothing. My affliction wasn't public knowledge, and if there was any way to keep my secret, I would. "Can you just get him to cut the ties?"

"Of course." Rox moved to stand behind me with Shorty.

My flight reflex kicked in, making my wings flare slightly.

"Relax," Rox said. "We're not going to hurt you."

"Says the man who just bought me from a gangbanger," I said angrily.

He didn't say anything, but when I looked at Grace, she appeared irritated. As if she couldn't believe she was in the middle of this situation. Everything about these three was odd. They looked like every other group of college-aged roommates who spent their time drinking beer and eating pizza while wasting their days away in front of a computer or game station. But I got the impression they hadn't exactly had the opportunity to go to college.

The zip ties snapped and suddenly I was free. I clutched my still-burning hand with the other one, placing both in my lap.

"Don't do anything stupid," Rox said. "The fact is we really don't want to hurt you or keep you restrained, but we can't let you leave until you hear us out."

I frowned, totally confused. "I'm sorry. Are you saying I'm not exactly your prisoner? That once I hear what you have to say, I'm free to go?"

Rox nodded. "Yes."

I got to my feet, frustration boiling over. "Then why the hell didn't you just come to my front door? Or to my shop? Or whatever? Jeez!" I cried. "I do talk to vampires, you know!"

Rox stepped back, rubbing his chin. "Yeah. We know. Your relationship with Laveaux has made that all too clear."

Now I was pissed. "David is just a friend. He's been protecting me."

Rox shook his head. "No, Ms. Rhoswen. He hasn't. Or at least that's not all he's been doing."

I stood stock-still, my attention riveted on the vampire. I'd had my trust issues with David all these months, and he still hadn't told me everything, like when he'd set me up to get involved with Lady Victoria and the fae shifter. My body went cold. "Tell me everything."

The vamp tilted his head, studying me for a moment. Then he waved a hand toward the office we'd walked through on our way in. "This way."

Trying to hide my trepidation, I strode through the door and spun, unwilling to keep my back to the vampires who'd just bought me from a gang member. I wanted to hear what they had to say, but I sure as hell didn't trust them. I trusted no one outside of Phoebe and Tal these days.

Rox sat at a big mahogany desk and swiveled to look at me.

I raised my eyebrows as if to say *Well? Get on with it.*

He pressed a button, bringing his computer to life. A few clicks later and the screen was filled with photo after photo of David, Harrison, and the two other guards Tal and I had healed that day. In each one, they were doing mundane things such as sipping coffee at the cafe a few doors down from my shop, walking the same mangy dog, reading a newspaper, and other things people might be doing out on the street in front of my shop. Like the one where Harrison was a road-crew worker, holding up a SLOW sign for traffic. Every single one of them was taken within a two-block radius of my store.

Okay, that was odd. I hadn't known all four of them had been keeping an eye on me, but I was aware Allcot had assigned me a security detail a while back. I shrugged. "So?"

"This is why we haven't been able to talk to you. Every time we get close, one of them strikes." Rox waited until I met his eyes. "It's fascinating what a surveillance camera can capture."

The picture changed. Harrison, stabbing one of the young vamps in the gut with a dagger. Blood had already blossomed all over the pale blue shirt. Another click. David again. His foot was crushing Vince's windpipe, whose eyes were bugging out as Harrison aimed a gun at another vamp's head.

My stomach turned and I fought to keep from gagging. I shook my head, trying to unsee the images.

Another click. This one was a group photo. Shorty, Rox, Grace, and the two who'd kidnapped me from the bar and three others I didn't know. Then, right there in the middle, was Beau, my brother. He had a huge smile on his face and had his arm around Rox. All of them were human.

Then the last picture, one set in the redwoods of California, featured Beau and Rox, whose physical appearance had changed dramatically. He was very clearly a vampire, and he was hugging Beau.

Rox clicked one last button, making the screen go blank. Then in a very low voice he said, "Laveaux has been keeping information from you and that's why he wouldn't let us meet. Beau was one of my best friends. He was there when I was turned."

"What?" The word came out in a squeak. Beau had been there? He'd seen vamps turned? How had I never known any of this? The sense of loss I always felt when I thought of my brother hit me hard, followed by betrayal. Beau had told me nothing. And neither had David. Even if Rox was lying about what David knew, he sure as hell hadn't told me about any of the altercations they'd had outside my shop. My heart hardened as yet another lie by omission crushed any remaining seeds of trust between David and me.

I took a deep breath and forced myself to ask the questions I didn't really want the answers to. "Why was Beau there? Who turned you?"

He waved to the other room, indicating the other two vamps. "We were supposed to be turned into daywalkers to be his security between the war Asher and Allcot are waging. Only Allcot got to him first."

Chapter 23

"Allcot?" I jerked. "You mean Asher, right?"

Rox sighed and shook his head sadly. "No. Though only because he got there first. Asher was closing in on him as well. The war those two have going—it's epic. They've been at it for decades. And because of the gift Beau had, he was caught in the middle."

My feet were moving backward before I could process what I was actually doing. "No. Allcot didn't even know Beau." But Carrie's face floated in my mind. His girlfriend—fiancée—was related to Allcot's consort. Allcot could've known him. It would also explain why Carrie disappeared right after Beau's death.

The thoughts tumbled through my brain at a rapid rate until my head was pounding. I grabbed my head at the temples and bent over, trying to block out the implications of what I'd just heard, but then I couldn't reconcile some of the past events. I stood up.

"Why would Allcot kill Beau and not me?"

He gave me a sad look. "Because, my dear, your brother was never going to turn him or any of his underlings into daywalkers. Allcot couldn't risk other vamps being turned that could be used against him and his employees. There was some speculation that you might have some of your brother's powers, but only enough to watch you. No one expected a female to inherit his gifts. After you turned Laveaux, Allcot decided to keep you in his stable, to get you to turn him and anyone else he wants. You're too valuable to him now."

I said nothing as I let that sink in. "Are you saying Allcot killed Beau because he didn't want Asher to have access to his abilities?"

"Yes. But what Allcot didn't realize is that Asher has always wanted to eliminate the fae of your line. What you've heard about him is probably true. Allcot had other plans. After he learned about your brother's gifts, he wanted Carrie to bring Beau to New Orleans to work for him. When Beau refused, Carrie warned him there would be consequences. Allcot always gets what he wants."

Rox was right about one thing at least—Allcot did always get what he wanted and he went to extremes to get it. But would he really have killed Beau? Wouldn't he just continue to manipulate him until he got what he wanted?

But Allcot had gotten what he wanted, hadn't he? Beau Jr. would end up loyal to Allcot for the rest of his life. Despair filled me and my breathing turned labored. I didn't know what to believe.

It was too much.

Suddenly I was very angry. What made this vampire any different than any of the others? How could I trust him? He'd had me kidnapped and tied up, for fuck's sake. I couldn't believe anything he said.

I stood up straight and stared him in the eye. I didn't even flinch as I said, "And what exactly is it that *you* want from me?"

His helpful demeanor fled, replaced by stone-cold determination. "You're going to complete the deal we made with your brother."

The other two vampires appeared in the doorway, arms crossed over their chests.

I glared at all of them. "And what deal would that be?"

Rox rose and loomed over me. "The only reason I agreed to be turned into a vampire was because I wanted to protect your brother. In turn, he was supposed to turn me into a daywalker. Like Vince and Talia."

"Beau changed them?" I whispered, barely able to breathe from the horror of this conversation... of the entire day.

"Yes. They offered to be the test subjects. But Beau couldn't change us all at once. He had to rest in between. By the next day he was dead."

Something flashed in his eyes I couldn't quite place. Frustration? Irritation? I couldn't tell, but it pissed me off even more.

"No."

"What?" His eyes turned red with off-the-charts vampire fury.

I sucked in a breath. Maybe I'd gone too far. I was the one outnumbered here. I did my best to keep my voice steady, free of censure, even though I wanted to rip his head off. Even if what he'd said about Allcot was true, that did not give this psycho the right to have me kidnapped. "It's been a long day. I need to get home to my magical tree to recharge. I couldn't change anyone tonight even if I wanted to."

He eyed me and then after a minute, he nodded. "Yeah. You're looking rough around the edges."

Rude-ass jerk. No matter what a girl looks like, a vamp wanting to be changed into a daywalker should probably try to stay on her good side. And that means keeping his unsolicited opinions to himself.

"You're not going anywhere, though," he said. "Not right now anyway. You can recharge here."

"But my tree—"

"Don't even try it." He cast me a disgusted look. "You forget I knew your brother. You can use the oak tree out back if you need your precious nature. But you're not leaving here until you turn me." He strode past me toward Grace and Shorty. Just before he disappeared into the back of the house, he said, "And don't even think about not bringing me back." He put his arm around Grace. "My girl here will torture you within an inch of your life and make sure you never forget her."

Grace looked at him with such love I almost vomited. God, they were twisted.

Shorty laughed and followed Rox into the back of the house, leaving me alone with Grace.

Immediately I noticed the lessening of vampire energy in the room. I still felt it, but it wasn't coming from Grace. I couldn't feel her at all. How was that possible? Unless… shit, she'd been turned too. Just like Vince and Talia. By Beau, and that was why their energy hadn't affected me. That had to be it.

She stalked forward and I couldn't help the flinch when she reached for my arm. It wasn't even that I was trying to get away from her fiery touch. It was that whatever was storming inside her terrified me more than anything her boyfriend had said. I hadn't seen it before, but it was there now. And she was the recluse among the crazy.

She stared at me, her lips twisted. "Don't want me to touch your precious skin, huh? Well, too damn bad." Her vampire hand clasped my upper arm. The heat combined with her bone-crushing grip weakened my knees, making me stumble as she dragged me across the room. "I'm taking you outside to fill up on nature or whatever the fuck it is you need to make my Rox whole again. I swear to God, if I have to stay indoors with him one more fucking time when I could be out in my bikini trolling for snacks, I'm going to lose my fucking mind."

Holy crow. It was as if she'd had a personality change now that their secrets were out. I had to find a way out of there. Fast. But I couldn't do it in my current state. If I could get outside to that tree, I could maybe form a plan.

We walked through an old kitchen that was covered in dust, not a dish in sight. There were fast-food drink cups piled in a corner along with empty bottles of cheap whiskey. No surprise there. Vamps couldn't exactly get drunk, not really anyway, but the strong bite of alcohol seemed to satisfy part of their hunger cravings.

"Go." Grace pushed me out the back door and then stood there watching me.

I placed my fists on my hips and glared at her. "What are you looking at?"

She eyed me pensively. "You're just so… vanilla. I can't believe you're the one with this power. At least your brother had a little bit of edge. You look like you should be working in a library or something." She wrinkled her nose.

Edge? Beau? He'd been a California fae who ate tofu and read labels for preservatives. He'd driven a Prius and had a kick-ass vegetable garden. I frowned. "I don't know what you're talking about."

"Look at you. All you need is a cardigan and you'd be ready for Bible study."

Well. That was going too far. Maybe I didn't push the boundaries with my wardrobe, but I was hardly a church mouse. I could kill her with my bare hands. Literally. But I decided to keep that to myself. If she wanted to underestimate me, then so be it. "I meant Beau."

She stepped out into the small backyard. "Oh. Right." A cat-that-ate-the-canary grin spread over her flawless face. "Let's just say that before he met Carrie, we spent some time together."

The image of Beau making out with this smug vampire made me want to vomit. Had she been a vampire already? Were Beau and I more alike than I'd thought? All this time I'd been thinking he'd hate my association with David and Allcot, and yet he'd clearly had his own circle of vamps.

And that's why he hadn't told me. I'd have acted exactly the way I'd expected him to act. Judgmental, disgusted, horrified. I didn't feel that way anymore. Or at least mostly, though this group was testing my patience. I backed up, resting against the oak tree. The cool energy filtered into me, easing the headache I'd been ignoring.

Grace stalked forward. "What? Nothing to say about my confession?"

I shook my head. "Whatever, or whoever"—I swept my gaze along her body, doing nothing to hide the contempt in my expression—"he did, it isn't my business."

She shook her head and laughed. "You're such a bitch. Too bad we need you or else I'd turn you right now. It's hard to find anyone with a backbone these days who's worthy of joining our little club. Can't take just anyone, now can we?"

Saliva welled on my tongue, and I had an insane desire to spit in her face. She was the worst kind of vamp. In it for control over other people, to terrorize and take whatever she wanted. Her perfect skin and perfect body were no substitute for the ugliness radiating from her insides. Had she been like that when Beau knew her? I couldn't picture it. Couldn't see him being friends with her, much less turning her into a daywalker. There was more to the story, and someone knew what it was.

Carrie. She had to know. Maybe even Allcot or David.

Frustration overwhelmed me. My brother had kept his secrets and now I had to pick up the pieces. "Go away," I said quietly.

"What did you say?"

"You heard me," I barked. "I'm well aware of a vampire's hearing ability. If you want me to get enough strength to turn Rox, I'm going to need some peace and quiet. I'm never going to reenergize with you looming over me, baiting me with your effed-up stories. I just need some damned sleep."

"If you think we're going to—"

"Grace?" Rox said from behind her.

She whirled. "What is it?"

"Come inside. Let the faery sleep. First thing in the morning she'll do as we ask." He held his hand out to her.

"You can't be serious." She tossed her long hair to the side in clear agitation. "We can't leave her out here by herself. She has wings, Rox." She spat out the last part as if she couldn't believe how stupid he was.

He just smiled at her and then waved at Shorty, who was eyeing Grace with pained desperation. He looked like he'd been punched in the gut. Did he have a thing for her? But as I watched him, the expression vanished just as quickly as it had appeared. "He'll keep an eye on her. Don't worry," Rox said and then turned in my direction, his gaze boring into me. "If she doesn't want anything to happen to her fae lover, she'll cooperate."

Fae lover? Did he mean they had Tal? I'd left him with Phoebe and Link. He was safe. He had to be. But they'd kidnapped me. Why not him? Or even Phoebs? Shit. I didn't know what to think.

Grace glanced between the two of us and my thoughts must have shown on my face, because she let out a bark of laughter as she took Rox's hand. She gazed up at him adoringly. "You always know just the right thing to say."

I sat in a patch of dirt at the base of the tree, eyeing Shorty. He was walking the small perimeter of the backyard in a continuous loop. Perhaps he was taking his appointment a little too seriously, because I hadn't moved in the past hour. In fact, I might have dozed off for a while there.

"What do you get out of this?" I asked him, every nerve completely aware that he was behind me and ten degrees to the left.

He appeared in front of me in a flash of vampire speed. "What do you mean, what do I get out of this?"

"Exactly what I said. What's in it for you? Are you expecting to be turned into a daywalker? Or are you just the backup, like the minions who work for Allcot?"

His eyes clouded over with uncertainty. After a moment he glanced at his feet. "They're my friends."

My eyebrows rose. "How so?"

He scowled. "What are you trying to pull, faery?"

I held my hands up. "Whoa. I'm not trying to start anything here, I'm just curious. I mean, if I'm going to be tied to this little group, I'd like to know what I'm getting into."

"You're not going to be tied to anything. Once you change Rox, he'll make a trade and we'll be free of you and the rest of this bullshit."

Trade? Trade what? Me? To whom? Allcot? Asher? Some other effed-up group I didn't know about? "Free to do what?"

"Live!" He shouted the word at me. "Ever since your brother up and got himself killed, we've been in this fuckin' limbo of hell, Rox and Grace fighting about what to do next, Asher calling all—" He stopped and stared at me, wide eyed. "Never mind. I just want to be done with this nonsense. I don't want to be involved in a political war any longer." He stopped pacing and slumped down onto an old stump.

I pressed my lips together tight, willing myself to stay quiet. It was hard, though. I had a lot of questions. But something told me the minute I asked him anything else, he'd clam right up. Instead, I made what I hoped was a sympathetic noise in the back of my throat.

He sighed and ran a hand down his face. "But it's not going to end, you know."

I waited a few beats, but when he didn't elaborate, I asked, "Why not?"

"Your nephew." He let out a long-suffering breath. "Even if you died today, there'd still be a battle over him once he comes of age. And because he's under Allcot's protection, it's going to be epic. Asher will never let that go."

Ice-cold dread shot straight to my heart. Beau Jr. He was at the center of all this. Not me. Yeah, they wanted me to do their bidding, but in the end, the war would be waged over my nephew. The reality of it settled over me with a hard finality. I'd known all along he was in danger, but I'd only been focused on keeping him hidden. Safe. Alive.

I'd reluctantly accepted that he'd be safest under Allcot's care, but I could see so clearly now that keeping him there was a surefire way of losing him faster than anything else.

As long as Allcot had access to the fae who could turn vamps into daywalkers, Asher would never give up. The last thing he'd do is let Allcot gain any more power.

I had to get Beau Jr. out of there. Had to find a way to end this power struggle between the two master vamps. The only problem was I had no idea how to do that.

And I sure as hell couldn't do it while being held captive by Shorty and company. I turned to him. "What would you do to end this right now?"

He stared at me, startled. "I don't…" Frowning, he rubbed his forehead. Then his expression brightened. "I'd work both sides against each other until the water boiled over, and then I'd skip town and let the pair of them battle to the finish."

"Hmm. Interesting." That definitely wouldn't work for me since Asher had already tried to kill me a few times. But his words combined with the look he'd had on his face right before Grace had left us for the evening did give me an idea. "So…?"

"Yeah?" He plucked a stray blade of grass and fingered it.

"Why haven't Vince and Talia shown up?"

He looked startled at the question, but then shrugged. "They do their own thing now. Only come around when Rox has a job for them."

"So it's just you and Rox and Grace usually?"

His eyes narrowed in suspicion. "Why?"

I waved a hand, trying to look casual. "Just curious is all. I was actually wondering if you had a girlfriend."

His expression went flat and then he cut his eyes to the house. "She… left."

"Oh," I said sympathetically. "Breakups are hard."

"No, that's not what I meant. We didn't break up. She just left one day. Went out and never came back."

Yikes. He looked so dejected I actually felt a pang of sympathy for him. "Do you know why?"

He was completely silent as he stared at the back door of the house. The night was still as I listened to myself breathe, waiting for him to answer.

Finally he turned to me, his eyes full of fury. "Because that morning she walked in our bedroom and found Grace crawling all over me. Naked."

Bingo.

Chapter 24

Shorty was vibrating with barely repressed rage. I wanted to reach out and soothe him if for no other reason than to calm my own nerves. I needed him to keep talking, but if he was going to lose his shit on me, it wouldn't do me any good.

Fortunately he got enough of a grip on himself that the tension drained from his face and he sat back down on the stump, pretending he wasn't upset. It was enough for me.

"Ah," I asked carefully. "Had you invited her there? Grace, I mean?"

He turned steely eyes on me. "No."

Short and to the point. And interesting. Had Grace and Rox had issues at some point, or was she just a troublemaker in general? I was going with the latter. "Did your girl know that?"

He shrugged. "I guess not."

"You didn't tell her?"

The look he gave me could've melted iron. "I would have if she'd come back."

"Oh." The word hung in the air between us. Finally I said, "I see."

His head snapped in my direction. "No. You don't see. Not at all."

I stayed silent, waiting for him to continue.

He stared me dead in the eye and said, "It wouldn't have done any good anyway. Because that bitch"—he pointed to the house—"she'd been fucking with the two of us for months. Undermining our relationship. And that day, Grace startled me. Caught me off guard. I actually thought she was my girl at first. So... there you have it. Grace got what she wanted. Like she always does. So do yourself a favor and just turn Rox. Maybe then she'll leave you the fuck alone."

I stood, pleased to realize my body was stronger, even if my eyes did feel like sandpaper. I needed to get some rest at some point, but at least I had some strength back. The tree had done its job. I reached out tentatively to Shorty.

He jerked back. "Don't even think about it," he barked.

"What?" I asked confused, then realized he didn't want me to touch him. Did he think I was going to drain him? I could, but then I'd be useless again with no hope of escaping. "Oh, sorry. I wasn't thinking. I was going to say that maybe you should stand up for yourself. Don't let Grace have so much control over your life."

He snorted. "Right. You have no idea what you're talking about."

"You sure about that? I have a boss and certain vampires trying to tell me what to do on a daily basis. But you know what? One person can only take so much, human or vampire. If you're miserable, what's the point in living?"

My words resulted in the exact opposite of my desired outcome. His shoulders slumped forward in defeat.

Son of a... How pathetic was he? I couldn't take it anymore. "Stand up for yourself, man! What she did is complete bullshit and you know it."

"What do you think you're doing?" Grace's sharp voice came out of the darkness. She was on me before I could even get my hands up to defend myself. "Are you trying to turn him against me?"

She let out a growl as one hand squeezed my neck, cutting off my airflow.

Panic rendered me absolutely still. *Can't breathe. Can't breathe.* The words filtered through my consciousness while my body tried to catch up with my brain. My world was dark, filled with foggy, colorless clouds.

I was quite literally the deer in the headlights as the raging vampire squeezed harder, sucking out my newly recharged energy.

But then everything came into clear focus and all I saw was the enemy trying to choke the life out of me. Pure hatred roared to life from deep in my gut. I'd be damned if I let that crazy vampire bitch get the better of me.

With my nerve endings screaming in pain from her contact and my body already trembling, I reached out and grabbed her perfect face, pulling in her tainted black vampire energy.

My legs wobbled but I didn't let go as she screamed bloody murder.

"You bitch. Get off me!" Suddenly I was lifted off the ground by my neck and flung backward right into the oak.

"Oomph." I heard a loud snap, followed by a sharp, blinding pain in my left arm. My body fell in slow motion down the trunk of the tree until I collapsed in a heap at the bottom. Tears from pure shock blurred my vision as I clutched at my limp arm. That bitch had broken it.

Oh. My. Goddess. It hurt.

There was a scuffle going on somewhere in the small backyard, but I couldn't focus long enough to make sense of anything. Most likely it was Grace and Shorty.

"Stop!" someone shouted and then more rustling commenced followed by accusations and threats from Grace and Shorty. She was berating him for being a pushover and letting me get to him and he was threatening to tell Rox about them.

"What's he going to say when I tell him where you've been spending your Tuesday nights? You think he's going to keep you around? You know him. And you know he'll throw your ass out," Shorty said.

"You wouldn't dare. He'd rip your dick off." Her voice was low and controlled.

But when he laughed in her face, she flew at him, clawing at his eyes as he used one arm to try to fend her off. She kicked out, hitting him in the knee, and they both fell to the ground, going at each other with such fury there was no doubt in my mind that they were crossing the lines of love and hate. No one had that much passion for someone they were lukewarm about.

Holy crow. Were they having some kind of affair? It had sounded like Shorty hated her. But the way they were fighting, it looked a lot like pent-up passion.

I stumbled to my feet, wiping my tears with my free hand just in time to see a tall figure drop from the tree above. I let out a cry of surprise and stumbled, almost losing my balance.

"Whoa," a very familiar voice said as he wrapped a steady arm around me.

"Talisen," I breathed and clutched him with my good arm. "Where'd you come from?"

"Later." He glanced down at my cradled arm and frowned. "You're hurt."

I nodded.

"Can you fly?" The concern in his voice had me standing taller, forcing myself to be strong.

Eyeing the two vampires trying to kill each other, I sucked in a sharp breath. "I will if I have to."

"Hold still," he said softly into my ear and then ran his magical fingers lightly along my battered arm. A cooling numbness took over, leaving behind a dull ache. "It's not healed, but it should be enough to get you out of here without too much pain."

He released me and scrambled up the tree from where he'd appeared. I followed him with my gaze, realizing he was headed for the neighbor's rooftop. Once again clutching my immobile arm, I thrust my wings and gasped at the sharp bolt of pain that shot through my arm. It wasn't as bad as it would've been, but it still made me see white spots. Despite the pain, I thrust my wings once more, determined to follow Talisen, to get the hell out of there.

Ten more feet and I'd clear the roofline, five feet. Three feet. I was so close, I stretched my good arm out for Talisen, but then a sharp pinch of pain pierced my ankle. Jerking my feet up, I pitched forward, losing my momentum. The night blurred around me as I was suddenly tumbling to the ground, my limbs and wings paralyzed.

Someone screamed. Maybe it was me. Nothing was clear, only the sudden and final impact of my body slamming to the hard-packed ground.

"Willow! Wake up." There was a faint trace of urgency in the faraway words. Talisen. He was calling to me. "Come on, Wil. You can do this."

I wanted to open my eyes. Wanted to look up into the green-emerald gaze I knew so well, but nothing was cooperating. My brain was sending the signal, but my body wasn't responding.

My breath came in shorter, more frantic gasps. I'd broken my neck. Or back. That's why I couldn't feel anything. Couldn't see anything. My insides were churning with the impulse to run, to cry, to lash out, but there was nothing. Only the sound of erratic breathing.

Was this death? I welcomed it, then. Didn't want to be in my frozen prison any longer. Everything would end. All my troubles with Allcot, Asher, and even the Void. Talisen could move on and have a normal life without me. Link would go with him. Phoebe would get a partner who had more than one useless skill. Tami would take over the shop, maybe hire another magical baker. And Mom. She could focus on... Beau Jr.

My heart pounded harder at the thought of my nephew. What would his life be like?

"Willow, dammit!" A bolt of power rocketed through my veins and I shot straight up, my body humming with familiar healing magic. Tal's magic. I twisted and found him white-faced and clutching my hand in both of his. "Thank the gods," he said and wrapped me in his strong arms.

His redwood scent engulfed me. I took a deep breath, fortifying myself with the knowledge that he was real. That I was real and hadn't died from my twenty-foot fall.

Before I said anything, he stood and pulled me to my feet. "Can you walk?"

"I…" The words were stuck in my dry throat. I coughed, tried again, but then shook my head and pointed to my mouth, indicating I couldn't speak.

"You need to hydrate. Don't try to talk. Just put one foot in front of the other."

I did as he said, wobbling perilously. After a few steps, my balance stabilized, and I glanced around, noting the now-familiar backyard.

Things had changed quite a bit. Grace and Shorty were no longer fighting. Shorty was lying flat out, unconscious. What had happened to him? Link was there, pacing in front of Grace, his teeth bared and his hackles standing on end. He was seconds from attacking her. But she stood with her hands up in surrender.

Talisen had his hands on both of my shoulders, steering me back into the house. I glanced around one more time, wanting to demand that Link come with us, but I couldn't and he wouldn't, not as long as he had a vampire cornered.

Once inside the kitchen, Tal found a cup in the cupboard and rinsed it hastily before filling it with water from the tap. "Drink it all down," he said as he lifted it to my lips.

I reached up, clasping my hands over his to tip the cup higher. The cool water was a sweet relief to the dryness claiming my throat. I closed my eyes and sucked it down, not even stopping when it spilled down my chin.

"More," I croaked out when the cup was empty.

This time Tal removed his hand and when I was done, I turned to him with a renewed sense of clarity. "How did you find me?"

He leaned down and whispered, "Phoebe got a call from some gang kid named Jasper, who tipped her off. We were here ten minutes later."

Jasper? I'd been right. He hadn't wanted to leave me with the vamps. Maybe there was still hope for him. I nodded my understanding and cleared my throat. "Where's Rox?"

"In here," I heard Phoebe call.

I glanced at Tal questioningly. "She's here?"

"Of course. She took down that vamp in the backyard."

Without hesitation, he clasped my hand in his and tugged me into the next room. Phoebe was standing over Rox, the spike of her heeled boot pressing down on his chest just over his heart.

"You're lucky she's alive," Phoebe said in a cold, dispassionate tone. "If she hadn't survived, I wouldn't have had a reason to let you live."

I frowned. What did that mean? "Phoebs?"

"Come over here, Willow," she commanded.

I did as she said, limping a little from the pain still pulsing in my ankle. I glanced down and grimaced at the open wound just above the anklebone. It was red and swollen.

"It's where he shot you with the paralyzing dart," Tal clarified. "Looks and feels like the drug used on Harrison and the others. We're not leaving here without the antidote."

Crap! Tal didn't know how to fix this, and if they didn't give up the ingredients, then I'd be in a hospital bed right alongside Harrison. Unconscious. A shudder rippled through me. If Rox didn't talk, Tal would have to guess, and if he got it wrong, it could kill me.

I let go of Tal's hand and then moved to stand next to Phoebe, glaring down at Rox. There wasn't time to play his game, so I blurted out, "What is it you want exactly?"

"You know what I want. To be turned into a daywalker. Do it and I'll point you to the treatment."

Phoebe pressed harder on his chest with her boot. "Think again, vamp. I might not dust you until you give us the information, but I can cause some serious damage if you don't start talking."

He narrowed his eyes at her and his white face contorted into something dark and angry. "You don't understand, witch. I don't give a shit. Kill me if you want. My life is a living hell without the sun. If she doesn't turn me, I'll end myself."

"He's not lying," Grace said from behind us.

I spun, my eyes darting around for Link. "Where's my wolf?"

She waved a hand and gave me a self-satisfied, evil grin, exposing her blood-soaked fangs. "Outside. Bleeding out."

"Link!" I cried and sprinted out the back door, but Talisen beat me, and in no time he was kneeling beside Link, who was lying on his side still in wolf form. There was a large gash in his neck and his breathing was shallow.

I paused, not wanting to leave Phoebe alone with two vamps. But when I doubled back, I saw Rox was already unconscious as Phoebe and Grace circled each other.

"Go on, Wil. I've got this," Phoebe said.

I nodded once and ran back outside.

"It's not that bad," Tal said. "He'll be all right."

I fell to my knees on Link's other side, frantically scanning his body.

Tal was right. If it was bad, Link would've immediately shifted into Shih Tzu form. He was wounded, but upon my second inspection, the gash was superficial.

"He's in shock," Tal said. "Give me a minute or two and he'll be ready to walk out of here."

I ran a light hand over Link's head and stared into his golden wolf eyes. "Tal will take care of you, boy. It's going to be all right."

Link blinked and then closed his eyes and surrendered to Tal's touch.

I stood and stared down at my two favorite guys. As I watched sweat bead on Tal's face and Link wince from Tal's tender touch, an uncontrollable torrent of rage built in my chest. Selfish, entitled, useless vampire scum. She'd bitten Link. And they'd nearly killed me.

I spun on my good heel and stalked back into the house. Barreling through the door, I flung it with such force it slammed against the wall, shattering the glass insert. I didn't even flinch.

Neither did Grace or Phoebe. They were too focused on each other. Rox was still passed out in the corner of the room.

I could only assume Phoebe had spelled him while she dealt with Grace. Standing in the large kitchen, Phoebe was circling Grace, magic clinging to her palms.

Grace was turning with her, keeping her catlike gaze trained on Phoebe. "Drop the magic, witch."

Phoebe sent her a flat stare. "Never going to happen. Tell me what the drug was, or I'm going to burn you from the inside out."

"Do it and Rox will never tell you what you want to know. Your faery-bitch friend will slowly deteriorate right before your eyes, and there's nothing you'll be able to do about it."

I'd had enough. My frustration and anger boiled over, and I lost all my control, falling into a blind rage. I felt as if I were standing on the sidelines, watching someone else run straight at the vampire, arms outstretched.

We collided and went down in a tangle of limbs, my thumb digging into her right eye.

She screamed, but I barely heard her over the rush of chaotic images filling my mind. Two red blobs shifted and morphed into Grace and Rox. Rox was kneeling before Grace, staring up at her with adoring eyes. Then Rox shifted to Shorty, and he was on his feet, pressing Grace into the wall as his hands roamed over her hardened curves. They mauled each other in a sexual rage, each battling for power while Rox watched with pure jealousy consuming him from the inside out.

"Get off, you crazy bitch!" I heard Grace snarl in my ear.

But I wouldn't let go. Wouldn't let her hurt my friends to get to me. It was as if all the crap that had happened to me over the past six months and everything I'd learned about my brother had finally made me snap. I wasn't willing to stand by and let it happen anymore.

"No!" I cried, pulling her vampire energy into me.

Her body convulsed while mine trembled in protest. But I'd been here before. Knew I could withstand it long enough to render her incapacitated.

"Willow!" Tal suddenly yanked me off Grace, who was slumped against the wall, unmoving. I kicked out and flailed, trying to get back to her, angry he'd interrupted. "You're going to kill yourself." His voice was a focal point amid the storm whirling in me.

"She hurt Link," I said defiantly, straining to reach her as he held me around the middle.

"He's going to be fine." He continued to whisper into my ear as we both watched Phoebe contain the vampire with her special cuffs. She wouldn't be going anywhere now. Relief cleared my bloodlust haze, and I started to relax in Talisen's arms.

That is until my adrenaline wore off. My body stiffened from the shock of Grace's lingering vampire energy and I started to scream.

Chapter 25

My body was in a vise and heat boiled me from the inside out. I felt nothing, heard nothing. My whole world was pain. Thousands of needles tore at my nerve endings, leaving me in a state of frenzy. I clawed at my skin, gasping for air I couldn't breathe. Everything was going dark again when something ice cold engulfed my hand.

The relief was instant as I instinctively clutched my hand around the ice-cold stone.

"Let it all out." Tal's hoarse voice sounded in my ear. I could feel him pressing into my back, holding me to him. My skin was on fire, too raw to bear our physical connection, and I struggled to get away, to curl into a ball and wait for all the awful sensations to fade away.

"Willow. Release her energy," he said more forcefully and clutched me tighter. "Now."

On his command, I focused on the stone, gritting my teeth as my body slowly went numb. I slumped in Tal's arms, unable to feel anything. The pain was gone, but so was everything else.

"Well done," a deep male voice said from behind us.

Rox, fully recovered from Phoebe's spell, moved into the kitchen and stood in front of me, his expression full of interest. "That's what you do when you change a vampire, isn't it? You take their energy, mix it with your own, and force it back into them. That's what Beau did to her." He waved a careless hand at the limp Grace.

"Back off, vamp," Phoebe said, striding to my side. "If you even think about touching her, I'll dust your ass right here."

He held his hands up. "I don't want to hurt her." He glanced over at Grace, slumped against the wall. "In fact, I want to thank her. Grace's been a pain in my ass for months now. With her out of the way, maybe we can come to some sort of deal?"

"Deal?" Phoebe snorted. "You've lost your mind. Tell us what was used in the dart and I'll let you live."

I stirred in Tal's arms. All I wanted was for him to take me to my house and my tree.

"I would, but I don't know." He shrugged. "I got it from the vampire, Lady Victoria. Her companion made it."

"Fuck." Phoebe whipped her phone out and started texting someone, probably the Void agent who'd been questioning the fae and Victoria. So far, neither had answered any questions of significance. It was possible they'd even already been written off, eliminated by the Void. It happened when supernaturals went way out of bounds and were classified unredeemable.

"Let's go," Tal said and started to lead me toward the front of the house. I could barely feel my foot and the motion made me stumble. I automatically clutched at Tal, accidentally dropping the stone he'd put in my hand.

"It's okay. I've got you." Tal's hands clutched at my waist, keeping me stable. I watched the crystal roll across the floor and land at Rox's feet.

He stared at it, too.

Then, as if on cue, our eyes met and I saw in his expression the moment realization dawned.

"No!" I cried and pitched forward, ripping myself from Tal's grip. But Rox was faster. His hand closed around the crystal as I dove to the floor, the impact not affecting me at all. I was too wired to feel anything. Scrambling to my knees, I frantically lunged for him. He stepped back, clutching the crystal to his chest.

Dammit! The crystal was full of the mixed energy I'd taken from Grace. I couldn't be sure, but I had a gut feeling that if he managed to absorb its contents, he'd turn into a daywalker.

"Willow!" Tal grabbed my hand and pulled me back up.

I let him, but couldn't tear my eyes from Rox. The crystal was glowing brilliant orange and pulsing with energy I could feel deep in my core. "We need that crystal," I said, much more controlled than I felt.

Phoebe moved in, her sun agate raised, ready to dust him.

"Phoebs," I said in a low tone as to not startle her. "I don't think that's a good idea."

I was connected to that crystal, and whatever was happening with Rox, I could feel it deep in my bones. The numbness had vanished, replaced by tingling pressure. The more the orange light pulsed, the more intense the pressure got. I felt as if my magic was trying to burst from my cells, and suddenly my heart sped up as I imagined myself exploding into a million pieces.

"What's happening?" Tal asked, running his hands up and down my arms. There was no doubt he could feel my physical response.

"It's… the… crystal," I gasped out. "My… magic. He's connected to it."

Rox's eyes went huge and then he let out a gasp of his own as he stumbled backward into the next room.

Tal glanced between the two of us, debating what to do. It was obvious he didn't want to leave me, but he couldn't let Rox use the crystal. He spun, propping me up against the wall, and then vaulted after Rox. Through the doorway, I watched Tal tackle him, trying to pry the crystal from Rox's grip, but Rox was too strong.

Phoebe paced. "I could spell him unconscious, but other than that I don't know what to do."

I shook my head. "No. Not yet." All of her spells would have an impact on the vampire's consciousness, but they were entirely too strong for a fae to survive. Given the fact I was somehow magically connected to him, I couldn't be sure the spell wouldn't transfer to me.

"Dammit!" Phoebe glanced between Rox and me.

I stood there frozen as the magic spread out over Rox, engulfing him. Then my energy shifted and my insides went cold. My magic was no longer my own. It was flowing into him freely with no help from me. I doubled over, curling into myself.

He was stealing my magic and I had no way to stop it.

Clarity hit me hard. He could kill me without even trying.

I straightened my spine and with one thrust of my wings, I leaped and was beside Tal, my hands joining his over the crystal.

A small burst of my magic rushed from me to the crystal. I let out a cry of frustration and tugged forcefully on the stream, forcing it back in my direction.

What I got was a mix of Talisen's, Rox's, Grace's, and my own energy. It was a live wire of magic that made my back bow from the force. There was no pain. Only a heady sensation of sweet power. I craved it. Needed it. And for once in my life, I wasn't at the mercy of anyone.

The life energy flowed into me easily, without effort, fortifying me. It was euphoric. Intoxicating. Addictive. Until disjointed scenes started to flash through my head.

Tal and me on a beach near the redwoods, walking hand in hand. A small redheaded fae ran in front of us, giggling as she splashed through the shallow surf.

The scene flashed to Rox standing in Allcot's office. He was on the phone barking orders when Harrison and his crew walked in. The three of them bowed, indicating their loyalty. Pride and self-satisfaction along with insatiable greed overwhelmed me.

Then Carrie walked in with Beau Jr. Her eyes were wide with fear as he ordered her to kneel as well.

"Come here, BJ," Rox ordered my nephew.

Carrie clutched Beau's hand tighter and whispered for him to stay put. Beau Jr. stood tall, an air of importance radiating around him. He glanced at his mother with irritation and then ran to Rox's side.

"Good little fae. Now tell your mother what I told you earlier."

Beau stared at Carrie with dispassionate eyes. Then he blurted, "I'm Master Rox's son now. You've been replaced."

"No!" I cried and scrambled back, horror consuming me. Tal had said the scenes were the soul's deepest desires. If that was true, Rox was a power-hungry manipulator with no compassion. To take Beau, to use him and turn him against Carrie, turned my heart to stone. If Rox was turned into a daywalker, he'd do everything in his power to challenge Allcot.

And while the chances of his taking Allcot down were slim, if Asher did it first, a daywalker would have a significant advantage in the power struggle that would follow.

I stood on shaky legs and held my hand out to help Tal up. He was white as a ghost and appeared just as shaken as I was, but he got to his feet without any trouble.

"Willow?" Phoebe asked, tension clear in her tone.

I stared at Rox, who was lying motionless on the ground. I'd taken enough of his life energy that he wasn't going to be moving anytime soon. But he was alert. His eyes were open and he was watching me, waiting for my next move. He didn't have to wait long. Without breaking eye contact, I said to Phoebe, "Knock him out."

She didn't hesitate. Artificial sunlight lit up the dark room like a bolt of lightning. And in the next moment, Rox lay on the floor, staring up at nothing, his eyes empty.

I couldn't help myself. The image I'd seen with Beau Jr. was still too fresh in my mind. I took two steps and with a herculean effort, I kicked him as hard as I could in the ribs. Then his knee and then his crotch. It was petty. He wasn't even conscious to feel it, but it made me feel better.

"Uh, Wil?" Phoebe asked. "You okay?"

I met her concerned eyes and shook my head. "Just get these three into custody, will you?"

She nodded, looking troubled.

I reached out and squeezed her shoulder, knowing how much she must've hated standing on the sidelines as I struggled with Rox. "I'll see you at home."

"Tonight?"

I almost laughed at the question. There wasn't anywhere else I wanted to be. I gave her a short nod, then turned to Tal. "Take me home?"

"You got it." He held up his hand in a wait motion and then disappeared back into the kitchen. A second later he reappeared with Link in his arms. My wolf had at some point shifted back into Shih Tzu form and was now pressing his little body to Tal's chest. I knew exactly how my dog felt.

My heart swelled.

"Let's go." With Link in one arm and the other wrapped around me, Tal led us out into the night.

I limped along, holding on to him with everything I had left. And when he tugged me closer, I let out a little sigh of relief.

When we got to my Jeep, he helped me into the passenger's seat and handed me Link. I clutched the pup to my chest and looked up at him.

His eyes softened as he brushed my hair out of my eyes.

"Thank you," I said softly.

"You never need to thank me for loving you."

A lump formed in my throat. Instead of answering, I clutched his hand, pulling him closer. Our lips met in the softest kiss. The tenderness filled up every part of me, invading all my empty spaces. Tal's hand cupped my cheek as we breathed in each other, time standing still.

Love. It's the only word for what passed between us.

"I'm never leaving you again," he said on a whisper.

In response, I clutched at his shirt, unable to wrap my mind around the enormity of the emotions claiming me.

He'd come for me and had fought with me as an equal. Now he was going to walk with me through all the complications and trials. Deep inside, I felt the commitment solidify, and right there on the street on the edge of vampire territory, we became one.

Chapter 26

My bed called to me. The magical pull was almost too strong to resist, but instead of crawling in, I forced myself to shower.

It wasn't pretty. I stood in front of the full-length mirror dispassionately taking inventory. My left side was bruised from shoulder to hip. My leg just above the ankle was red and swollen. And my left arm was still weak and aching. It was likely I still had a fracture after Tal's hasty healing.

I took my time under the hot stream of water, reveling in the temporary oblivion. Then everything crashed down around me and I slumped against the wall, unexplained tears streaming down my face, my body wracked with sobs as the enormity of the day's events hit me hard.

I don't know how long I sat there, but the water started to chill and still I didn't move. Eventually I heard the shower door open. The water stopped. I glanced up, finding Talisen with a bath sheet open for me.

He kneeled, draping the soft cotton over me. "Come on, love. I've got you."

I let him pull me to my feet and dry me off in his gentle, unassuming way. I was bared to him in every way and had never felt safer. He was mine. And I was his. It was all that mattered to me in that one moment. I watched the deep emerald green of his intense, wise eyes as his healing hands inspected every bruise, scratch, and injury marring my body. I didn't care about the damage. I was alive and so was he. We'd get through everything else.

"Stop," he said lightly.

"Stop what?"

"Staring at me like that." He took a moment to cast his gaze down the length of my body once more, but this time he wasn't cataloging my injuries. This was a look of pure appreciation. "You're making me want to do more than just tuck you into bed."

His slow, playful grin coaxed a soft chuckle from my lips. "That's the Talisen I've always loved."

At the word love, he stilled. Pleasure lit his eyes as he threaded his fingers through mine and then brought my hand up to lightly kiss my knuckles. "I like the sound of that."

I'd meant to say *that's the Talisen I know and love* in an off-hand, playful way, but it hadn't quite come out like I'd planned. In addition to mixing up the words, my tone had been too throaty, too low, and entirely too serious.

I glanced away, trying to regain some composure. It didn't help that I was standing in the middle of my bathroom, wrapped in only a towel. Talk about being at a disadvantage.

"Wait here," Tal said and planted a kiss on my temple. "I'll be right back."

I heard the creak of my armoire door opening, followed by the slide of one of my drawers. The very normal sounds of domesticity brought me back to myself, and I turned to the vanity to finish my nightly ritual. When I was done brushing my teeth, Tal was there, holding a very skimpy camisole and matching bikini panties.

I raised my eyebrows in surprise. "Uh…?"

A faint blush dusted his face as he cleared his throat. "Sorry. I'm going to need to reach all your injuries if you want me to heal you. Bare skin is easier."

Right.

If I'd been thinking, I would've realized that. Instead, here I was being an idiot. Tal wasn't going to try anything. Not tonight. Not yet.

I took the clothes from him and nodded to the door. "I've got it from here. Thank you."

He gave me a wry smile and looked vaguely disappointed that he wasn't going to dress me.

Once again, I chuckled. "Check Link once more, will you? I just need a few minutes."

"Of course." He turned without hesitation and clicked the door shut, giving me the privacy I craved.

I pulled the panties on without too much trouble, but when I got to the camisole, I winced when I had to lift my arm over my head. Damn, that shoulder hurt. Gritting my teeth, I somehow struggled into the top, but not before I knocked my arm on the vanity, nearly making myself pass out from the sharp pain. By the time I was dressed, I was breathing hard.

I waited for my heart rate to slow and then walked into my room. The scene nearly gutted me from the adorableness. There on my bed, high in the magical tree, was Talisen lying on his back with Link draped over him. Tal had his hand resting over the healed wound on Link's neck. Both were breathing deeply, appearing to be fast asleep.

It was almost a shame to disturb them. Almost.

Instead of flying like I normally would, I climbed the stairs at the end of the bed and then gingerly took a place beside Tal.

As soon as he felt the bed shift from my weight, he repositioned himself, making a space for me next to him.

I grinned at Link, the ragdoll pup who hadn't moved a muscle. I crawled in, suppressing a groan in response to my entire aching left side. "I should've eaten a Hibiscus Healing bar. It would've helped. But now that I'm in bed, too late."

Tal popped up and Link woke, scrambling to the foot of the bed. "You want it, trust me. Otherwise you're going to be incredibly achy tomorrow."

I shrugged and closed my eyes, to blissed out on my oak tree's restorative magic to care.

"I'll get it, then," Tal said and disappeared, leaving Link to keep his spot warm.

I snuggled up to him and gave him a few kisses, letting him know what a good wolf he'd been. It wasn't his fault the vampires were batshit crazy.

"Here." Tal stood at the side of the bed holding out two cookies from an experiment I'd tried not long before I'd left for Eureka.

"How'd you know those have hibiscus in them?" I asked him.

"I can smell it," he said matter-of-factly, as if smelling ground seeds in cookies was a totally normal thing. That just anyone could do it. In fact, they couldn't. Not even me, and I'd made the darn things. It had to be because of his healing abilities.

I nibbled on one of the cookies as Tal climbed up and sat on the edge of my bed. Across the room on my desk something white caught my eye. "Is that my phone?"

"Huh?" Tal turned to follow my gaze. "Oh, yeah. Phoebs found it on the ground after the vamps abducted you."

"Thanks. I thought I'd lost it."

He nodded and then silence fell between us. Nervousness I'd never felt around him rose up and grabbed me. I averted my eyes, fingering Link's soft fur.

"Wil?" Tal said softly.

"Yeah?"

His lips were quirked up in a half smile as his easygoing nature returned. "Relax, huh?"

I shook my head but returned his smile. "I don't think I can."

"Sure you can. Lie down and I'll go to work on those bruises."

We'd been here before, me in my bed while he healed me. Only now everything was much more intimate. I took a deep breath, set the half-eaten cookie aside, and snuggled down into my bed. I sighed in relief as I rolled onto my stomach and closed my eyes.

After a few moments, I turned my head in Tal's direction, finding him gazing down at me intently. "Everything okay?"

"Just thinking."

"About what?" That coil of unease tightened in my gut.

"The first time I kissed you." His eyes turned even more brilliant green.

"Oh." My mouth went dry and the unease turned into butterflies.

He reached out and touched my jaw, his thumb grazing over my lips.

Peace settled over me, and I felt a real, natural smile spread over my face as I rolled to my side. "I thought you were supposed to be healing me."

He nodded. "I am. But I'm having trouble focusing when all I can think about is this." Leaning down, he cupped my cheek and stopped just before our lips met.

My heart thudded in my chest as I breathed in his clean scent of soap and a faint trace of redwood. I vaguely wondered when he'd had a chance to shower, but the thought flew out of my head when he closed the distance and brushed his lips lightly over mine.

My entire body sighed in pleasure. I shifted closer, wanting to feel his warmth over my barely dressed body. And then he gently pulled me up onto my knees, careful to not jostle my arm, and wrapped his arms around me as he captured my lower lip between his teeth.

I clutched at his shirt with my good arm, my fingers curling into the cotton, and flicked my tongue, tasting him.

A faint moan escaped from deep in his throat as his tongue met mine. Everything faded away except for the warmth of Tal's skin and the tingling sensations of his touch. He made all my aches and pains fade into the background. My world narrowed to him.

All too soon he pulled back slightly, winded, but he didn't let go. It took me a moment to realize we were both trembling. And when I did, I pressed my hand to his heart and said, "This is all I need."

His hand moved to cover mine, squeezing my fingers. "It's always been yours."

I kissed him, tenderly at first. Then I wrapped my good arm around him and sank into him, surrendering myself to all the pent-up passion of the past eight years.

He matched my fervor with his own, his hands tangling in my hair as he deepened the kiss, claiming me with just his mouth.

Waves of pleasure overwhelmed me, and when he pulled back this time, I kept a tight grip on him, unwilling to let him go.

He tilted his head and trailed kisses from my bare collarbone up to my ear, sending a shiver all the way to my toes. "I want you, Wil."

The words were a wildfire that burst deep in my core, heating me from the inside out. Goddess, I wanted him, too.

"But not tonight." His words were strained and full of regret.

Slowly, I sank down, sitting on my heels, trying to get a grip on my raging hormones. But the way he was gazing down at me with pure lust in his eyes made my nipples tighten with anticipation. And he noticed. His gaze lowered as his breath caught in his throat.

"Tal?"

"Yes."

He swallowed and ran a hand through his sandy-blond hair. It stood up in random mussed clumps. My hand twitched to smooth it, but if I touched him, I'd lose all control and I knew it.

"If you're determined nothing is going to happen tonight, it might be better if you… uh… gave me a moment."

"Umm… a moment?" His lips twitched.

"Not that!" I screeched and pulled the blanket up to hide in mortification.

He laughed and tugged the blanket down, exposing my face. "Good, because I wouldn't want to leave for that."

"Holy cripes." I pushed on his chest and chuckled. "Never mind." Still laughing, I crawled back under the covers and patted Link, who was curled up near my pillow, snoring softly.

"Now I need a moment." He winked at me and hopped off the bed. "I'll be right back."

The room felt empty somehow, which was crazy considering my bed was suspended in a giant magical tree. It was the loss of Tal, even though I could hear the creak of his footsteps against the old hardwood floors.

I shook myself, trying to ignore the eerie feeling that something ominous was going down. It was just the lingering effects from being kidnapped and battling crazy vampires. If anyone I loved was in danger, I would've gotten a phone call. I cut my eyes to the desk where Tal had dropped my phone and noted the white cord of my charger was attached. Good. No doubt the battery was low.

Tal reemerged, two water bottles in his hands. He cracked the top of one and handed it to me.

"Thanks," I said and sucked down a third of it before I came up for air. "I needed that."

"Drink it all." He took a swig from his own bottle. "It will help with the healing."

I did as I was told and watched him as he stripped out of his shirt. His well-defined chest was tan and lean from hours of working the nursery and climbing the trees of the forest. I couldn't keep my gaze from lingering on his hips and his low-slung jeans. Jeez. He was gorgeous.

He stood still, letting me get my fill, and when I finally realized he was watching me, I felt the flush climb up my neck. "Sorry."

"No need to apologize." Smiling, he climbed back up onto the bed, wearing nothing but his jeans, and gently turned me so I was lying on my back. His magic was already pooling at his fingertips, fortifying me. Gently, he took the hand of my injured arm in his and ran the other hand from shoulder to wrist. It was a tickle of magic at first, growing into a constant irritant the deeper it went into my cracked bone.

I bit down on a pillow, fighting back the sharp sting of tears. I could get through this. One way or another. When Tal's magic was pulsing to almost unbearable levels, he wrapped both hands around the fracture point and poured more magic into me.

"Stop!" I cried, gasping for breath. My chest was tight and my vision turned black as my head swam.

A second later, Tal's magic vanished. My body went limp as if I'd suddenly been released from a vise.

"Holy crow," I whispered.

"Are you okay?" Tal asked, concern radiating from him.

I flexed my fingers, testing gingerly. Not even a twinge of pain. "I think so. Just need a moment."

I focused on the air filling my lungs, letting the world come back into focus as I slowly worked my arm. A small smile claimed my lips when I realized it was completely healed. "Tal?"

"Yeah?"

I lifted myself up with my other arm and kissed him softly. "Thank you."

"Don't thank me yet, love. We still have a lot of work to do. And I doubt it's going to be pleasant." His eyes focused on my shoulder and then my leg as he handed me one of his crystals. "Here, take this. It will help take the edge off."

I opened my palm and accepted the amethyst stone. The effect was immediate. My muscles relaxed and a blissful numbness soothed me.

"Are you ready for this?"

"Yes." I lay back down and closed my eyes. "Work your magic."

Chapter 27

Talisen was right. His healing magic was painful despite the healing stone he'd given me. Not because of his magic, but because of the depth of my injuries. When he'd healed the bone-deep bruise on my shoulder, piercing pain left me gasping for breath. And the rest of my bruises, the healing for those took much longer than ever before. Neither of us really knew why. At least not until he'd gotten to my ankle.

My calf and ankle were still numb. It was the only reason I'd been able to walk, stand, or heck, even sit on my knees while Tal and I had been kissing. I just didn't feel anything. Or I didn't up until Tal went to work on the wound. At first there was only a bit of pressure but no pain. Then when it was clear his efforts weren't making progress, he sucked in a breath and poured everything he had into the affected area.

The change was immediate. Every part of me vibrated as if I were about to burst. My leg stiffened and my calf cramped, ripping an uncontrollable scream from my throat. I reared up, clutching at my leg.

"Willow!" I heard Tal's frantic cry, but I couldn't see him through the white spots swimming in my vision.

Then everything stopped and my leg went numb once more. I flopped back down on the bed, panting.

"Jesus, what happened?" Tal asked, clutching my hand.

I stared up into the canopy above us and shook my head. I didn't have a clue. It was his magic.

The mattress shifted and the next thing I knew, Talisen was stretched out beside me, tucking me close to his body. "I'm sorry. So sorry," he whispered, tenderly stroking my arm.

"It's not your fault," I said when my breathing returned to normal. "It's just like with the guards. You can't fix it because of the poison. We'll need the antidote."

He didn't say anything at first, but then he nodded. "You're right. My magic is only a temporary fix, though you seem to be holding up better than they are. Probably because our magic is mixing."

"Maybe," I said weakly, my eyes heavy with sleep.

"Get some rest, Wil. First thing in the morning we'll work on it. I'll be right here in case you need me." He kissed the top of my head with a gentleness that would have made me cry if I'd had anything left to give.

I nodded, or at least I tried to, but darkness had closed in, and I fell into sweet oblivion, wrapped in Tal's arms... again.

A loud crash made me bolt upright from a dead sleep. Commotion reigned around me as Link, in full wolf form, leaped from the bed, snarling, his fangs bared. Talisen followed Link over the side of the bed, fully tensed in fight mode.

I sat frozen, still wearing the skimpy camisole, and stared into the stricken face of David. His eyes shifted from me to Talisen and then back to me. A chill crawled over my skin, and I yanked the blanket up to cover my almost-bare body.

"What the hell are you doing, Laveaux?" Talisen demanded.

David ignored him, still staring at me.

Tal took a step forward and Link, taking his cue from Tal, charged forward and circled David.

"Link!" I cried, startled out of my shock. "No. Sit."

My wolf glanced at Talisen for confirmation.

"Dammit, Link. I said sit!"

He promptly sat back on his haunches, but he didn't take his eyes from David.

I wrapped the blanket around myself and fluttered to the floor to stand beside Tal. "What is it?" I asked David.

As the vampire watched me, his face slowly morphed into his expression of stone, the one he wore when he was hiding his pain.

Guilt mixed with sadness and unease made it hard to breathe. Even though David and I hadn't been together officially, we'd danced around the possibility long enough. He deserved better than finding me in bed with Tal. I had to talk to him. And soon. But right then, I could tell by the set of his shoulders there was something much more pressing. Otherwise he would've never burst into my room the way he had.

"Get dressed," David said to me. "You need to get out of here. It isn't safe."

He turned to go and was at the door when I ran forward and placed my hand on his rock-hard arm. "What happened?"

He turned slowly, a haunted expression claiming his face. "Fire. At The Red Door and Father's mansion. Both are destroyed. Threats have been made against your house and your shop. Your staff is already being evacuated."

Shock had me clinging harder to his arm. I'd heard what he said about the threat on my home and the store, but I didn't care about that. There was only one thing that mattered. My nephew lived in an apartment above The Red Door. My words came out in a panic. "Beau? Carrie? My mom?"

He glanced down at me, his expression hard and unfeeling. I nearly jumped back from the coldness radiating from him. But my hands were fused to his forearm, my nails digging into his skin. I wouldn't let go until he answered.

"They're fine," he said. "Father went in and got them out." Allcot saved them himself? "Is he okay?"

"He will be." With that, he shook off my hold and strode to the door. He paused, plucked my phone from the desk, the charger cord dangling from the adapter. It was obvious the charger hadn't been plugged in, which meant my phone was dead and explained why he'd burst in instead of calling.

Son of a… Damn.

David stuck my phone and the charger in his pocket and then left without saying another word.

Unable to move, I stared at the empty doorway. Allcot had saved my family at great personal risk to himself. Fire and vampires do not mix. It was one of their greatest threats. And one Phoebe almost never used because it was so unpredictable, especially in New Orleans, where so many old wooden houses stood.

I vaguely registered Tal's footsteps behind me, only coming out of my trance when he draped my robe over my shoulders. "They're okay," he said softly and rubbed my neck. All the pain from the day before was gone. Tal's magic had worked better than ever. The only area that wasn't healed was my completely numb foot and lower leg. It didn't matter right then anyway. I could fly.

I turned and hugged him, needing to connect with the warmth of a loved one. He held me close, stroking my hair, but didn't say anything further. There wasn't anything to say.

It took less than ten minutes to get dressed and pack a few essentials. When Tal and I got downstairs, David was standing at the window, staring out at the park across the street.

"We're ready," I said.

He pointed to my phone. He'd plugged it in and it was charging on the entry table. "You don't want to forget that."

"Thanks," I mumbled, uncomfortable. Having Tal and David in the same room was too much for me. But then I pushed the thoughts out of my head. My silly love triangle was nothing compared to two massive fires and my small family almost being burned to death.

The phone buzzed and vibrated on the table.

Phoebe. *We found a vial of the drug they shot you with. Bring Talisen to the Arcane ASAP. We have the ingredients.*

"Let's go," I said and hitched my bag over my shoulder. "We need to stop at the Arcane."

Link jumped and ran ahead of me while David let out a huff of impatience. "No. We're going straight to the safe house."

"Not if you want to cure Harrison and the guards. We've got the info Tal needs to make an antidote."

"Phoebe can bring it," David barked. "You can't be seen roaming the city. It's too dangerous."

"No. The antidote is too important." Tal spun and stood directly in front of David. "If you weren't so pissed at her right now—"

"I'm not pissed at *her*, fae." David's tan face turned red from barely suppressed rage.

Tal just raised an eyebrow. "Fine. But you are pissed." He didn't need to clarify at who. It was obvious David was ready to rip Tal's head off. "But if you'd actually taken a second to look at Willow, you would've noticed her limp. She was shot with that poison last night, and if we can't heal her leg soon, it's going to get a lot worse before it gets better. So I strongly suggest you get on board with stopping at the Arcane. Otherwise, we'll go on our own. I'm not letting her suffer any longer. Not to mention I don't know how long Wil and I can keep the guards from slipping back into nonresponsive states. The best bet is to get the information, concoct the antidote, and then go to whatever mansion Allcot has to stash us all away in."

David narrowed his eyes and loomed over us, his fists clenched tightly at his sides. I wanted to smack him. He was right back to where he was before—ordering me around as if I belonged to him. It didn't matter that I knew he was only trying to protect me. It still grated.

"We have to go." I held up the phone, revealing a message from the director.

Your presence is required. Report to headquarters immediately.

"Fine." David stalked to his car while Tal and I headed for my Jeep. David let out a growl of frustration. "I was going to drive you."

I took a deep breath and prayed for patience. "But then I'll have to rely on you if I need to go anywhere. This will just be easier on both of us."

"Willow, dammit. You're going to be in our custody until this crisis is over. You don't need your car."

"Are you saying I'm being taken and held against my will?" I stood with my hands on my hips, my chin jutting out. "Because as much as I appreciate your concern and the effort you and your father have gone to for my family, I'm still my own person with my own commitments. And trust me, I understand how serious this is." I softened my tone and my stance. "I've been living with this since the day Beau died. But you can't put me in a box until the world stops trying to hurt me. Haven't you figured out that isn't ever going to happen?"

Tal put his hand on the small of my back in a gesture of support.

David's eyes locked in on the connection and his lips formed a thin, tight line. When he finally looked up at me, he let out a slow breath. "I just want you to be safe."

"I know." I closed the distance between us and slipped my arm through his, pulling him toward his car. Tal stayed behind with Link. We stopped at the driver's side. "Sometimes a person has to save themselves. I appreciate everything you've done for me and continue to do for me, but I can't sit around and let everyone take care of me, especially if there's something I can do to help. Please let me do what I have to, otherwise all I have is fear."

"And a fae, it seems." He glared over my shoulder at Tal.

I resisted the urge to scowl. It had been because of Allcot that Tal had left in the first place. But I doubted David had known about that. "Can we talk about that later?"

"Are you sure there's anything to say?" The words weren't an accusation, more of resigned acceptance.

"Yes." I touched his arm lightly. "I need to explain."

"No, you don't."

He reached for the door handle, but I stopped him.

"David." I waited until he looked at me. "Yes. I do."

The ice melted from his brilliant blue eyes. "Okay. Later, once we're back at the house."

"Thank you." I let my hand slide off his arm as I walked away and tried to swallow the ache in my throat.

"You okay?" Tal asked when I climbed into the Jeep.

I nodded. "Thank you."

"For what?" He put the Jeep into gear and took off down the street.

The fact that he'd given me space and had even asked how I was doing meant the world to me. He had every reason to be jealous, but he wasn't letting himself go there. At least not now. And I couldn't have appreciated it more. "For just being you."

Chapter 28

David followed us to the Arcane building and waited outside while Tal, Link, and I disappeared inside. He could've come with us if he'd wanted to. He'd been there often enough for the testing in the past three months. No one would question why he was there. But he'd said he wanted to watch the building just in case.

I was pretty certain he just didn't want to see Tal and me working together.

Phoebe, dressed in fresh jeans and a black T-shirt, was waiting for us in the lobby. Her short dark hair was slightly curled and pinned with a silver barrette.

"Did you come home last night?" I asked, taking in her appearance. She looked incredibly rested for someone who'd been working all night.

"No. I was here. Come on, Director Halston is waiting for you both." She pushed the gate open and Tal, and Link, and I followed her in. No magic neutralizer. Thank the goddess.

"You stayed here? But you look so… put together."

She cast me a mischievous grin. "I have a friend nearby who had a free shower."

"And you just happened to have some clean clothes at *your friend's* house?"

"Yeah." She glanced over her shoulder and winked at Tal. He laughed.

I shook my head. "Phoebe doesn't ever talk about her boyfriends. That's all we're going to get."

"Damn straight." Phoebe quickened her pace and rounded the corner.

The director was waiting in her doorway when we got there. "Good. You're all here." Her frizzy gray hair was piled up into a haphazard bun, and her linen suit was wrinkled as if she'd slept in it. Seems the director didn't have a friend nearby. She waved us into her office and then called to her assistant, "Hold all calls. I'm in an important meeting."

I raised an eyebrow at Phoebe. The director had never given us that kind of consideration before. Usually we were summoned, barely acknowledged, and then dispassionately dismissed with nonnegotiable orders. This was new.

"Have a seat." Her wings flexed as she bustled to the front of her desk and leaned back, casually crossing her legs at the ankles.

I sat in the middle, with Phoebe and Tal flanking me, Link in his Shih Tzu form at Tal's feet.

"It's good to see you again, Director. Though I wasn't expecting to be back so soon," Tal said courteously.

"You too, Mr. Kavanagh. It's a shame you no longer work for the Void, but I appreciate your cooperation in this matter."

He glanced at me and then nodded. "I appreciate your willingness to share your resources."

"Well, unfortunately we're forced to work with Allcot on this one." Her tone changed to one of irritation. "After the incident at the burlesque club, I'm tempted to cut all ties. No one puts my agents in danger without consequences. But it appears humans' lives are on the line. So we will do what we have to until this situation is resolved."

I didn't disagree with her there. I was ready for some distance from Allcot and his crew, too… after Asher was neutralized.

"Anyway…" She stood up straight and met Tal's gaze. "We have a situation. The female vamp Kilsen brought in last night cut a deal with the higher ups. In exchange for her freedom, she's given us a solid lead on Asher's second in command. It seems he followed Ms. Rhoswen to town."

"What? Are they insane? Grace's way too dangerous to be walking the streets," I said, furious.

"A lot of vampires are dangerous, Rhoswen. In this case, the powers that be decided she isn't a direct threat to society and let her go." She picked up a pen and marked something off on her paperwork.

Phoebe shook her head in exasperation. No doubt she'd seen more than her fair share of vamps freed in exchange for intel.

The director cleared her throat and focused on me. "Word is Asher's pissed as hell about the vamps you've turned into daywalkers, and he's put the order out to have you and your nephew eliminated immediately. If his people fail, it's likely he'll find you himself."

"He's welcome to try," I said, my tone full of anger. No one was going to hurt Beau. Not Grace. Not Asher. And certainly none of his lackeys. I'd kill them myself.

"I like that fire, Rhoswen," she said with an appreciative smile. Then she made eye contact with Tal again. "If we can get to Asher's second, we'll find Asher. He's never far behind. Hunter's meeting you here in"—she twisted to look at her clock on the wall—"twenty minutes. You'll join him and his team to track down and eliminate all of Asher's minions. The goal is to weaken his circle enough that when he shows his hand, we'll be right there to take him down."

Tal sat back and eyed her with curiosity. "Of course I'll do whatever I can, but my cover's been blown. Are you sure you want me to serve in that capacity?"

She waved an impatient hand. "We're way past that. In light of the fires earlier this morning, we're in all-out war." Casting her intense gaze on Phoebe, she said, "You've got your orders?"

"Yes. You already know I want Willow and Link on my team. If I'm going to hunt daywalkers, I'm going to need a little help."

I opened my mouth to speak, but the director cut me off.

"Yes. That's why they were summoned. Here are the files." She handed Phoebe a manila folder. "Rhoswen?"

"Yes?"

"Did you get a chance to investigate the fae we have in custody?"

I stifled a groan. After yesterday's events, I'd forgotten all about him. "No, not yet. I was pretty battered after the run-in last night."

"I want you or Kilsen to make that a priority. He isn't talking, and I'm certain he has useful intel. After the fires this morning, Allcot decided to share what he knows. I've been informed the fae was loyal to Victoria, and she's been recently cast out by Asher. Seems she liked biting humans too much to remain under his roof. Apparently she thought bringing you to him would put her back in his good graces." She scanned my body with a long, lingering look. Then she turned to Tal. "She looks to be healthy enough. Your work?"

"Yes, ma'am, but before we do anything, I need the ingredient list for the poison that was found last night." He leaned in closer to me and pointed at my swollen leg. "I need it to treat Willow's ankle and a few of Allcot's guards."

Her nostrils flared as she glanced at me and frowned. "Is it serious?"

"It's just my leg," I said, not wanting to appear as vulnerable as I was. Everyone preyed on the weak in this town. "As soon as Tal makes the antidote, I'll be fine."

A contemplative look came over her face and she unconsciously smoothed her suit jacket. I recognized the movement. It was her tell that she was calculating her next move. And it could be anything.

"Is there a problem, Director?" Tal asked, and I noticed a small twitch in his right eye. He was seconds from losing his cool. All he wanted to do was get in the lab to take care of business.

I was used to her, so her seemingly unreasonable behavior didn't faze me. We'd do whatever we needed to do regardless of what she said. We always did. For better or for worse.

"No." She shook her head, frowning. "Nothing's wrong. Take Rhoswen to the lab and see what you can do. We can't have her injured while she tracks daywalkers. When you're done, come see me to get the whereabouts of Hunter."

"Sure thing." Tal stood and held out his hand to me.

I picked up Link and joined him, waiting for Phoebe.

"I'll be in my office." Phoebe tucked the file under her arm.

"You have an office?" I stared openmouthed at her and the director.

"You both do." The director handed me a key. "You're sharing. Kilsen has been pushing for it for a while now. Since she's our highest-ranked tracker, it seemed she was due."

I almost laughed at the turn of events. It was no secret I was the redheaded stepchild of the Void branch. And I'd gotten a coveted office out of association. That was fine. I'd take it. Not that I ever spent that much time at the Arcane building. But having a dedicated place to work wasn't too shabby.

"This way," Phoebe said. "It's on the way to the lab."

A few minutes later, we were in our joint office. I couldn't stop staring. It was huge and luxurious. I'd never imagined the Void would consider us worthy of such grandeur.

"Phoebs?" I said with no small amount of suspicion. "What's going on? The director doesn't even like me."

"It's come to her attention that we're both very valuable to her cause. Especially you."

"Huh?"

Tal slipped his arm around me and whispered, "You're at the center of everything because of Asher. And even if it wasn't Asher, it'd be some other warlord vamp looking to exploit you. You're important in the Void's war on rogue vampires."

"So?"

"You're an asset... and a liability," Tal explained. "She's trying to keep you close so she always knows what you two are up to. Why else would she put your office on her same floor? No one else's is here."

Phoebe nodded. "Tal's right. This is about her keeping you and me happy and where she can watch us. But since nothing ever really happens in the office, I don't give a crap about that.

All we'll be doing here is analyzing and planning. Nothing too earth shattering. But the best part is we'll no longer need to go through the magic neutralizer. If we're trusted enough to have offices, we're trusted enough to keep our abilities." A triumphant grin lit up her face.

"Score!" I said and gave her a high five as we laughed.

"Okay, time to work." Phoebe handed Tal a list. "Take Willow and start on the antidote. She knows where the labs are."

I shuddered at the word "labs." I sure as hell did know where they were. My mind had all the unpleasant memories burned into it. My jaw tensed as I clenched my teeth, trying to let the emotions go. But they wouldn't.

"Willow?" Phoebe asked, concern radiating from her.

I waved a hand. "I'm fine. Let's go, Tal. We'll meet Phoebe back up here and then deal with David." The mention of David reminded me he was waiting for us. "Phoebs? Before we take off on our mission, I need to go to Allcot's to see Mom and Beau Jr."

"I figured." She sent me a sympathetic smile. "I'm sure they're fine."

"They are, but I need to see for myself."

"Of course."

Tal slipped his hand into mine and I instantly felt calmer. "Let's do this."

"This way." I took a deep breath and led him into the stark white hall that had become my personal hell.

By the time we got to a decently stocked lab, I was panting from the panic trying to claim me. Tal had sent ripples of his healing energy into me, but it was about as good as an aspirin for a migraine.

The fluorescent lighting didn't help, either. My vision had white spots of panic blinding me.

"You need a Calming cookie." Tal pulled me closer and tucked my body against his.

"You can say that again." I breathed into him, instantly feeling better.

Link prowled around the lab three times, his nose to the ground, before he stopped at my feet. He clamped his muzzle shut, showing the most awesome underbite ever, and then growled.

"What is it?" I asked him. But he only got up and sniffed at my leg. My bad one. "I know, little buddy. Tal's going to fix it."

Link sat and stared up at Tal, his tongue hanging out in undisguised adoration. *Get in line, dude.*

"Hey," Tal said, looking up from the file the director had given him.

"Yeah?"

"You doing okay now?"

"As good as I can be, I guess." There was an ache radiating from my ankle that I'd been trying to ignore for the past hour.

He pulled out a stool for me. "Take a seat while I work."

I did as he said and watched as his brow furrowed in concentration. He made a bunch of notes, scratched some out, and made a few more. Then he sat back and rubbed at his jawline.

"What is it?" Absently I massaged my calf, wincing when the pain intensified.

Tal jumped up from his place at the table and crouched down in front of me. His gentle fingers stroked the red area around my wound. "It hurts again?"

I gritted my teeth and nodded.

He cupped his hands over the swollen area. The soothing tingle started at once, but then intense fire erupted, burning me from the inside out.

"Ouch!" I cried and yanked my leg back, tears stinging my eyes. The force of my withdrawal knocked me sideways, and I slipped right off the stool, landing with a thud on the concrete floor. "Ow!"

"Wil!" Talisen dropped to his knees and scooped me into his arms. "I'm so sorry."

"What happened?" I all but whimpered, still shaken from falling so spectacularly.

"The wound is too advanced for me to even numb it. We need the antidote *now*." He gazed down at me, lost in thought. "If you're up to it, I think your magic might help."

"How?" I inspected my leg, noting the heat radiating from it. It reminded me of a giant spider bite—red, swollen, and hot to the touch. Thank goodness it didn't itch.

"I…" He touched his chest just above his heart. "When our magic mingles, it's soothing. There's a peace that fills me up that isn't present when I work my magic on my own." Moving his hand to rest over my heart, his lips turned up in a wry smile. "And I think that might be true for you as well."

My mind immediately recalled the scene of Tal and me together and the feelings of complete joy. I could feel the emotion bursting to spring forth. I nodded, afraid to speak.

His fingers were a whisper of a touch as he stroked them along my collarbone. I closed my eyes and took in the sensation, never wanting it to end.

All too soon he whispered into my ear, "Give me a few minutes."

I pulled my good leg up and wrapped my arms around my knee while Tal stood at the lab table, measuring and mixing unfamiliar ingredients. Finally he glanced down at me and wiped his brow. "It's done."

I stood and hobbled the few steps to his side. The liquid was putrid green and slightly chunky. "Oh yuck… you've got to be kidding!" I stepped back, covering my mouth.

"Sorry, Wil." He gave me an apologetic look. "You don't want to know what I had to use to counteract the poison."

"Battery acid?"

"That might have been preferable."

"Ugh." I stared at it and almost hurled. "You want me to drink this?"

He hesitated and then nodded.

"Can I dress it up? Add something to make it less… awful?" I was grasping at straws and we both knew it.

"If we had more time, I'd be happy for you to experiment with it, but I can't imagine anything you add to this version is going to make it taste better."

"An injection maybe?" I was desperate now. My gag reflex was already kicking in at just the thought of choking that crap down.

He frowned. "That's possible, but it would take a lot more precision and some careful testing to put it in the bloodstream. If we want quick, the best thing to do is swallow it."

"Cripes." I squeezed my eyes shut, praying for strength.

His warm hand closed over mine. "First we need to infuse it with our magic."

My eyes popped open. "Our magic? You sure about that?"

"Positive." He tugged me forward until we were inches apart. I leaned into him, needing to feel him against me.

Taking my hand, he pulled out his healing stone and placed it between our palms. "All I need you to do is pull a bit of my magic from the stone, let it mix with yours, and send it back in. Can you do that?"

"I'll try. Stones aren't my specialty. You know that." I could take in life magic, but stones? It wasn't like they were living, breathing things.

"Good enough. I'll let you know when I'm ready. Just hold tight."

I wasn't going anywhere. Leaning against Tal was calming me in a way I couldn't explain. It wasn't magic. Not that I could tell, anyway. It was something else. A sense that I was where I was supposed to be. Tal was my go-to person and the reason I'd been so miserable the past few months. Not having him in my life had left a crater-sized hole in my heart. Now the hole was gone.

Under Tal's ministration, the stone warmed and started to vibrate. His body went stiff with his effort as the power that radiated from him glowed brilliant white between our palms. The crystal heated to almost unbearable levels, and I flinched.

But Tal's grip tightened around my hand. "Now, Wil."

My heart raced from the residual magic in the air, and I was fully aware of every inch of Tal. Focusing was near impossible. "I don't..." I let out a whoosh of breath and stared at our joined hands.

"You've got this." Tal's soothing voice penetrated the chaos trying to overwhelm me.

My pulse slowed to normal levels while I focused on the heat of the stone. It turned hot, singeing my skin. Under normal circumstances, I would've abandoned the transfer, but after watching Tal and the amount of effort he put into the spell, I couldn't give up. I focused as much for him as I did for myself.

The magic pulsed right at my palm, resistant in a way my plants never were. It was more like when I changed a vampire into a daywalker, though a little more elusive, like the magic was slipping out of my grasp. I tightened my hand over the crystal and squeezed Tal's fingers, trying to keep the magic from sliding away.

"Relax," Tal said softly. "The more you try to control it, the harder it will be. Just let it flow into you as if I were directing it."

"Oh," I breathed and stopped trying altogether. I just focused on connecting with Tal's magic and let it come to me. He'd healed me so many times it was second nature. His tingling magic concentrated at my fingers, and with a will of its own, it filtered into me. My world morphed. I was standing in my bedroom next to my bed, Tal staring down at me with love in his eyes, my fingers poised to undo the top button of his shirt. There was excitement sparking between us along with a heightened anticipation of something more happening. Something intense and wonderful and long overdue.

I blinked and the world shifted again. The stark walls of the lab came into view, anchoring me in reality as the stream of Tal's power flowed into me until I was almost bursting.

I wanted to live in that moment forever, with Tal's magic swirling inside me. It made my head swim and my heart pound. It was like being one with him in a profound way.

"Now, Willow."

Only when I heard his voice urging me did I harness the magic and send it back.

It bent at my will, and within moments, the crystal was filled again, leaving me with an empty ache in my chest. I slumped forward, trying to catch my breath.

"Willow?" Tal placed his hand on my back.

"I'm okay," I gasped out. "I sent a little more than I meant to, I think. I'll be fine in a moment."

"You sure?"

I nodded. I hadn't expected the magic to be so easy to manipulate. When I worked with plants, it took more effort, and a whole lot more effort when changing vampires to daywalkers. What had just happened was totally unexpected.

Tal's warm hand moved down my spine, sending shocks of his magic into me.

I sent him a grateful smile then stepped away, frowning slightly. "Thanks, but you didn't need to do that."

His eyebrows arched in surprise. "Why not?"

"I would've been fine," I said, struggling to not fidget. I didn't want to seem ungrateful, but I couldn't always rely on him to fix me. "It takes a moment for my magic to restabilize, but it does. I just don't want you depleting yourself too much. You're going to need your strength when you work on the guards."

"But it's a basic need to make sure you're okay. I can't really turn it off," he said lightly.

I understood that all too well. He was only trying to protect me. That was the problem. And what David always did. Placing my hand on his arm, I said, "I know, but I have to stand on my own two feet sometimes."

"Why? In this case I mean. Do you know how hard it is to watch you suffer, especially when I know I can do something about it?" He was dead serious now.

When he put it that way, how could I argue? "I just don't want to deplete you. And I guess I don't want to appear weak. I hadn't thought about it from your point of view. I get it."

"You're not weak," he said, steel in his voice. "Anything but weak, actually." Grabbing my other hand, he turned me until we were eye to eye. "I'm not trying to dominate you. I know other people in your life do that. What I want is a partnership. I'll do whatever I can to keep you safe and whole. And I hope you'll do the same for me."

I couldn't say anything at first. He was everything I'd ever wanted.

"Why are you looking at me like that?" he asked, his lips turned down.

I rose up onto my tiptoes and kissed him softly. "I'm just wondering what I did to deserve you."

He chuckled. "No telling. But you're mine now, got it?"

"Got it." I saluted him. "Just as long as you remember who *you* belong to."

"Are you kidding? I've already ordered the business cards." He winked. "Now let's get this leg healed."

Chapter 29

By the time Tal was done, my leg was completely healed. If I was honest, I'd never felt better. He was right about the peace part of the magic. It had soothed every inch of me. And even though I was still dying to see for myself that my family was safe, the panic had ebbed, and I was ready to take on anything.

After checking in with the director, we stopped by the office Phoebe and I now shared to see if Hunter had shown up yet.

"No," she said as she slid a magical ring onto her right ring finger. "But I expect him at any moment."

Tal and I glanced at each other. David was still waiting. I cleared my throat. "We need to make a quick run before we start hunting."

"Going to Allcot's?" she asked.

"We kind of have to. Meet us there? Or somewhere nearby?"

She frowned. "You know he's going to lock you in. We have a mission."

"We won't let him," Tal said with conviction. The look on his face made me regret that we had to go there at all. "But Willow needs to see her family, and I'm sure they want to see her. Besides, we need to give the antidote to the guards before they get any worse."

Phoebe pursed her lips. "Yeah, I suppose so." She pulled a silver pen from her bag and slipped it into Tal's pocket. "Twist it if you want me to hear whatever's going on."

I smiled. She was always coming up with new items to

magically bug. "Thanks. I'll call you when we're done and then we can decide where to meet."

"Be safe."

"We will," Tal said and took my hand. "It'll be a quick trip."

Tal and I disappeared back into the hall with Link in tow. My dog had a pep in his step that hadn't been there this morning. It was as if he knew I was better.

We found David pacing the garage, his phone pressed to his ear. He spotted us and quickly ended the call. "Better?" he asked me.

I nodded. "Tal has the antidote."

Talisen stopped behind me, his hand on my back. "The sooner we can administer it to the guards, the better."

David gave Tal a sharp nod of acknowledgement and stalked to his car.

Tal leaned down and whispered, "Maybe you should ride with him. It'll give you a chance to talk."

I turned slowly, unable to believe he'd just suggested I ride with my ex. "Are you serious?"

He nodded. "I know you have things to say. And once we get to the house we'll be too busy."

"But…" I didn't complete the thought, unsure of what to say.

Tal smiled down at me. "I'm not worried, love. The sooner you're able to settle things with him the easier it'll be on you. Go ahead. Link and I will be right behind you."

I hesitated, not wanting to separate from Tal or Link. There were too many unknowns, too many different groups coming after me. I wanted to keep those I loved as close as possible. But Tal was right. I needed to settle things with David, and once we got to the safe house, the opportunity would be lost. Nodding, I gave him a quick hug and then jogged to David's car.

The pictures Rox had showed me of David and his crew were fresh in my mind, and I considered asking David about them. But in my heart, I didn't really believe David had known about Rox and Beau's friendship. David had only been keeping vampires away from me and my shop. And of course he hadn't told me about them. He probably thought he was handling them, just like he'd handled Clea, a female vamp who'd tried and failed to assassinate me last year.

David raised both eyebrows in question when I slipped into the passenger seat.

I gave him a sad smile. "There are things I need to say."

His hands tightened around the wheel as he pulled out of the garage and onto the streets of New Orleans. "You don't have to say anything, Willow. I think it's obvious what's going on."

I clasped my hands in my lap and forced myself to look at him.

Once he stopped at a light, he turned and met my determined gaze.

"I'm sorry, David." My words were barely audible and gravelly through the lump clogging my throat. "I didn't mean for any of this to happen this way."

"Forget it." He turned to stare at the traffic whipping through the intersection while we waited. "Nothing happened. You got back together with your ex. End of story."

I let out a sigh and tried again. "It's not the end of the story. You and I, there was something there. I don't want to pretend there wasn't. That's not fair to you."

"Life isn't fair, Willow," he snapped and pressed on the gas. "Forget it already. We both knew our relationship was never going anywhere. Fae and vamps don't mix. Right?"

His face and tone were so cold I almost cringed, but forced myself to not react. It was obvious he needed to put up a wall between us, that he didn't want to hear that I cared for him, that I had loved him in my own way. "Yeah. I guess so."

"That's what you've always told me." He took a sharp right turn and then a left, speeding faster than he normally did.

"David—"

"Let it go, Willow." He swerved past a line of cars and merged onto the freeway, heading toward the west bank.

I slumped in my seat, feeling worse than ever. This had been a bad idea. I stared out the window for the next twenty minutes until we turned onto a deserted-looking dirt road and stopped in front of a large white farmhouse, which was concealed from the street by large moss-covered oaks. Cypress trees and swampland stretched out behind the house. The isolation was both comforting and terrifying. It was hard to believe Asher's people would find it. But at the same time, if they did, where would everyone go?

David stormed into the house as soon as we parked while I waited for Tal and Link, who'd been right behind us.

"How'd it go?" Tal slipped his arm around my waist and gave me a kiss on the head.

"Not well." I stepped back, putting distance between us. "Can we keep the PDA to a minimum for now? I don't want to make things worse."

Tal glanced at the house and back down at me. "Yeah. Sure."

I placed a light hand on his arm. "Just until we leave here? I don't want to make him feel worse than he already does."

Tal gave me a sympathetic smile. "Trust me, Wil. Nothing's going to make him feel worse than losing you, especially to me. But I agree. No need to rub his face in the fact. Let's just get to work, okay?"

Rough wood floors and a banister with peeling paint met us in the entryway. This was Allcot's safe house? I had to give him credit. Every other building he was associated with was high-end in the extreme. No one would ever believe this place was his.

"Why is it so quiet?" I whispered to Talisen, not wanting to disturb the unnerving silence.

He shrugged. "No idea, but we can't stand here all day."

I nodded and moved ahead of him into the parlor. An old, saggy brown couch took up one wall and a plain-wood side table filled the other. A single bulb hung from the ceiling, illuminating the cobwebs in the corners. Jeez. The place looked like it belonged in a horror movie.

"There you are," Allcot said from the top of the stairs. He glared down at us, his eyes full of fury. "I sent Davidson to get you hours ago."

"We were working on the antidote for your guards," I said evenly, trying not to engage in his anger. "Thank you for taking care of my family. Can I see them?"

His gaze narrowed in on Talisen. "You work for me now. I expect you to follow orders when given."

Tal stared at him, his expression blank. "Like Willow said, we were working on the antidote. I have what I need to cure them. We'll discuss my *employment* at another time."

My fists clenched, and I wanted to deck Allcot. Employee. Right. More like indentured servant. Tal had been sold to Allcot. It was outrageous.

"My family?" I asked again.

Allcot tore his icy stare from Tal and cast me one of irritation. "Your mother is waiting for you in the kitchen."

I took off toward the back of the house, not caring what else Allcot had to say. I appreciated his help, but it was more and more clear to me he was only doing it out of his own selfish motivation. He'd own me too if he could figure out a way to do it.

"Mom!" I cried, bursting into the kitchen. She was sitting at a butcher-block table, her head resting in her hand.

"Willow?" She stood, a stark streak of black ash on her face making her appear paler than usual.

"Mom," I said more softly and wrapped her in my arms. "Are you all right?"

She nodded, hugging me back fiercely. "Yes. My lungs feel a little singed, but other than that I'll live after some rest."

"Oh, no." I hugged her tighter, an ache forming in my chest. "I'm so sorry. Tal is here—I'm sure he can help."

I felt her nod again, and then we stood there just holding each other. When she finally let go, I sat with her at the table.

"Where are Carrie and Beau?"

"Sleeping," she said and poured out a cup of tea for me.

"How are they doing?"

Mom took a breath. "Beau is fine. Allcot got him out first."

My heart swelled with gratitude that Allcot had been there for my nephew even if I would never be entirely sure about his ultimate motivations when it came to Beau Jr.

"He went back in for Carrie, but by then she was already passed out from the smoke inhalation and her leg was burned pretty badly."

I stood, ready to get Tal immediately, but Mom grabbed my hand, not letting me go. "Allcot brought in a healer. She's okay."

I sat back down, eyeing her. "But he didn't send the healer to you?"

She shook her head. "I declined. I'll be fine."

"Mom, you're wheezing."

"You know how much I don't like enduring another fae's magic," she said stubbornly.

I sat back and crossed my arms over my chest. Yes, I knew. Mom was suspicious of everyone in the supernatural world, and it took a lot to gain her trust. That seemed reasonable to me. She'd lost her husband and her son because of their gifts. And one never knew what powers someone had hiding under a seemingly friendly smile. "Well, Tal is here. After he's done, he can give you a once-over."

She took a sip of her tea. "All right. Did he find an antidote?"

"Yes." I stood, intending to go find him, but my phone buzzed. I pulled up a text message from Phoebe. It was a picture of four people: Meredith, the fae from Eureka we'd turned over to Allcot; the fae who'd been with Victoria and was currently in the Void's custody; Rox, the vampire who'd tried to force me to turn him the night before; and finally the power-hungry third guard Talisen was currently curing upstairs.

Phoebe: *Found this at the fae's residence along with a bunch of half-formed plans for infiltrating Allcot's residences. Allcot's guard is a mole.*

Chapter 30

Son of a... Tal had been right. The images we'd seen when we'd healed the guards had been their heart's desire.

"What's wrong, sweetie," Mom asked. "You look like you're ready to pass out."

"Who all's here?" I asked her while texting Phoebe with the address and asking her to come immediately.

"Allcot, David, Pandora, Nicola, the sick guards, and that female fae David brought back from California. Why?"

Panic took over as foreboding weighed down on me. Had the guard been strong enough to give away our location? "Oh, God. I have to find David."

"Honey?" Mom stood. "What's going on?"

"Our location has been compromised," I called as I ran out of the kitchen. The entire bottom floor of the house was deserted, and it wasn't until I got to the top of the creaky stairs that I heard voices. I followed them into a dimly lit bedroom to the right.

Nicola, a witch and Pandora's half sister, was pacing. Her blond hair was piled high on her head and she wore glasses low on her nose as she scribbled something on a pad of paper. Pandora was sprawled on a chaise lounge, her eyes closed. Blackout shades covered the two windows, but it was clear that being awake during the day was taking a toll on the vamp.

I cleared my throat. "Uh, hi."

Nicola spun, clearly startled. "Oh, hi, Willow. When did you get here?"

"About twenty minutes ago," Pandora said without opening her eyes. "Her and her fae."

"Have you seen David?" I asked.

Pandora waved a listless hand. "He's probably with Eadric, forming some sort of a plan."

"We can't stay here." Nicola turned to me. "It's not safe."

"No, it isn't," said a female voice I didn't recognize.

I spun and found Meredith standing in the doorway, wearing the same clothes she'd had on when I'd met her in the forest. Only now they were a bit tattered. She stood tall with her feet shoulder-width apart, ready to attack.

"What are you doing out of your shackles?" Nicola demanded, magic already bursting at her fingertips.

"Change of plans." Meredith opened her palm, revealing a small vial of gas. Then with an evil smile, she tightened her fist around it and the glass shattered. Gray mist engulfed her.

What the hell? I moved forward but froze when she sucked in air, breathing in the entirety of the mist. Her lips turned up in a self-satisfied smile.

"What did you just do?" I demanded, trying to still my fluttering wings. My flight instinct had kicked in. Whatever she'd done, I knew deep in my bones it was not going to turn out well.

"This." She lifted her upturned palm to her lips and blew. The gray mist turned into a familiar thick fog.

"No!" I cried, throwing my hands up as if that could shield me from the intoxicating magic.

"What the hell?" Nicola threw a blast of magic that shattered a hole in the plaster wall when Meredith ducked.

The fog encompassed me and my entire body relaxed. All my worries fled as I sank into a threadbare chair.

"That's it, fae. Curl up in that chair for a while. Don't worry about anything while I take care of a few things."

As soon as the fog reached Nicola, she stumbled backward and flopped down on the bed, her arms spread wide. "I think we need to nap," she said. "We've been working too hard."

Meredith laughed. "Yes, witch, I think that's a fine idea. Just close your eyes and get some rest."

"What the fuck is going on?" Pandora jumped to her feet in lightning vampire speed. "What did you do to them?"

I watched Pandora in fascination. Her blond hair fell in long layers down her back. The dim light bounced off her glossy locks, and I found myself wishing I weren't a redhead.

"They're under my spell. They'll do whatever I wish as long as I ask nicely. Won't you, girls?"

Nicola and I nodded. In the back of my mind there was a nagging doubt that something was off, but I didn't care. The fog had created a utopia I didn't want to leave.

Pandora growled. "Reverse it this moment before I rip your goddamned head off."

"Restrain your sister, Nicola," Meredith commanded.

Nicola turned without hesitation and cast a spell that stopped Pandora dead in her tracks. She appeared to be frozen in place by the magic.

"That's impressive," I said.

"Thanks." Nicola turned to smile at me. "I've been learning a lot from my lessons with Phoebe."

"Nicola! Reverse the spell this minute," Pandora cried.

"You will do no such thing. Leave your sister where she is," Meredith said softly. Then she gestured to me. "The pair of you, follow me."

Nicola and I did as we were told, ignoring Pandora's demands to release her from her invisible prison.

"This way, ladies," Meredith sang and glided out of the room and into the hallway. We followed her halfway down the hall until she stopped at another door. "Willow, this is the room your nephew is in. Please retrieve him so we can take him away from this vampire lair."

My nephew. Yes. That's who I'd come here for. I nodded, and with bold determination, I strode into the quiet room.

"Auntie!" Beau called and ran toward me.

"Willow?" Carrie sat up on the bed and rubbed her eyes.

"Hi." I waved at her as I squatted and engulfed Beau Jr. in a giant hug. "Mind if I spend some time with the little guy?"

She lay back down on the bed with a soft sigh. "Sure. I'm glad you're here, actually. I need to sleep and I've been too afraid to take my eyes off him ever since the fire."

I stood, holding Beau's hand. "Aw. Get some rest. We'll come back and check on you a little later."

"Thanks, Wil."

"No problem. I'm glad you're okay."

She nodded and closed her eyes.

"Let's go, little guy." I tugged on Beau's hand and together we slipped back into the hall.

"Well done, Willow," Meredith said. "Time to go." She spun and took off down the stairs. Nicola, Beau, and I followed without complaint.

We'd just hit the bottom of the stairs when I heard Talisen call, "Willow?"

Grinning, I turned and waved. "Hey, Tal. How'd the treatments go?"

His expression turned from one of confusion to complete outrage. "What's going on?"

"She's mine now, Kavanagh," Meredith said and placed a firm hand on my shoulder. "So is the boy."

"I don't think so." His green eyes turned the color of coal as fury radiated off him.

"It's okay, Tal. I've got Beau. Everything is going to be fine now." I felt an odd sense of confusion filter through me. It felt right to follow Meredith's lead, but now that Talisen was questioning what was going on, I hesitated. Why was he so upset? I knew the answer was buried somewhere in my memory, but I couldn't find it.

"She works for Asher!" Talisen ran down the stairs, headed straight for me. "She tried to kill you two days ago."

Meredith raised her palm once more and blew more mist in Tal's direction.

He stopped, his eyes wide with surprise. Then he scrambled over the banister, out of the way of the fog. "Shit."

"Laveaux, Allcot!" Talisen bellowed. "Security breach!"

There was a commotion at the top of the stairs as footsteps pounded on the old floors.

"Outside, now," Meredith commanded us. Even though I didn't want to go, my feet moved on their own as if I didn't have a choice.

Once I was on the porch, the bright sun hit me full in the face. Momentarily blinded, I squinted and rubbed at my eyes.

"Auntie?" Beau tugged at my hand.

I kneeled beside him. "Yes, love?"

"Who are all those people?"

"What?" I shielded my eyes just in time to see Harrison coming straight for me... No, not me—Beau. On instinct, I pulled his small body to me and wrapped an arm around him. "Harrison? What's going on? Why is everyone outside?"

"K.C. ordered it." He jerked his head in the direction of the third guard. The power-hungry one. They both appeared to be completely healed. Talisen had wasted no time with his antidote.

My memory snapped into place. The mole! He couldn't be trusted. I snatched little Beau up in my arms, holding him against my side. He clung to my neck, his legs wrapped around my waist.

"Auntie?" he said again, and this time fear radiated from him as he trembled.

"Give him to me, Willow," Harrison said.

"No." I stepped backward toward the house. "Tal!" I called, but he was nowhere to be found.

"Stop, Willow," Meredith commanded. "Give the boy to Harrison."

My arms encircled Beau tighter as I tried to fight off the compulsion to release my nephew.

"Do it!" Meredith blew more gray mist at me. "Harrison will take care of him now."

A sense of calm settled over me. This was Harrison. He'd been a part of my security detail and had been guarding Carrie and Beau for months. Of course it was okay to hand Beau over to him. He'd be safe with him.

As soon as Harrison reached for Beau, shouting started from behind me, followed by a small group of people materializing from the trees.

"Willow, don't!" David's voice came from behind me, causing me to hesitate. I clutched at Beau as David launched himself at Harrison, tackling the guard.

Meredith swore and ordered Nicola to neutralize David.

I spotted Talia, Grace, and Vince stalking toward me from the trees. And right there between Grace and Vince was the vampire Asher himself.

Compromised! The word flashed in my mind. Suddenly everything became clear again. I knew I was drugged to bend to Meredith's will and that the only way to break the spell was to incapacitate her. But I had Beau Jr. in my arms. There was nothing I could do until he was safe.

I had to give him to a vampire. They weren't affected. Everyone else already was. It was the only explanation for Harrison's behavior. Oh Goddess. That left Allcot or David. Pandora wasn't a daywalker.

But where was Allcot? I glanced around, seeing him nowhere.

"Willow!" Tal called and bounded out the door.

"Rhoswen," Meredith ordered.

But before she could finish, I clutched at Tal's arm and pleaded, "Whatever happens, get us inside."

"Stop right there," Meredith ordered. "Give me the child."

My feet stuck to the porch. Part of me ached to do as she said, but that little voice was keeping me immobile.

Thank the gods, Talisen didn't hesitate. He picked Beau and me up and hauled us both back inside. I still felt the urge to join Meredith outside, but I was able to fight it off.

"It's her spell," I huffed out. "Compelled."

"I know." Tal set me down and gently took Beau from my arms.

My nephew started to whimper, his face scrunched up in panic.

"I've got him," my mom said and took Beau.

"Stay as far away from the fae as you can," Tal told her. "Go upstairs with Pandora. Whatever you have to do, but don't leave her side."

Mom nodded and ran up the stairs two at a time.

"Where's Allcot?" I huffed out, trying to fight the urge to go back outside.

"I don't know." A tingle of Tal's magic zapped through me but did nothing to alter Meredith's magic.

I sighed, frustrated. I couldn't focus.

"You have to attack her," Tal said.

"Who?" My mind was full of static. No coherent thoughts. Just a buzzing that wouldn't go away.

"Meredith."

I stared at him blankly, not able to process what he meant.

He let out a frustrated breath. "Never mind. Just stay right here. Don't move." Tal flung the front door open and disappeared out onto the porch.

I stood there, totally helpless. The pull of what was waiting for me outside was too much. I had to get to Meredith. Reluctantly, I pulled the door open and once more stepped out onto the wide wraparound porch.

Chaos greeted me. David was currently battling Harrison and the other two guards. They had him pinned and were struggling to put him into vampire cuffs.

Tal was circling Meredith, doing whatever he could to avoid her mind-altering fog. Vince, Grace, and Talia had disappeared.

But right there in the middle of the yard were Asher and Allcot in a one-on-one fight to the death. My eyes widened at the sight.

I was transfixed, unable to look away… right up until Nicola started throwing spells in Allcot's direction. Meredith must've ordered her to do it.

Oh, crap on a cracker. He was going to be taken out by his sister-in-law. Nicola's magic was slowly leeching Allcot's energy, giving Asher the upper hand. With Allcot neutralized, Asher would plow right through the rest of us to get to Beau.

I spun and focused on Meredith. She had to be taken down. I had to do whatever I could to help Tal. She was so focused on trying to bait Talisen with her magic that she didn't notice I'd reappeared. Good. I needed the element of surprise, or I'd be right back where Nicola was, doing the bidding of my enemy.

Tal glanced in my direction for a split moment and to my horror, Meredith's gaze followed. Our eyes met. This was it. She was going to order me to do something awful. Determined to stop her, I thrust my wings, heading straight for her.

Her mouth opened and she got out something inaudible just as Talisen jumped her from behind, clasping his hand over her mouth. They went down in a heap of arms and legs. It was all I needed.

A second later, I was on them and wrapping my hands around Meredith's neck. It was a savage move, meant to keep her from speaking, but as soon as my hands touched her skin, I instinctively pulled on her life energy.

My blood ran hot with horror from the reality of what I was doing. There was no help for it, though. If I allowed her to remain conscious, she'd continue to use Nicola and me against our loved ones.

I stared down into Meredith's face, dispassionately watching as her skin tone turned ashen. She'd tried to take Beau. It was all I could think about as her tainted life energy filled me up, nauseating me. My stomach was turning and my limbs vibrating when her eyes finally rolled into the back of her head and her body went limp.

I knew she'd passed out, but still I didn't move. I continued to stare into her unseeing eyes, wanting more than anything to end her.

Then Tal was there, his gentle voice coaxing me back to myself. "Wil? It's okay, you can let go now."

"She tried to take Beau," I said. "She tried to make me give him up." It was the horror of that realization that made me want to vomit more than anything else.

"But you didn't, love. You didn't. Let go now." Gently he pried my hands from Meredith's limp body and tugged me to him. "You're fine now."

I leaned into him, grateful for the physical support. My body was shaking from the fae's energy still trapped inside me. "I have to let this out."

"Here." He spun us and led me to a nearby tree. "Give it back to the earth."

I clutched at the bark and felt instant relief as it took everything I poured into it. The poor tree. It would be in a bit of shock for a few days, but the giant oak would recover faster than I would've had I kept Meredith's poisonous energy.

"Better?" Tal asked.

I nodded.

"Good, because we need you right now." Tal turned me toward the battle in the middle of the yard. Nicola had retreated and was sprawled on the grass as if she'd collapsed there. Her eyes were open and she appeared aware, but I couldn't be sure. She'd been using a lot of magic.

David had somehow managed to knock out Harrison and the second guard and was currently grappling with K.C., the power-hungry one. It was clear he hadn't needed to be spelled in order to fight on Asher's side.

That left Asher and Allcot, still going at each other's throats. Asher appeared to have a slight advantage on Allcot, no doubt due to Nicola's magic.

"We should help him," I said.

"Who? Laveaux?" Tal asked.

I glanced at David and shook my head. He was a little worn around the edges, but he'd take down the guard in no time. "No. Allcot."

Talisen focused on the epic battle of two vampire leaders. Neither seemed to be slowing down, each battering the other in blow after blow after blow. The only difference was Allcot had burns from Nicola's magic that had to hurt like a bitch. Asher didn't. Nicola had some damn fine aiming skills.

"Shit," Tal said.

"Exactly."

His hand tightened around mine. I knew that was his way of asking me to stay out of it, but I didn't think I could. If I got my hands on Asher, I'd weaken him and maybe even end this battle right then. I'd made up my mind to do just that when Asher twisted and got Allcot into a headlock.

Before anyone could move, Asher's fangs extended and he viciously tore into Allcot's neck, sending blood gushing everywhere.

Someone screamed. It might have been me.

I stood there, horror consuming me. Blood sprayed in an arc. No one could survive that sort of epic blood loss for long, not even a vampire. If someone didn't stop Asher soon, he'd drain Allcot dry and end him forever.

But David was still battling the human guard. They were rolling around on the ground, each struggling just as much as the other. The guard had to be under the influence of Tal's elixir in order to be holding his own with a vampire. There was no other explanation. And Nicola was passed out in the grass.

I made a snap decision. "Tal, help David. Do whatever you have to in order to get the guard off him. He's obviously hopped up on your drug. I'm going to stop Asher."

"Wil, no!" Tal grabbed both of my hands. "It's too dangerous."

"It's too dangerous if I don't."

Our eyes met and Tal's worry reflected back at me.

I reached up, smoothing the wrinkle on his forehead. "We don't have a choice if we want to keep Beau safe."

Tal's shoulders slumped in defeat and he gave me one short nod. "Just get to him before he gets to you. Promise."

"Promise." I gave him what I hoped was a reassuring smile and turned my attention to the master vampires. Asher had weakened his hold on Allcot, and Allcot was starting to slump against him. It was now or never.

I chose now.

Chapter 31

With one thrust of my wings, I was high in the air. The only way this was going to work was if I caught Asher by surprise. Otherwise the vampire could break my neck before I even had a chance to register he'd caught me. I flew high above the pair, grateful Asher was too focused on Allcot to pay any attention to me.

I was directly over him, ready to descend, when a shout came from the second story of the farmhouse.

"Asher, look out!" It was Grace, standing on a small upper balcony, and to my extreme horror, she was holding Carrie upright by the neck. My friend had passed out... or worse.

"Carrie!" I cried and switched course, intending to do whatever I could to help her. But then Talia appeared right behind them and sank her teeth into Grace's pristine white neck. Carrie crumpled to the deck as Grace let out an inhuman howl and tried to buck Talia off.

"Rhoswen!" Asher growled below me.

Shit! My element of surprise was completely blown. Everything in me screamed to go after Carrie, to help her. I moved toward the balcony and blinked when Talisen appeared behind the two fighting vamps. He dropped to his knees and pulled Carrie to him. His eyes met mine for one agonizing second, and then he jerked his head, indicating I should go finish what I'd started.

Asher. He was mine.

I glanced down at the son of a bitch, and with cold determination, I flew right at him.

It was a suicide mission. Asher was waiting for me, his expression full of bloodlust. He would kill me. It was written all over him. I only hoped I weakened him enough that someone else could take him down.

My world narrowed to only Asher, taking in his nondescript features. He had a medium build, light-brown, short hair, a round face—no real distinguishable traits. There was nothing about him that said vampire lord or evil leader of a misguided cause. No wonder he'd flown under the radar for centuries. Nothing about him was memorable.

But he'd messed with the wrong fae this time around. No one hurts my loved ones and gets away with it.

"Yes. That's it," Asher said, inflecting false charm into his English accent. "Come to me, Willow Rhoswen. Meet the same fate as your misguided brother." There was glee in his dull brown eyes.

With those words, he confirmed what I'd known all along—he'd killed Beau, not Allcot.

"Go to hell, Asher!" I cried and dove for him, my hands stretched out in front of me. All I needed was contact, and I'd do my worst. I was a about a foot from him when he leaped up, grabbing my ankle. Heat and fire shot through my leg, straight to my heart, and I lost all control and tumbled forward.

"Stupid fa— Oomph!" A loud growl cut him off, just before Asher was tackled by my giant wolf.

The three of us landed in a pile in the middle of the yard, Link on top of Asher, savagely going after his neck. There was blood everywhere. Link's muzzle was covered with it, his teeth flashing with more determination than I'd ever seen.

I'd landed about a foot away and scrambled to my knees, my gut churning when Asher reached out and wrapped both hands around Link's neck. It would only take a second before he crushed Link into pieces.

"No!" I flung myself at them, both hands grabbing one of Asher's arms. My world turned into a fiery inferno of pain. I welcomed it. Willfully I took in the red-hot agony of a thousand knives carving me up from the inside out. With every bit of vampire life I stole from Asher, I was one step closer to ending him forever.

"Let go!" Asher demanded and tried to shake me off, but I dug my nails in, holding on harder.

I kept my brother Beau, Beau Jr., Carrie, and Tal all in the forefront of my mind, clinging to their memories while I did what I had to for those I loved most. This was for them. For everyone else who'd ever suffered at the hands of the twisted, self-appointed savior of humans. He was no better than the gangbangers who killed for territory or rogue vampires who ate whomever they liked just because they could.

Asher wanted to stop daywalkers because he believed there would be too much of a power shift and humans would suffer. But in my limited experience, daywalkers became more sympathetic to humans. Even Asher. Who was to say if they were all daywalkers, had a part of their humanity back, that there wouldn't be less conflict, not more?

It didn't matter. Not to me. Not then. All I wanted to do was keep those around me safe.

Asher's energy flowed into me, raw and unbearable, but I shut my mind down. His death would be the beginning of a new chapter. One that didn't include a war focused around my nephew. As long as Beau Jr. had the opportunity for a seminormal life, it would all be worth it. I'd give up any life I had for him. For my brother.

"Willow! That's enough." I recognized the feminine voice but couldn't place it. Couldn't even move. My hands were locked around the vampire's arm as if they'd melded there. I saw nothing but red, felt nothing but pulsing agony. My body was starting to shut down. Commands from my brain no longer worked, and I imagined myself slowly fading away into a world of darkness. It would be better there. Cool. Peaceful. A place to finally rest.

A flash of light filtered through my haze, and then I was lying on the grass, staring up into the face of the vampire—no, fae—I'd met a few days earlier. Hunter.

"Willow?" he asked, concern in his voice. "Are you all right?"

I blinked and glanced to the side, finding Asher gaunt and unconscious. "We have to end him," I croaked out.

"We will." Phoebe came into view. They must have just arrived together. "We needed to get you and Link out of the way."

"Do it. Now!" I cried in a panic, not lifting my head or moving any other part of my body. It was too painful. It felt as if fire ants where crawling beneath my skin. I was trembling and so hot I was certain I'd combust right there. They had to end Asher before he woke up and touched me and stole his energy back. Because I couldn't contain it much longer. It was out of my control.

Phoebe nodded to Hunter and the pair of them disappeared from my field of vision. I turned my head, eyeing the source of all my angst for the past year. And deep in my soul, I knew I wanted to see his undead life end. Needed it on a purely base level in order to feel safe again.

And then my best friend and the fae who'd spent years as a vampire tracking Asher down did what no one else had been able to do. They raised their arms and together they cast a blinding red bolt of fire magic at Asher. His body bowed as the magical flames engulfed every inch of his skin. It crackled and popped like sap in a pinewood log. And then all at once, the fire magic exploded.

All that was left was ash.

I felt the hot streaks of tears on my temples. He was gone. Finally. Beau Jr. was safe. For now.

"Wil?" Phoebe dropped to her knees beside me. "You're shaking. What do you want me to do?"

I stared up at her, not knowing what to say.

"Willow?"

I opened my mouth to tell her I need to unleash Asher's energy, but it was eating me from the inside out and I couldn't speak.

"Talisen!" Phoebe cried, glancing back at the house. "Hurry!"

I felt his footsteps in the yard before I saw him. His worried expression when he crouched down next to me only made the tears come faster.

I'm okay, I tried to say, but still the words wouldn't come out.

"She needs to release the vampire energy," he said as he scooped me up into his arms and bounded into the house.

I curled into myself, barely able to stay conscious from the agony claiming my flesh. Each jostle, each footstep, each brush of skin on skin was pure hell. Even Tal's normally cooling touch didn't help. It only made things worse.

Finally he stopped and ever so gently laid me down on a bed. I was too far gone to even open my eyes. A hand covered mine, irritating the fire ants that were burrowing away beneath my skin.

"No!" I got out as I tried to steal my hand back. But the grip on it tightened.

"Here," Tal said softly and pressed my hand to a cold, hard stone. "Release Asher's energy. Do it now."

The ants fled through my body, pooling in my palm. Heat and ice mixed at the connection of my hand to the stone. I could taste the release, but I wasn't strong enough. The energy wouldn't budge.

"Take a tiny bit of her energy into yourself, Wil," Talisen said.

Her? Had he assigned gender to his stones? It didn't matter. I was beyond caring. All I wanted was the energy gone. Pulling the will from deep in my gut, I connected to the stone and pulled.

White-hot streaks of life seared through me. I gasped, sucking in a startled breath. Tal's stones never felt like that. It was then I realized I wasn't taking energy from a stone. It was a vampire. A female one.

I turned my head, squinting to focus on the blond beauty beside me. Pandora. Oh, Goddess. She wasn't moving. Someone had killed her.

The sight of Allcot's consort and Nicola's sister made me want to cry. She was one who'd always been nice to me. I didn't want to see her dead. I forced myself to roll over and placed both my hands directly over her heart. Then I squeezed my eyes shut and willed the energy back into her. This time there wasn't any barrier. Her energy, along with all of Asher's, rushed into her so fast it made my head spin.

Pandora sat straight up, knocking me to the side, and let out a loud gasp of her own. "What happened?"

"Pandora!" I heard Nicola cry, but it was Allcot who was beside her instantly, his arms cradling her against his chest.

His deep gray eyes met mine, his expression a combination of wonder and relief as he clutched his partner. His expression turned soft and vulnerable when Pandora's arms went around him. "Thank the gods you're okay," he whispered into her ear, never taking his eyes off me.

I gave him a tiny smile, pleased to see he really did have a heart underneath all the power and arrogance.

He returned my smile with a grateful one of his own and mouthed, *Thank you.*

Chapter 32

The injuries and destruction were great. By the time I was functional enough to survey the damage, Allcot and his people had either eliminated or restrained all of Asher's supporters. A group of us had gathered in a large den on the second floor.

Pandora, a new daywalker, was standing on the outside balcony, her face turned to the sun. Allcot stood just inside the room, keeping one eye on her and another on David. His neck wound was raw and puckered, but no longer bleeding. David was lying on a long couch, his leg elevated. He had a long, ugly gash from his hip to his knee.

"What happened?" I asked sitting in a chair next to him. Link, still in wolf form, lay down at my feet, keeping an eye on me.

"Vince. He was trying to take Beau Jr." David moved to sit up, but I held up my hand, indicating that wasn't necessary. His wound was ugly.

"He wasn't successful," I noted, glancing at Beau Jr. playing on a blanket in the middle of the room.

"No. He wasn't." David's words were hard and full of contempt. "And he paid for it."

I raised my eyebrows, curious what that meant.

David grimaced. "He's ash now, courtesy of Hunter. We destroyed an entire room trying to kill each other. Finally, when both of us were losing so much blood and neither had much strength, Hunter arrived and ended him."

David sounded pissed about that.

"And you wanted to be the one to do it?"

He shrugged. "Not necessarily. But I do like questioning my enemies before deciding to terminate their existence."

Normally I'd balk at the idea of ending the life of anyone, including a vampire, but in this case, I held only gratitude for Hunter. These vampires would've never stopped until they got to Beau Jr. And that was unacceptable.

"It doesn't matter," Carrie said in a tired voice. "We got all the answers we needed." She was sitting on the floor across from Beau, keeping a sharp eye on him. Bruises had blossomed around her neckline, but other than being exhausted, she appeared to be okay.

"And the answers are?" I glanced around the room. I'd been out of it for quite a while after I'd changed Pandora. Talisen had been with me for most of that time.

Hunter cleared his throat. "I guess I'll start at the beginning."

I nodded. "Seems like a good idea."

He stood and started pacing. His dark hair was wet, as if he'd just gotten out of the shower, and there was an ugly scratch on the right side of his face. "You know your brother and I were friends in high school."

"Yes, but you didn't go to our school, did you?"

"No." He ran a hand over his head. "I went to a private school that was integrated with fae and humans. I had a human girlfriend a couple of years older than me who'd been turned into a vamp." He glanced at Talia, who was leaning against the far wall, staring at her feet.

"Talia?" I asked.

Her head snapped up. "Yes. It was me. I was turned against my will."

My heart broke for her. It was one of life's worst invasions, having your life stolen from you. I suppressed a shudder. "Was it Asher?"

"No," she said quietly. "But he found me shortly after, and because of my anger at being turned, he used me for his cause—to protect humans from being harmed by vampires. From there I recruited Hunter and Beau."

"Beau?" The question came out in a gasp. "He willingly worked for Asher?"

"Yes." Her tone was apologetic. "Because he trusted me. The thing is, Asher had an unnatural interest in Beau, and I never knew why. Not until the night Asher killed me, or tried to, and left me where Beau would find me. It was a test to see if he could in fact turn vampires into daywalkers."

Holy crow. Asher had set him up. If Beau had never met Hunter or Talia, would he still be with us today? It was possible, but I wasn't naïve enough to believe nothing would've ever happened. The gift was too strong a lure.

"After that, it became apparent Asher was after Beau," Hunter continued. "We set up a plan to turn a group of vampires into daywalkers as his security team. But Asher got wind of it and picked them off one by one until he gathered enough information to get to Beau himself."

I sat back, horrified. Poor Beau. He'd been so young and all his resources had been new vampires. I turned to Carrie. "Did you know about all this?"

She shook her head. "Not at first. Not when he was aligned with Asher, anyway. Beau knew my sister was a vampire and didn't want to upset me. He felt strongly about protecting humans but didn't want to fight about it. It wasn't until he knew he was in real danger that he told me. I was already making a plan to get us out of Eureka when Beau was killed."

The familiar ache in my heart throbbed. I missed my brother more than words could convey. And today, with my defenses so blown apart, his absence hit me harder than it usually did. I glanced at little Beau and took comfort in the fact my brother had left such a beautiful gift behind.

"So he turned Vince, Grace, and you into daywalkers?" I asked Talia.

"Yeah, and Victoria."

That explained why I hadn't felt her vampire energy, either.

"He'd planned to turn a few others but never got the chance." Talia's tone was sad as she continued. "After that, I made it my mission to take Asher down. But he went into hiding and no one knew where he was. I teamed up with Hunter, and we've been looking for him ever since. We got close once or twice, but it wasn't until he recruited Rox, Grace, and the others recently that we got a real line on him."

"Why?" I asked, genuinely curious. "You could've just gone off and lived your lives. Especially after four years of false leads."

She met Hunter's gaze and an unspoken communication passed between them. Hunter nodded, and Talia took a deep breath. "First, if it wasn't for me, Hunter and Beau never would've been involved with Asher. I felt responsible."

"I did, too," Hunter added.

Once again, the knowledge of Beau's dangerous secret life made my heart ache. Why hadn't he ever said anything? *To protect you,* the thought ghosted through my mind, and I knew it was true.

Talia cleared her throat. "But mostly I did it because it's my fault Asher found Beau. I was the only one who knew where he'd be at all times. I was supposed to trust no one, because we knew someone was feeding Asher information. But I was scared and needed someone to talk to. I told one person. Grace. She was quiet back then, with an air of honor about her. She was always talking about right and wrong, trying to live a moral life." She let out a huff of sardonic laughter. "I was so gullible. Within two hours, Beau was gone." Her eyes misted with pink-tinged tears.

I frowned. "But yet you continued to work with her undercover this whole time?"

"No," she said forcefully. "I actually went solo for a long time and only infiltrated their group after I started working with Hunter again. That was a few months ago. Yesterday when you were kidnapped from the bar, I had no idea Vince was going to do that. It was supposed to be a recon mission, which was fine for undercover work, but by the time I realized what he had planned, it was too late. I did everything I could to get you away from him."

I narrowed my eyes, not sure I could believe her. "How do I know you're not lying to me?"

Allcot spoke up for the first time since I'd entered the room. "Everyone has been given Truth Clusters. Her story meshes with the information we've ascertained from the remaining prisoners."

Oh. Right. He'd placed an order at my shop recently. I stared at him. "Did you suspect someone on your team was disloyal? Is that why the emergency order?"

"Yes, Ms. Rhoswen. And as it turns out, I was correct. Our guard, K.C., was a mole. He's been eliminated, along with the vampire Vince. The other vampire and that traitorous fae will undergo more questioning before we decide their fate."

He was talking about Meredith and Grace.

"I see," I said, trying to suppress the desire to find Grace and end her. It was her fault Beau was gone. My only consolation was my certainty that Allcot wouldn't show her any mercy. A small twinge of guilt twisted in my gut, but it was hard to feel bad about it after all we'd been through.

Phoebe entered the room, her brilliant blue eyes scanning as they always did. "Everyone okay in here?"

There was a murmur of agreement. "How is everyone else? Harrison? And Mom?" I stood suddenly. How had I forgotten about Mom? "Where is she?"

"Relax. She's tending to Harrison and the other guard. David levied some impressive blows on them while they were under Meredith's compulsion magic."

David frowned. "It's not like I had a choice. They were trying to kill me. And hell, at that point, I had no idea who was on what side."

"You did what you had to," Hunter said.

"But Harrison is… dammit. He's our most loyal guard and my best friend." David blew out a long-suffering breath. He must have been in a lot of pain still, but just about the only thing that would help him now was fresh human blood. And he wouldn't accept any from the humans in the house.

"He's right," Carrie said quietly. "Harrison won't hold it against you."

Beau chose that moment to run over to David, a toy truck still in his fist. "Uncle David?"

David's expression softened as he smiled at my nephew. "Yeah, little man?"

"You're hurt." Beau dropped the truck and climbed up on the couch to sit next to him.

"I'll be okay." David smoothed Beau's red hair down ever so gently.

"I can hep," he said, his toddler lisp adorable, and then he turned toward Carrie. "Right, Mommy?"

Carrie smiled at her son and then at David. "We've been working on a few healing spells."

"Beau has magic?" I asked, surprised I hadn't heard about this before.

"Of course he does," Carrie said lightly. "How could he not with who is parents are?"

I laughed. "I was just surprised it's already surfaced. It's a little early, isn't it?"

Carrie shrugged. "We haven't had a lot to do considering we've spent the majority of our time indoors these past few years."

That made my heart hurt and it must have showed, because Carrie gave me a reassuring smile. "Don't worry, Wil. Things should get better now that Asher's out of the picture. Right?"

There was a cautious murmur of agreement around the room. Asher's second in command was still out there somewhere. But Carrie was right. The main threat was gone and we had a solid lead on Asher's second. With any luck we'd have him in custody soon. Hopefully Beau would have a relatively normal childhood now.

"I can fix Uncle," Beau told his mother.

"Sure you can, baby," Carrie said, humoring him. She cast David a questioning glance to see if he was game.

He shrugged slightly and nodded.

"It's just a simple healing spell. He's practiced on me a few times. Pretty harmless. It might not even work on you."

"Nothing could be worse than this." David waved at his leg and chuckled. "Go ahead, little man. Let's see what you've got."

Beau grinned up at David, then furrowed his brow as he focused. He ran his small hands along David's leg, parallel to the wound.

David stayed totally still, giving Beau his undivided attention.

"Ready?" Beau asked David.

"Ready." David made a show of closing his eyes as if to prepare for the sting of Beau's magic.

Beau bit his lip and scrunched up his face in concentration. "By the magic of the sea, I give you what you need to be healed by me." Magic burst from Beau's fingertips and latched onto David's skin, skittering across his large body until David glowed with it. The magic brightened into a flash of white light and then it vanished.

David's wound was completely healed.

Beau let out a loud laugh and clapped his hands together. "I did it, Mommy. I did it!"

Everyone in the room was completely silent as we gaped at David.

"Mommy?" Beau asked, suddenly self-conscious. "I fixed him, didn't I?"

"Yeah, baby," Carrie said softly. "You fixed him."

I stared at David, taking in his tired eyes and softer physique. His features were less defined and his marble-like frame had vanished. Beau had fixed him all right. Totally.

The vampire was gone.

David was once again the man I'd dated—a human.

Chapter 33

One Week Later

I stood behind the counter of The Fated Cupcake, blissfully filling the case with a new batch of Hibiscus Healing bars. It was my fourth day back in the shop after spending three days filling out reports and sitting for interviews for the director of the Void regarding the events surrounding Asher's demise. Phoebe and Hunter had apprehended Asher's second in command and, thankfully, the case had been put to rest. Phoebe and I were both on a much-deserved break from everything vampire related.

"Willow?" Jasper called from the register.

I stuffed the rest of the bars in the case and smiled at my newest employee. I'd asked Phoebe to track him down to come talk to me. The fact that he'd sent Phoebe after me after I'd been sold to Rox had weighed heavily on my mind. He hadn't willingly chosen the gang life. He'd been born into it, and I'd wanted to give him a hand up. So I'd made him a deal. Leave the gang for good and he had a full-time job with me for as long as he wanted. If there was ever even a hint of trouble, he was out. No second chances.

He'd accepted on the spot. Today was his third day, and I was confident in saying I'd never had a more willing or eager employee. Especially one that was willing to show up at six a.m. for the morning shift.

"What do you need, Jas?"

"There's a delivery for you." He nodded to a woman holding a thick envelope sealed with wax.

"Thanks," I said absently.

Oh jeez. It had to be from the Cryrique. The old-fashioned grandeur was their thing. I rolled my eyes. What did Allcot want now? Officially, I was no longer tied to them in any way. Talisen was, though. I bit my lip and signed the form, indicating I'd gotten the letter. The courier nodded and moved to the counter to order a Mocha in Motion.

I stuffed the envelope in my pocket and went back to stocking the shelves, preferring to remain blissfully unaware of whatever it was Allcot wanted. But after a few minutes, my curiosity got the better of me.

What if it was about David? What if whatever Beau Jr. had done to turn him human had caused side effects? We'd collectively decided to tell the Void that the fae Meredith had turned him back to human with some unknown magic so Beau would be protected from any testing or interrogation. With Meredith safely locked away in Allcot's care—or worse… I didn't want to know what he'd ultimately decided to do with her—no one would ever know Beau's ability. It wasn't something we wanted to explore. Not right now.

The envelope started to burn a hole of curiosity in my jeans, and finally I touched my assistant's arm.

Tami paused from filling a pastry box. "What's up, boss?"

"I'm going to my office for a bit. Can you keep an eye on Jasper in case he needs anything?" I'd decided to be the one to train him, considering his checkered past. But he was doing so well I didn't think letting Tami take the reins was going to be an issue.

"Sure thing. I'll call you if we need anything."

"Thanks." I knew she wouldn't unless the place caught on fire or something. I grimaced at the unfortunate thought. The Red Door and Allcot's mansion would be undergoing construction for the next few months to repair the damage Asher had caused. In the meantime, I'd heard they were all staying at David's house in Mid-City.

I stepped into my office and was instantly cheered by the man sitting at my desk. "Hey," I said. "When did you get here?"

Tal stood and opened his arms wide. "About forty minutes ago. You seemed busy with the new kid, so Link and I just slipped in and got to work."

I moved and wrapped my arms around Tal as he tugged me to him, his embrace perfect and warm. I glanced over his shoulder at Link. He was curled up in his dog bed, blissfully sleeping. "Looks like someone is well on his way to a productive day."

"Lucky dog." Tal chuckled.

I felt the rumble in his chest and decided I could get very used to that. Tal had been staying at my house the past week. Mostly we'd been sleeping a lot, trying to recover from the toll taken on both of us. During the day he'd started to come into the shop to work on some healing spells until he could find his own lab.

"I've been thinking," I said.

"Yeah?" He pulled back slightly and glanced down at me. "What's that?"

"There's extra space here. There's a storage room that's just full of extra junk. Why don't you use it as your lab? Maybe even team up with me to work on a few things?"

His eyes sparkled with interest. "Like?"

"Oh, I don't know. Maybe something like Intoxicating Fusion or Heart's Desire dollops. You know, something that helps people see what it is they really want out of life? But I can't really do that on my own, I don't think."

"No?" His lips turned up into a sexy little smile.

"No. There's a secret ingredient I'm missing, but I think you can help me out with that."

In answer, he bent his head and kissed my neck, his lips moving slowly up until they closed over my earlobe. "Hmm," he murmured. "I kind of like the sound of this idea."

I let out a giggle and then turned to capture his lips with my own. Our bodies melded together in all the pent-up desire and longing we'd been burying the past eight or nine years. Soon our breathing became labored, and I knew I was moments from ripping his shirt off and mauling him right there in my office.

Instead, I kissed him softly once more and stepped back. "I think we need to put this on hold until later tonight."

Passion smoldered in his vibrant green eyes. "Is that an invitation or a promise?"

I swallowed and smiled shyly. "Both."

Tal had been sleeping in my bed the past week, holding me tightly while we slept. It had been a week of healing, but today felt different. Like we were both ready to let go of the past and finally embrace our future. There was only one thing standing in our way.

Allcot.

I sighed and pulled out the letter. "This came today."

Tal swore.

"I know."

He wrapped his arm around my shoulders and gently tugged me over to the loveseat I'd placed near Link's dog bed.

I handed it to him. "You open it. I don't think I can stomach whatever it is he wants."

Tal took the letter from me, and without ceremony, he tore it open. The envelope fell to the floor as he opened the folded piece of paper. His expression shifted from annoyance to downright shock. After a moment, he held it out to me.

"What does it say?" I asked him, wanting to hear it from Tal. Allcot's orders were entirely too condescending.

Tal shook his head. "Read it."

I took a deep breath and scanned the letter.

> *Dear Ms. Rhoswen,*
>
> *It is probably not a surprise to you that there are very few people in this world whom I treasure. I'm sure you well know one of them is Davidson and*

the other is my dear Pandora. Last week's event marks the second time you have saved someone dear to me. I will be forever in your debt.

I have asked Davidson what it is I might do to show you my appreciation for sacrificing your own health and well-being for the people around you, in particular for the people I treasure. Davidson informs me there is nothing more important to you than freedom. As you well know, the Void is unwilling to sell your tenure with them. However, you also might be aware I purchased Talisen Kavanagh's contract not long ago. In exchange for your self-sacrifice in healing Pandora, I am hereby granting the freedom of one of your loved ones. I have enclosed the release-of-duty certificate for one Talisen Kavanagh. He is no longer required to be of service. If this is not an acceptable exchange, please inform me at your earliest convenience.

I'm in your debt,

Eadric Allcot

I let out a loud gasp and picked up the fallen envelope. There it was. Talisen's release-from-service form. "I can't believe it!"

Tal took the piece of paper from me and read it carefully. Twice. Then he stood and grabbed me, twirling me around as I laughed.

"I still can't believe it. Allcot did something that wasn't completely self-serving."

Laughing, Tal set me back down on my feet and kissed me hard. "This calls for a celebration."

I grinned up at him. "What did you have in mind?"

"You'll just have to wait and see. What time do you get off today?"

I glanced at the wall clock. "Six."

"Good. I have plenty of time to arrange everything." With one last kiss, he winked at me and then snapped his fingers. "Let's go, Link. We have work to do."

"Hey!" I called as he opened the side door to my office.

"Yeah?"

"You never answered me about working here for a while."

His smile turned mischievous. "Are you sure you can handle having me around all the time? I might become a distraction."

"That's what I was hoping for."

The gleam in his eyes brightened. "In that case, Ms. Rhoswen, you're on."

The shop was empty with only few minutes left before closing, and I'd already let the rest of my staff take off early. I was crouched down, organizing the extra stock of boxes and cups, when the bell rang indicating a customer. "Just a sec," I called.

"Take your time," a familiar male voice called.

I popped up. "David?"

He flashed me a lazy smile. His human one. I hadn't seen him since that day at the farmhouse. He'd been in total shock. We all had.

I slipped out from behind the counter and stood in front of him. "How are you?"

He shrugged. "Good, I guess. It's a huge change."

"I can imagine." I waved toward one of the tables near the giant mural covering the wall. "Want to sit?"

"Sure." He pulled out one of the metal chairs while I flipped the Closed sign and locked the front door.

"Want anything?" I asked as I sat across from him? "A Kiss Me chocolate?"

It was an inside joke and I was happy he laughed. It was the first thing he'd ever ordered from me and was what I'd brought him when we'd restarted our friendship after Tal had left.

"No, I'm good. I just wanted to talk to you for a minute."

"Sure," I said. "I'm really glad you came by. I've been worried."

"You have?" There was true interest in his expression.

"Of course. We're friends, right?"

He nodded. "Always have been."

"Good."

We stared at each other until an awkward silence stretched between us. I shifted, not sure what to say or do next.

Then he cleared his throat. "Did you get Father's letter?"

"Oh. Yes, I did. That was—"

"The least he could do?" David asked with a kind smile.

I laughed. "I was going to say generous."

"You're too nice, Willow." David's expression turned serious. "Honestly, I think it's not enough considering everything you've been through."

I shook my head. "I'm not looking for anything. Your father looks after Beau and Carrie. All I've ever wanted is for them to be safe."

"And to live your life as you see fit," he added.

"Well, that, too. You were right about me wanting freedom. I have what I need now. Please thank Eadric for me. I saved each of you for my own reasons, so payment wasn't necessary, but I appreciate it all the same."

David nodded. "I'll tell him."

I studied his decidedly human features, loving the softness around his eyes and the small scar above his eyebrow that hadn't been there as a vampire. "Can I ask you something?"

"Anything."

I swallowed, not wanting to upset him. But I had to know. "Are you happy being human again?"

He frowned, but not unhappily. More as if he was considering the question. "You know, I'm not sure. I don't think I've fully come to terms with it. It's hard to say."

That was interesting. "So you don't want to be turned back into a vampire?" Allcot could do it. Would do it anytime David asked him to, I suspected.

David met my gaze, his brilliant blue eyes suddenly intense. "I really don't know. I wasn't happy as a vampire. Life got better once you turned me into a daywalker. I don't think I want to live in darkness again."

I bit my lip. "What if I agree to turn you again? Back into a daywalker, I mean."

He sat up straight. That had certainly gotten his attention. "You'd do that?" he asked, skepticism clouding his tone.

"Well, yeah. It's not something I'm dying to do, but you've suffered a lot of changes in your life because of me. If you loved being a daywalking vamp and wanted to be one again, I think I would be on board to help you out."

He reached across the table and clasped my hand in his. "That's very generous of you."

I frowned. "Why do you say that?"

He chuckled. "I know how you feel about vampires."

It was my turn to laugh. "No. I don't think you do. I admit, I was a prejudice pill about vamps before. But one of the things I learned through all this is that not all vampires are created equal. There are good and bad and everything in between. Just like every other race and creature on this giant planet. You were one of the good ones." I squeezed his hand. "At this point, David, I only want whatever will make you happy."

The brilliant blue of his eyes dimmed slightly but then brightened as he smiled at me once again. "I think I need to figure out what it is that will make me happy. Then maybe we can talk about it."

Before I could say anything else, he stood and kissed me on the top of my head. "Good night, Willow. You know where to find me if you need anything."

I stood and walked him to the door. "The same goes for you. And I meant what I said. If you want to be changed, all you have to do is ask."

"I know you did. And thank you."

I watched him walk down the street to his silver Mercedes. He slipped in and then waited. Just like he always did. I smiled, knowing he wouldn't leave until I was safely in my car and on my way home.

The house was silent and dark when I walked through the door that night. "Tal?" I called and flipped the deadbolt on the door.

"Upstairs," he called back.

I wasted no time bounding up to the second floor but stopped dead in my tracks when I got to my bedroom door. Candles, what appeared to be hundreds of them, were placed all around my room on every flat surface. The soft glow bounced off the shadows and illuminated Tal, who was sitting at a small table right in the middle of the room.

"What's going on here?" I asked, walking slowly toward him.

He stood and held out his hand. "We're having a romantic evening for two."

I glanced around, noting Link hadn't met me at the door. "Does Phoebe have my dog, or did you rent him out for the evening?"

He chuckled. "Phoebe does have him. They're holed up in her office doing paperwork."

"Poor dog," I said, smiling.

"Yeah, he's really broken up about it." Tal pulled out my chair for me.

I sat and glanced around my room. It had been turned into a magical wonderland. "Did you do all this yourself?"

He shrugged.

"You did, didn't you?" My heart swelled with more love than I thought possible.

"It's a special occasion. We're celebrating, remember?" He picked up a chilled bottle of white wine and filled my glass. While I sipped, he dished a helping of seared tuna onto my plate.

"Nice." I couldn't help the grin from claiming my face. He'd picked my favorites. I stabbed one of the slices and was getting ready to take a bite when I stopped and eyed him. He was staring at me with an intensity I didn't recognize. Tal was almost never serious. And definitely not when we were eating.

I put the tuna down. "What's going on?"

He swallowed. "Nothing. I…"

"You're nervous," I said, noting the bounce of his right leg. "Why?"

"Shit." He chuckled. "This wasn't how I wanted this to happen."

"For what to— Oh."

He slipped out of his chair and dropped to one knee. In his right hand was a small blue velvet box.

"Oh," I said again, my heart ready to pound out of my chest.

Ever so slowly, he opened the box, revealing a large round diamond surrounded by sapphires. Ones the same color as my eyes. Tears started to fall before I could blink them back.

Was this really happening?

"Willow." Tal swallowed again and then blinked hard, forcing back his own tears.

I let out a small laugh through the lump clogging my throat.

His hand squeezed my fingers tightly, and he looked up at me with so much love my heart nearly burst. "Wil, I've been in love with you for nine years. Nine glorious and frustrating years. There's never been anyone I've ever wanted the way I want you, the way I crave you. You're my other half, my partner, and the one I lie awake at night aching for."

"Tal—"

"I don't want to be apart from you again." He pulled the ring from the velvet box and moved it toward my left ring finger. "Will you—"

"Wait." I pulled my hand back, needing a moment before he finished the question, and immediately hated myself when I saw the hurt flash through his eyes. "No, it's not what you think. I want this. I want this more than you could ever know." And dammit if that wasn't God's honest truth. My heart was cracking from just that small moment of uncertainty I'd caused.

"Then what?" Tal got to his feet and sat in the chair opposite me, but he didn't let go of my hand, and for that I was grateful.

"I need to tell you something first."

His lips thinned and I wanted to kick myself again.

"I'm messing this all up." I sent him an apologetic smile. "It was a beautiful proposal and as soon as we get through this, if you still want to ask me, I promise my answer is yes."

Now he looked confused. "I think you better start explaining."

I let out a nervous laugh and pushed my hair off my face. It was best to just rip the Band-Aid off. Put it right out there. I took a deep breath and then said, "David came to see me tonight. He's still human, but if he decides to turn vamp, I offered to turn him back into a daywalker."

Tal just looked at me, his brow furrowed. "And?"

"And nothing. He hasn't decided what he wants to do."

Tal's frown deepened. "Okay."

"Okay? What does that mean?" I was frustrated now. Why was he being so dense?

He lifted one shoulder. "It means okay. What were you expecting me to say?"

I tilted my head and studied him. Then I downed the rest of my wine. With a laugh, I put the empty glass back on the table. "I guess I expected you to get mad. Or at the very least try to talk me out of it."

"Why would I—?" He stopped midsentence as realization dawned on him. "Oh." Then his face relaxed and he gave me a real, genuine smile. Standing, he tugged on my hand and pulled me with him. "When I made up my mind that I wanted you as my wife, I came to terms with the fact that you are a very strong woman. And yes, that means that sometimes you are going to do things that I don't want you to do, but that's also one of the many reasons I love you. You come with gifts most people can't even fathom. To think you'll never use them is a fool's game."

"So you don't mind, then?" I asked, holding his gaze and loving the intensity I saw there.

"I wouldn't say I don't mind. I'll worry. There's no getting around that. But I also know that to try to hold you back is not my place. You are your own woman. And I expect you to be nothing less."

"Tal," I breathed and leaned into him, overwhelmed by his affirmation. "I love you so much."

I felt his shoulders relax beneath my fingers. "Is that a yes, then?"

I pulled back and sent him a teasing smile. "Did you even ask the question?"

His eyes turned serious, and when he spoke again, his tone was low and full of love. "Willow Rhoswen, would you do me the honor of being my wife?"

I was frozen in his embrace, the tears rolling uncontrollably down my cheeks. Unable to speak, I nodded and clung to him.

He pulled me into a tight embrace, one of a desperate man. "Thank you, love. Thank you for loving me."

I choked out a laugh and clung tighter.

After a moment, he whispered in my ear. "Say yes."

Swallowing the emotion choking me, I forced out, "Yes."

He pulled back and gently took my left hand in his. The ring fit perfectly, and once it was on, he pulled my hand to his mouth and kissed it.

My knees nearly melted right there.

"Tal?"

"Yes?" He leaned down and kissed the corner of my mouth, sending waves of anticipation through my core.

"I want you."

"You already have me." His fingers glided up my neck, making me shiver with undisguised desire.

"All of you," I whispered.

His index finger found my lips, pressing ever so gently. That is, until a small moan escaped me. Then his lips were on me and we were all heat and passion and everything light. Our hands were everywhere, exploring each other in ways we never had before.

By the time he pushed my shirt up and over my head, my body ached for him in ways that were too delicious to deny.

Moments later, our clothes were left in a pile on the floor and we were lying on my bed. Tal gazed down at me with molten desire, making me pulse everywhere.

"Are you sure?" he asked just before kissing me with the intensity of a starving man.

When we broke apart, gasping for breath, I answered by cupping my palms over both his cheeks and kissing him with all the love bursting in my heart. "I'm sure," I whispered.

Then he lowered himself and together we became one.

Epilogue

It was a late fall day when I stood under the giant water oak in Coliseum Square, the park across the street from the house Tal and I shared. I was dressed in a formfitting silk dress, Tal in a gray seersucker suit with white pinstripes.

Link, in full wolf mode, sat at our feet watching over the ceremony. The past six months hadn't been entirely drama free. There'd been a few vampire attacks and some political shenanigans at the Void, but nothing we couldn't handle. Link was in wolf form only because he was being protective of the two people he loved most in the world. Me and Tal.

I stared up at my bridegroom and smiled. He was so utterly handsome I nearly burst with pride. And he was gazing down at me as if he were the luckiest man alive.

Harrison, who'd just performed the ceremony for us, was announcing us as Mr. and Mrs. Kavanagh, even though Tal and I both knew I wasn't likely to change my name. Tal caught my eye and winked. I laughed up at him, and then we both turned and waved at our guests. Everyone we loved was there. My mom, Phoebe, Hunter, Eadric, Pandora, Nicola, my entire staff, Carrie, and Beau.

And as I stood in front of our small crowd, I spotted one other guest I was surprised to see. David. He was standing off by himself under a tree. I hadn't seen him since that day we'd talked in my shop. The day I'd offered to turn him back into a daywalker.

Our guests started milling around us, hugging and wishing us their heartfelt congratulations. After a while, Tal squeezed my hand and nodded in David's direction. "Why don't you go invite him to the party?"

I glanced up at him, my heart nearly bursting. "You're a great man, you know that?"

He pulled me to him and kissed my temple. "That's what you keep telling me, Mrs. Kavanagh."

I giggled and tugged him down to show him what a real kiss looked like. We didn't part until the catcalls and whistles started in.

"Get a room!" someone called and everyone cheered.

Reluctantly, Tal let me go and then nudged me toward the tree David had taken refuge under. David was sitting down, leaning against the trunk, when I finally made my way through the crowd of well-wishers.

"Hey there," I said. "Want some company?"

He glanced up at me and smiled. "What are you doing over here, Willow? Isn't your groom going to miss you?"

I turned to find Tal laughing with Phoebe and Hunter. "It looks like he's doing okay."

David raised his eyebrows. "You didn't answer my first question."

"Oh, you mean the one about what I'm doing over here? That's easy. I'm here to bring you back to the party."

He got to his feet and shook his head. "No. I shouldn't even be here."

I frowned. "Why not?"

He pressed his lips into a tight line. "I wasn't invited."

Laughing, I shook my head. "What? Of course you were. I sent you an invitation. Didn't you get it?"

He shook his head. "No. I didn't. But I moved from the Mid-City house, so maybe that's it. But seriously, why would you invite me? I'm your ex. Hasn't anyone ever told you that's bad etiquette?"

His move made sense. He hadn't turned vamp again. And

he had good reason. I glanced over at Carrie and met her worried gaze.

"If it's such bad etiquette, what are you doing here?"

He sighed. "You know I'm keeping an eye on Beau."

I scoffed. No one had heard even so much as a rumor about anyone going after Beau since we'd destroyed Asher. "That's not the only reason, David," I said gently and placed a light hand on his arm. "I already know about you and Carrie."

His sucked in a surprised breath. "How? Did she…?"

I shook my head. "No. Phoebe saw you two a couple of weeks ago."

"And you're not… I mean, you don't mind?"

I gave him a warm smile. "Of course I don't mind. I just got married. I'm blissfully happy and ridiculously in love. And the only thing that will make me happier is to know that everyone else I love is here with me to celebrate. Now come on. Come back with me and join Carrie like you should've in the first place."

He shook his head in disbelief. "You're really not upset?"

"Do you love her?"

"I think so."

"Then I'm not upset. You're a good man. You'll protect her and my nephew. What's to be upset about?"

He smiled down at me. "Will your husband blow a gasket if I give you a hug?"

"Only if you cop a feel."

Laughing, he folded me into his arms and said, "Thank you."

When he released me, I took his hand and tugged him over to where Carrie stood with my nephew. Carrie looked at me in surprise, but I just pulled her into a hug and said, "Take care of each other."

There were tears in her eyes when I let her go. "We will," she said and wrapped her fingers around David's.

"There you are, my gorgeous bride." Tal came up behind me and wrapped an arm around my shoulders as he held his other hand out to David. "Good to see you, man."

"Congratulations," David said, pumping his hand. "You're a lucky man."

"So are you," Tal said with a grin and nodded toward Carrie.

Then with a wink at me, Tal whisked me away to the temporary dance floor. And as the music started up, he held out his hand and gave me a half bow. "Will you do me the honor, Ms. Rhoswen?"

"Dance with you, Mr. Kavanagh?" I asked and took his hand in mine. "Always."

About the Author

Deanna is a native Californian, transplanted to the slower paced lifestyle of southeastern Louisiana. When she isn't writing, she is often goofing off with her husband in New Orleans, playing with her two Shih Tzu dogs, making glass beads, or out hocking her wares at various bead shows across the country. For more information visit her website at www.deannachase.com.

Made in the USA
San Bernardino, CA
13 November 2016